Jillian

Book 1 of the Women of the Fellowship Series

Julia A. Royston

Edited by: Claude R. Royston

BK Royston Publishing, LLC
Jeffersonville, IN

BK Royston Publishing
P. O. Box 4321
Jeffersonville, IN 47131
502-802-5385
http://bkroystonpublishing.com
bkroystonpublishing@gmail.com

Published by: BK Royston Publishing LLC
Cover Design: Jonathan Snorten
Cover Models: Mr. & Mrs. Marcus Maclin
Cover Creative Director: Shenique Calhoun
Layout: BK Royston Publishing LLC

ISBN-13: 978-0692528068
ISBN-10: 0692528067
LCCN: 2015914715

Printed in the United States of America

Dedication

This is dedicated to my father, Dr. Jack C. Foree. I really didn't think I could write a full novel. My dad always told me, "If there is something that you want to do, make sure Julia Ann that human beings do it. If a human being can do it, you can do it too." Thanks Daddy…

Acknowledgements

I thank my Lord and Savior Jesus Christ for giving me another opportunity to introduce more people to a gift that you have given to me. I thank you that you have entrusted this gift to me. Lord, let your Spirit move, guide and empower through this book to the people who will read it.

To my husband, Brian K. Royston, the love of my life for loving and cheering me on so much that I can be and do all that God has placed in me. I love you...

To my Mom, Dr. Daisy Foree, my greatest supporter and best friend. To my Dad, who is in heaven, that I know is proud of me and always encouraged me to 'go for it.' Thanks to all of the rest of my family for their love and support.

A special thank you to Rev. and Mrs. Claude R. Royston for all of their love and support. Papa, thank you for using your fine tooth comb to edit yet another book for me and this time maybe blushing a little bit.

Love, Julia A. Royston

Introduction

God is love. He loved us first. He then commanded us to love Him and love one another. Love is wonderful. I love being loved each and every day. There are all types of love, but there is something quite special about romantic love. I am a romantic at heart. I have always desired to write a romance novel of my very own and here are my words of love to be shared with you.

Have you ever known or been a woman who waited a long time to get married? It seems you've done everything. You have an education, a career, a house, a car, in pretty good physical condition, attractive and spent years of service to your church or community. But, where is the love?

Jillian Forrester was no different. She comes from a great family. She has served in her church in many capacities and is a role model to many. She has gone to school, graduated and built her a thriving business. Where is her husband and her true love? When will it be her turn?

Byron Randolph is a childhood friend. He is good looking, has a twin brother, comes from a loving family and has built a successful corporation. Why isn't he already married? Where is his girlfriend? What has held him back from love?

The season has come. The opportunity is here. The time is now. Introducing, Jillian Forrester.

Table of Contents

Jillian

Chapter 1

"Jillian, you are as big as a tank. You are getting so fat that if you keep eating the way you do now, you are not going to be able to fit into any of your clothes. One day we are going to just get a sheet and cut a hole in the top and drape it over your head," Jillian's father John yelled. Hearing the commotion, Jillian's mother Delores ran up the stairs and swung open the door immediately after hearing those words to her oldest baby girl.

"John, don't say that to her!" Jillian's mother Delores yelled back.

"No, Delores somebody's got to say it. She just keeps eating and eating. She's getting bigger and bigger. I am concerned about her health and future." Turning back to Jillian, her father took a deep breath and in an unusually low voice said, "Don't you want to be like the other young ladies who can fit into their clothes nicely and wear little cute clothes? I will spend $500 on a new wardrobe if you lose 50 pounds, okay?"

Jillian stood with her head hanging down and thought, 'oh no, not this again. It's the same 50 pounds and the same $500 wardrobe that he promises all of the time.'

Unlike her sister, Jillian was never one to talk back to either of her parents for any reason. She just kept standing there in that same spot on the carpet. The tears were rolling down her face speaking volumes that her voice couldn't and wouldn't utter. The words of her father cut like a knife into her heart and ripped it into shreds. Inside Jillian wondered, 'will anyone ever love me for me? Will it always be about how I look and never what is going on inside my mind? I am fun. I am not ugly. I am a good student. I have no boyfriends, but plenty of friends. Will my dad ever be proud of me for the things I do and not just how much weight I lose or how I look? Will I ever be good enough?'

John and Delores stood quiet for a short time waiting for a response to all that had been said, but there was none. The words had feverishly unpacked to take residence. Emotional baggage waited its turn at the door to move in, it was suddenly too crowded. John left the room. Delores paused for a second not knowing what to say either. She couldn't take back the words of her husband, but this was still her baby. Delores prayed that God would be able to comfort Jillian in a way that she felt inadequate to do so now. Giving up, Delores slowly left the scene of the crime and closed the door behind her. The white walls of Jillian's bedroom seemed to close in on her. In an effort not to faint from the emotional roller coaster ride, Jillian propelled her body hard onto the bed. Her self-esteem fell all of the way to the floor along with her heart. Jillian's five feet three body shrunk to 2 inches. The five foot part of her was all gone. It was the 1970s, thin was in and Jillian was certainly not thin. She was five feet two and most of her life, wore a size 18-20 dress and at the height of her weight was a 24-26 dress size which she knew was just too large. Plus-size models were unheard of back then. Lane Bryant and Sears were the only plus size outlets.

The clothing was functional, fit well, but only occasionally stylist. For a teenager, stylish clothes were a must, but not found frequently enough for a plus size teen. Some years she was smaller and other years she was larger. It all depended on how well she did on the latest diet craze. Diet drinks, walking, starving, meetings and weighing in was all a part of Jillian's life. Those words by Jillian's father that day were supposed to motivate her to stay on one of those diets. Jillian's dad was her hero, but that day he hurt her more than he would ever know. Those words caused Jillian to never look at herself the same. Jillian's future would involve going from one bad relationship to another. She doubted and second guessed every guy who came in her life. She was constantly looking for a guy who would love Jillian for who she was and not just what she looked like, who she knew or what she could do. Those who met Jillian would probably describe her as pleasant, fun, out-going, talented and intelligent. As a pre-teen, Jillian had a body well beyond her years. With large breasts, a small waist and a large behind, Jillian always attracted the wrong guy looking to have some fun and use her body to fulfill his latest fantasy. Jillian may have had low self-esteem or a poor self-image, but high morals. Years of love and support from her mother and the teachings of her church, "New Life

Christian Church," these were the things that kept her grounded. The public school taught sex education class in the sixth grade. Seeing that birthing video helped to keep Jillian walking in the straight and narrow. No man was just going to use her body and then walk away. That woman's screams from the video solidified that. She was saving herself for marriage. For the God sent, educated, hard-working, God fearing man who was going to support, love and protect her as they walked together into destiny. At forty years old, Jillian was still praying that God would send Mr. Right and the devil would stop sending those "Mr. Right Now and Mr. Wrong."

Jillian snapped out of her day dream just as Patricia, her assistant, walked into her office. Jillian turned from the window in her corner office, atop the spacious tenth floor in her now named, "The Forrester."

"Jillian, here are those Taylor & Edwards renewal contracts to sign. When you have signed them, leave them on my desk and I will messenger them over in the morning. Remember, you have to be at church at 7 for rehearsal and the national conference meeting tonight. It is now 4 o'clock. Boss, after 10 years, I know you. Don't let the view distract you. Are you alright?" Standing five foot ten, well dressed as always, red dreads and a beautiful red dress to match, Patricia commands a room without saying anything. Patricia took off her reading glasses and looked at Jillian intently waiting for an answer. Patricia knew Jillian too well. She could easily tell when and if

Jillian's mood changed. She was usually all business and professional, but her boss seemed suddenly melancholy.

"Thanks Patricia, I am fine, I started looking out at the view and got caught up. I love this time of year because I reflect, review and renew my commitment to a great future. What's up?" Jillian asked.

"Well, I have placed some papers on your desk that need your attention. There's no rush." Patricia quietly left the room realizing that Jillian needed a few more minutes to herself. As Patricia sat down at her desk, she thought about the years she and Jillian had worked together. She had worked with Jillian long enough to know that she sometime worked too hard and felt lonely at times because she desired a man to love and complete her life. Jillian had a full life with work, church on the local and national levels and music, but it wasn't quite complete without love. She secretly prayed that Jillian would find that special man to fill the love piece of her life's puzzle. Patricia had enough love going on with the multiple men she dated and didn't want to be tied down, settle down or be down with any man for too long. That just wasn't Patricia's style. She was more comfortable with, 'keep them waiting, wanting and wishing they could be with me.'

Patricia Johnson had been Jillian's friend and assistant since she began the Forrester Information Management Company in the living room of her small condo on the north side of the Queen City of

Cincinnati, OH. Patricia was initially friends with Jillian's sister, Monica. Monica knew that Jillian was going to need help with her business and mentioned it to Patricia who needed some part-time work to make ends meet. Jillian met Patricia and seemed like the perfect assistant to help her get Forrester moving in the right direction. Jillian was right about Patricia and after coming on board became an important part of the Forrester team and Jillian's life. Back then, Patricia worked for Jillian while she was completing her doctoral education. Jillian had big goals, dreams and plans. She just needed someone to help her with the details and day to day operations to keep her on task. Jillian had saved her money in preparation of needing an assistant. The pay wasn't much, but Patricia believed in Jillian and was willing to help her fulfill her plans. Jillian always encouraged Patricia to fulfill her dreams also and not just be her wonderful assistant. Jillian asked on several occasions if Patricia wanted to go back to school, start her own business or had some other plans. She assured Jillian that she didn't want the pressure of her own business and was fine working for her. Patricia was now listed as the Office Manager which was an invaluable key position to Forrester's operations, success and Jillian's sanity. Patricia's strength was her organizational and administrative skills keeping Jillian organized, on task and meeting deadlines for each project. Today was one of those days that Jillian needed Patricia to get her back on track. Jillian was never diagnosed with ADD as a child, but some days she could get easily distracted. Jillian needed to stay focused to move Forrester forward. Forrester was now one of the major players in the research and information management companies in the Midwest.

Forrester Information Management Company had long since moved out of the condo living room and was now located in the heart of downtown Cincinnati. It is within walking distance from the *Procter and Gamble* twin towers, Kroger Co. building, the Courthouse and easy access for lunch to the famous Cincinnati's Fountain Square on Vine Street. Access to the business district was essential to the growth and customer service of Forrester's business of research and information management services.

Jillian found the pile of papers that needed her attention. She picked them up and walked to her assistance's desk. "Patricia, I'll get these signed and place them on your desk for you in the morning. Are you headed out?" Jillian was slightly waving the papers at Patricia to let her know that she saw the ones that needed her attention.

"Yes," she looked up from her desk toward Jillian's voice, "I am about to take off as soon as I straighten up my desk. Is there anything else you needed from me before I go?"

"No, I'll be fine; I will see you in the morning. Have a great night, Patricia."

"You too, see you in the morning," Patricia said over her shoulder as Jillian walked back into her office and closed the door softly behind her. Jillian reviewed the papers thoroughly and signed them quickly and placed them on Patricia's desk. Jillian was CEO of an information management company. Information was her thing and knowing it best was her game.

Jillian gathered her things, turned off the lights, locked the door and headed toward the elevator. She needed to get home, change and get to the church for the rehearsal and the conference meeting. Jillian stepped on the elevator when it arrived and as the doors closed, she could see her full five foot three, 200 pound frame in the reflection. Turning slightly to the left, she could see her behind sticking out. She was looking good in that size-18 knit suit that she loved so well. Navy blue was the color of the day and the pumps always matched the suit which matched the purse. Jillian loved clothes and especially for them to match.

As the elevator continued to descend, Jillian prayed 'Lord I thank you for helping me get everything done today in my work life. Be with me tonight to get something accomplished in this meeting at church.' Jillian knew that she was going to need it working with the members of this conference planning committee. She temporarily put that out of her mind as the elevator door opened and she walked onto the first floor. Jillian noticed that Marvin, the security guard, was on post as usual. Marvin was a very polite, fine, six foot four brother covered with chocolate skin and a body built to take anyone down.

He looked up and saw it was Jillian and said, "Good night, Ms. Forrester."

"Good night Marvin and be sure to tell your wife I said hello and kiss that new baby for me," Jillian replied.

"I will," Marvin said with a smile while he looked at the picture of his wife and new baby on his desk.

Jillian saw him looking at the picture before she went through the door of the garage. She smiled and thought to herself, 'Lord, that wife of his is blessed to be married to that fine brother right there. If you could make another one that fine, Jesus send him my way.'

Jillian was still smiling and shaking her head as she pushed the button to unlock her car door and drive away. Cincinnati traffic wasn't that bad at this time of day and she didn't live too far away from the office. While maneuvering through the garage, Jillian thought about how God had been good to her since the early days of starting her company and attending graduate school. Jillian remembered how proud her parents were on graduation day. Since graduation, she had paid off student loans, built the company and now lived in a spacious 3 bedroom, 2-bath condo in one of the new high rise complexes conveniently located minutes from downtown. Jillian stopped to get a light dinner and proceeded to her condo. Jillian's condo was on the 12th floor so she could see the Bengals' and Reds' stadiums from her balcony. She could also see traffic build on the highway from her bedroom window before leaving the house in the morning.

Her condo was complete with simple furniture, neutral colors for the walls and carpet with a splash of color on one wall and accented with the décor.

Jillian was not a decorator by any means. Decorating was her sister, Monica's department. She was an interior decorator and image consult. Monica could turn a cave into a show place, any woman into a model and any professional into a superstar. Monica had the gift. Monica decorated 'The Forrester' office building and received rave reviews for the design, layout and decor. Jillian knew what she liked, but couldn't pick it out to save her life. Thank God for Monica. Jillian could tell Monica what she wanted, give her the budget and it would be done in no time.

As she walked in her condo, Jillian kicked off her shoes, set down her purse and laptop bag as she walked in the door. She quickly looked at her phone for any messages and realized that there were none so she turned her attention to food. As she sat down, she wondered, 'will I always eat alone or will there one day be a good looking guy like Marvin sitting across from me?' She put that thought out of her mind, turned on her 67 inch TV to Channel 9, WCPO to watch a few minutes of the news from the day. After putting her trash away, the fork and glass in the dish washer, she headed to her bedroom to change into more comfortable battle clothes for her meeting with the conference planning committee. 'Lord, help me tonight,' she told herself as she headed toward the elevator back to her car.

Thirty minutes later, Jillian was pulling in a parking space at the New Life Christian Church. She could see several cars in the parking lot that she recognized so she knew that the majority of the committee was inside ready for battle. It was that time again for the Christian Church World Fellowship Conference. This year, thousands of Christians would be descending upon Cincinnati in less than six months for the conference. Each year the conference was held in a different city and all roads were leading to the Queen City. New Life Christian Church had requested to be the host for this year's conference. Of course, Jillian was on the conference committee as well as a member of the music and administrative staffs of the conference. Jillian's family had been a part of the Christian Church World Fellowship for four generations. Jillian's mother, Delores Forrester was a national board member of the Women's Ministry. Jillian's father, John Forrester was a national board member of the Christian Education Department. It was Jillian's turn to carry on the legacy of working on the international conference committee. Jillian had been a part of the children's, teen and young adult conferences growing up. At 40, she was well prepared to work on the adult conference committee. Jillian knew all of the preachers, their wives, children, church names and regional areas by name. With a global conference, you had to know all of the players, history, scandals, political history and family connections their likes, dislikes and preferences. As Jillian entered the church, it was all abuzz. It was Tuesday night which was rehearsal and meeting night. The children's, youth, young adult and adult department singers, dancers and drama departments were all meeting simultaneously. It was convenient and the church was used to its fullest capacity. All of the rooms, sanctuary, rehearsal halls, corridors and even the hallways were used to accommodate all of the activity. Jillian loved to see the church productive, active and moving forward in its purpose. As she passed each area, she noticed how the children and young people had grown up, taking charge and now using their gifts in church. She answered several greetings of 'Hello Ms. Jillian or Sis. Jillian.'

Other children gave her some updates on their personal news 'Sister Jillian this happened to me at school today or Sis. Forrester I now have this toy or that activity I will participate in or can you sponsor me for that project or fundraiser?' Although Jillian loved children, she never really imagined herself having her own children. She was always proud to see anybody's children doing well in and out of church. Jillian headed up the stairs and could hear the discussion before she opened the door. Mother Williams was at it again. She hadn't realized that we were well into the 21st century and not 1940 when black people couldn't eat in most restaurants and during conferences, bought a meal ticket to eat at the church.

"I don't know why we can't serve dinners at the church instead of the people going out to all of these restaurants," said Mother Williams. "Back in the day, they used to line up for my fried chicken, greens, macaroni and cheese, homemade rolls and peach cobbler so good it made you want to slap your mama. Chile' those was the days," Mother Williams was making her point by pointing her finger into the faces of each of the committee members.

"Yes, Mother Williams those were the days. Now, people have their own cars, can eat in the restaurants in the hotel or anywhere else they want to go to instead of being forced to buy a meal ticket and go to the church. The church doesn't need to incur that expense for food when there are so many other alternatives," said Sis. Pamela Jenkins.

Mother Williams was the oldest member of the church at 95 and still remembered as well as wanted to continue the good old days. Pamela Jenkins was the church financial secretary and knew all too well the current church and conference budgets. Jillian walked in right after that spirited exchange.

"Good evening to everyone. I am sorry to run a bit late," interrupted Jillian. "Where are we now on the agenda Sister Pamela?" Jillian said as she placed her purse on the table and sat down in the chair closest to the door. She knew that she would be called to go to the music department rehearsal at 8 so she needed to move the meeting along. Sis. Pamela Jenkins was the committee secretary and assigned to keep the meeting agenda, minutes, the committee on task and not veer into unnecessary or unproductive side bar conversations. Sis. Pamela was a good friend of Jillian's, efficient and punctual. She can get a job done as well as keep accurate notes.

Sis. Pamela reviewed her lap top and began running down the list. "Well, we heard from Jasmine with what's going on with hospitality and that looks like everyone will be in place." Jasmine Rucker was another one of Jillian's good friends. Jasmine was very friendly, giving, helpful and cordial to everyone. Jasmine was perfect for hospitality department. Jillian loved her friends because they would follow through even though they were her friends. Jillian knew how to pick team members.

Pamela continued, "We still need to hear updates from transportation, media and technology, vendors, music and any other instructions you have for us Jillian, from the National Conference Committee members."

"That's a long list," said Jillian. "I will be speaking to them tomorrow night. I will send Pamela an update from the co-chairs and she will forward any new concerns or requests to the individual department chairs. Pamela, I probably won't be back before this meeting ends. Could you send me a copy of your minutes as well as any concerns we have to Vernice?" asked Jillian.

"Will do, Jillian," said Pamela.

"'We have approximately six months from now until the conference. I was told that the only way to eat an elephant is one bite at a time. So let's get to it," said Jillian while organizing her notes.

"Before we get started, Jillian," interjected Linda Smith, "I have an update on the conference speakers. We have confirmed Bishop Norman James from Columbus, Ohio for Tuesday night, Bishop Nathan Gentry from Los Angeles, California for Wednesday night, Bishop Robert Johnson from Cincinnati, Ohio on Thursday night, and Bishop Clarence Randolph from Indianapolis, Indiana for Friday night to close us out." Linda was in charge of the daily worship service and stage coordination. The Worship Coordinator made sure that all participants were in the right place at the time so that each service flowed well.

There were pleasant gasps of agreement all around the table from the other committee members.

"Wow Linda, Bishop Randolph has agreed to come as well. That's fantastic! I love them all but; I am really looking forward to seeing Bishop Clarence Randolph. I used to have so much fun with that entire family over the years, especially his twin sons, Byron and Myron. Oh well, I digress," Jillian smiled as she thought of Byron Randolph. 'Lord, I wonder who he married?' She thought.

"Didn't you have a crush on one of the twins, back in the day, Jillian?" said Linda. Jillian swatted with her hand at Linda for her to hush. It seemed like Linda could read her mind about Byron Randolph.

"Girl, that was way back in the day. This is church business and don't be telling all of my personal business. By the way, don't let me get started on your many conference crushes, you too Pamela while you are sitting over there all quiet as a mouse not saying nothing," Jillian added.

"I was trying to be invisible and keep my mouth closed. I'm just waiting on the Lord," added Pamela bowing her head and suddenly looking at the floor.

"Ladies, let's get back on task, you young single girls always trying to get a man. Just let me pray for you. Let's finish planning this conference and then maybe God will send your husband to you. He that "findeth a wife" is what the good book says. Ya'll shouldn't be looking anyway," said Mother Williams with a huff.

"Yes Ma'am," said Linda, Pamela and Jillian simultaneously. Both Linda and Jillian were forty, professional, no children and very single. Pamela was forty as well as professional but had a son from a previous marriage. Pamela had been through divorce and other financial issues. Linda made it with the help of God, her family and a great church family. Pamela's son was now 18, a star on the football team and headed to college at the end of the school year.

All three women looked at each other smiling at the motherly rebuke.

"We're sorry about getting off task for a brief moment. Linda that will make your marketing and promotions efforts much easier with that great

Line-up of speakers. Hopefully people will make an effort to come to the conference. Furthermore, we need to make sure that we are prepared and can adequately accommodate the crowd that is sure to come," said Jillian.

Everyone agreed with Jillian that this would be a great conference with the speaker line-up. Jillian had a sudden flash back and an ADD moment to being young at the conference and running the halls to get to the concerts or other youth activities with the Randolph twins and many other preachers' kids. 'I wonder how they are doing these days. Are they both married or single, with children or childless?' Jillian pondered these and other questions in her mind forgetting totally that she was still in the meeting. Fortunately, she heard her name being called by Linda.

"Jillian are you with us?" Linda asked.

Jillian brought herself back to the moment and to the task at hand. "Oh, I'm sorry I had an ADD moment there, but I am back. Linda where are we on the agenda?" The conference committee jumped right into the agenda and decided on the issues that needed attention, made a list of those issues that needed further information and raised even more issues and concerns for the next meeting. At eight o'clock, John poked his head in the door to remind

Jillian that the music department was waiting on her to go over her song with the praise team. She excused herself and went down to meet with the music department. Jillian was tired and ready to go home. As soon as this rehearsal was over. Jillian was blessed with many talents. She loved singing, leading worship and event planning for the church and other organizations even more. If music and event planning were as lucrative as her information business, she would leave Forrester, travel, plan and sing full-time. Jillian realized that she is able to donate her time, talent and treasure to the church because *Forrester Information* did so well. Jillian greeted the praise team, the musicians cued her song and they sang it perfectly in one take. That was the final song of the night, so Jillian stayed for the dismissal prayer with the praise team.

When Jillian opened her eyes, Pamela was bringing her purse and notebook into the rehearsal hall. "Thanks Pamela. So, how did everything go after I left?" asked Jillian.

"Fine, girl," said Pamela. "You know how everybody goes back and forth over little petty issues, but overall we were able to get a lot accomplished. We are getting short on time with only six months left. We have to make some concrete decisions and stop debating. I will send out an email with the minutes from this meeting, the agenda and date of the next meeting. Things are moving right along as always. It is time consuming, but we'll be ready. I will wait to hear from you about any changes or additional issues once you talk to the National Conference co-chairs."

"I am going to place a call tonight when I get home."

"Great," Pamela said.

"So, Pamela, you got your 'man getting' clothes planned out yet for the conference?" asked Jillian, teasing Pamela.

"Girl, you are a mess. I have scoped out some cute dresses in the catalogs for spring. I am going to have to save my pennies to be able to buy a few unforgettable pieces. I hope to be razor sharp, as my mother would say, for the conference. I must admit that at times, I go back and forth between being open for a new relationship and just closing myself off to anybody new. I am leaning toward remaining open about a new relationship though. My baby is getting older and will be gone to college next fall. What am I going to do sit home alone? I think not." said Pamela.

"I know that's right. You can't let what happened in that relationship carry over into the next one. You just never know what God has in store," interjected Jillian.

"I know. I have to remind myself of that when men approach me in the grocery store or anywhere else that I am attractive and I do deserve love. My son is a young man and not a child. He is about to start creating his own life with an education and one day a wife and children of his own. I am believing that God will send me a good man that loves Him first, then me and also my son. I don't need a daddy for my son, he has a daddy, but I will take a good role model," Pamela's face formed a smile.

"Amen, Pamela. I've had my share of pain, but ready to love and be loved. God's best could walk through the front door of the *Duke Energy Convention Center* and I want to be ready on the inside and out," said Jillian passionately as they walked out the door to the parking lot.

"Preach on my sister," said Pamela.

"I'm no preacher. You just never know what could happen at the conference, if you are ready," added Jillian with a wink and a smile.

"Yep, you never know. May the force of the Holy Trinity be with us. This prayer request calls for God, Jesus and the Holy Ghost," said Pamela in her deacon prayer voice. The two women laughed.

"Let's get out of here, go home and get some rest before another work day tomorrow," said Jillian as she gathered her things heading toward the door.

"Exactly, Jillian. Good night."

"Good night Pamela."

"It's your mother on the phone, pick it up. You can't run from me, I know where you live." That was the sound of that annoying and loud cell phone ring tone down in the side of her purse that her niece picked for her. Jillian was turning the key in her front door and hurrying to get to the phone before it stopped. 'I must have my niece change that ring tone, it drives me nuts,' thought Jillian. Mrs. Delores Forrester was Jillian's 71 year old mother and her best friend in the world.

"Hey mama, what's up?" Finally getting to the phone, Jillian pressed the pickup button.

"Hey baby, how are you doing? Are you home yet?" Jillian's mom said.

"Yep, just coming in the door," said Jillian. "Hold on and let me put down my things real quick." Jillian put her purse down, kicked off her shoes and headed to the couch. She knew this would be a few minutes so she shifted her phone to a more comfortable position and propped up her feet. "Okay I'm back. How was your day?" Jillian asked.

"Same 'ole same 'ole. I met with the sewing circle this morning and ran some errands this afternoon. I went by the nursing home to visit a few people. I ate a late dinner and I'm doing some crocheting." Jillian knew that her mother stayed busy each day running errands and doing volunteer work since her father passed away 2 years ago. "I really called to see how the conference meeting went tonight. Is Ruby Williams still trying to take over and run things?" Her mom asked.

"Yes, Lord. Mama are you praying for us? She is getting on our nerves. She wants to take us back to

1940 when the conference sold meal tickets, prepared meals at the host church and black people couldn't eat in a regular restaurant. I love having the conference historian on our team, but we are trying to have a conference in the 21st century, not the 19th. Praise God, we can eat in any restaurant that we choose and can afford to." Both women laughed as they thought about Ruby Williams and her antics. Jillian continued, "The meeting went well. I had to leave to go to Praise Team rehearsal. Other than that, things are moving right along with the various committees," Jillian's mom was laughing the whole time just thinking about what Jillian was going through.

"Glad to hear that Ruby hasn't changed. If anybody can handle her, it's you and the rest of your team. My prayer is that the conference will be a success, but that maybe you can get a date and find a husband. You know our preference for you to date someone in the Fellowship." Jillian's mom said proudly.

"I know, I know and I've been waiting patiently. I'm not getting any younger mom." Jillian said.

"I'm just saying that God blessed me with a good husband for fifty years and two lovely girls, the best any mother could ask for."

"Thank you Mama," Jillian almost wanted to cry, but didn't.

"I have been praying that God send you a man so good that you forget those other two."

Jillian rolled her eyes to the ceiling and said, "Lord, Mama, please don't go there. I hate it when you bring them up." She knew exactly the two, Roger Hart, the lawyer from Oklahoma and Jeremy Garrett, the Engineer from Dallas. Roger cheated on her and Jeremy was boring, uninterested in Jillian and wouldn't commit.

"I'm sorry, but just telling you my prayers," her mom reiterated.

"I know and thank you for your prayers. I hope one day that the subject of those two will finally die." Jillian's voice trailed off as she remembered that very disappointing night. Roger had been calling her and trying to sweet talk her back into his life for months. One night Jillian woke up about two o'clock in the morning and a voice said, 'she's pregnant and he's going to marry her.' The next time Roger called Jillian told him what the voice said. Roger was confronted and demanded to know who told. Jillian simply said, 'God told me.'

Jillian remembered Roger shouted, 'God told you what? Girl you are crazy!' With that said, Jillian quietly hung up the phone without another word. Roger was supposed to be a Christian and so super holy. We all found out that he wasn't that holy just one month before the wedding. All of those gifts were re-wrapped and returned. Jillian was so humiliated. After that, here comes man number two, Jeremy. He was fun, but after five years of dating, wouldn't commit to more than dinner and a movie.

"Mama, I looked up Jeremy on Facebook last month and his information page still lists him as single. He will probably always be single. Mama you know that old saying, 'get off the pot or...' Well, he just wouldn't get off the pot. He's still waiting on what I don't know. I asked him was it my size, my hair, my degree that made him not commit? He didn't have an answer. Oh well, I can't worry about that now." Jillian said.

Jillian knew how many mistakes she had made with men. She tried so hard to make them love her. She lost weight, gained weight, weaved in hair, took hair out, bought new clothes and got rid of old clothes. She was available to listen to the guy when they called. Not too available, as her sister Monica warned, because you appear needy and anxious. It was a mess in every effort. Jillian was tired of trying to make somebody love her. The level of emotion and commitment that she placed into each relationship still plagued her today. Not to mention, the expense of dating. The investment in the right clothes, every hair is always in place and not to mention making sure your nails are done. Jillian knew expensive it was to maintain nails when you spent the hours daily typing on a computer keyboard. When was somebody going to love her for her? When is somebody going to take me as I am and let me be me?

"Baby, I think both of those guys couldn't have handled your success anyway. I spent 50 years working and living as a wife and partner with your father. I was brought up in a day that emphasized the man being the head and in control. Your father and I were partners. He asked my advice on a lot of things. We worked together. I helped your father build, run and work in his business, take care of you girls, keep a neat house and still work in the church. Jillian, when God brings your husband, he will be able to deal with and celebrate all areas of your life. You won't be his trophy. You will be his helpmate, friend, lover, partner, advisor, cheerleader and wife. On top of that, he will love and be attracted to what you look like on the inside and out." Jillian's mom, Delores stated.

Jillian fought tears.

"Thanks mama for that advice. You are my best friend and I love you very much," Jillian said quietly.

Just then, Jillian's house phone rang. "Hold on mama." The caller id said, Vernice Washington. "Mama, this is Vernice, I better take this."

"Okay, talk to you later. Have a good night." Ms. Delores said as she hung up the phone.

Jillian quickly switched calls. "Hey girl, what's up chickie? How are you?" said Jillian lightly. She was glad to hear from her friend.

"I am fine girl," said Vernice.

"I was talking to my mama on the other line"

"I thought so. How is your mama doing?" Vernice asked. She loved Ms. Delores. She was a mother to so many.

"She's fine and going strong. You know my mama is going to enjoy life until she dies and goes to heaven. She keeps busy. She cracks me up saying she is visiting the senior citizens when she is in fact a senior citizen herself." Jillian let out a small laugh as she sat back down on the couch to talk to her longtime friend.

"I know that's right. I have known your entire family all of my 40 plus years and your mom has not changed a bit. She was always outgoing and fun to be around; not like those other mean older ladies. Not to mention looking forward to each Sunday and what big hat she was going to wear. I looked up at her in those beautiful hats and thought, 'how is she keeping that big thing on her head?'

"You too? I was in the house with her and saw her put the hats on and still wondered. My mama always and still does love her hats. My daddy liked to see mama in those big hats too."

"I know you miss him."

"Yep, you know I do. I am a daddy's girl in spite of it all. He's was my daddy, my hero." Jillian recalled.

"Listen girl, I just called to touch base. I got your email that you were having a conference committee meeting tonight. How did it go?" inquired Vernice.

Vernice and Jillian discussed the night's meeting and then Vernice's cell phone beeped, "Jillian, hold on a minute."

Jillian loved talking to Vernice because she was so fun, lighthearted and easy going. She hated when Vernice moved away to Chicago when she got married. They both celebrated about the wedding and the marriage, but Jillian missed her friend. Jillian took a brief look around her living room and began thinking of all the things that she should be and wanted to be doing right now. Take a hot shower.

Have some raspberry sherbet. Get in the bed and watch T.V. She enjoyed talking to her friend, but the bed was calling her name.

"Sorry about that Jillian, but that was Sister Erma on the phone."

"Vernice, why don't you call her back and conference her in?" Jillian asked.

"Okay I'll try, but you know how I am. Hold on and I'll give it a try," Jillian waited a few minutes more while her friend worked with her phone to get all three women on the call.

"Jillian?"

"Yes, I'm here."

"Sister Jamison?

"Yes, I'm here too," Sister Erma answered.

"I did it! I just can't believe it. Jillian knows that I can be technology challenged with my phone and have cut people off and didn't mean to." All three women laughed.

"How is everything in Houston, Sister Jamison?" asked Jillian.

"Chile' the same ole, same ole. God is still good, the devil is still a liar and people are still crazy," said Sister Jamison with a laugh.

Jillian and Vernice both chimed in with, "I know that's right."

"One thing for sure, things are the same everywhere then. I was telling Vernice that we had a team meeting tonight and had some additional logistical questions. Pamela is going to email the questions to Vernice and look for a response later this week," said Jillian.

"You know Jillian, I have been doing these conferences for 35 years and know where I am best suited. My expertise is on the phone prior to the conference and on the ground during the conference. You young ladies will have to handle the technology and let me know what I need to do. I will await a call from Vernice for any details that I need to move forward on my end," said Sis. Jamison.

"If only more people were like you Sis. Erma. People need to be doing what they should be doing and the world would be a much better place," added Jillian.

"Child you have said a mouthful right there," added Sister Jamison.

"Listen, I'm getting sleepy, I have to ask Sister Erma, how are your children and grandchildren doing?"

"Jillian, physically they are great and doing well. Pray for me and them, is all I can say. Emotionally and spiritually they get so easily off target and make me work so hard encouraging and praying them through. I want them to grow all of the way up and be all that God called them to be," Sister Erma said.

"That's what I would want for my child," inserted Vernice.

"Don't let Sister Jamison fool you Vernice, she has spoiled her children rotten," Jillian stated.

"No, let's not say spoiled Jillian, just well taken care of," Sister Erma added.

"Okay, I'll let you have that Sister Jamison.

"Well, being a widow so young and raising them by myself didn't help matters none. I put all of my energies into three things, God, my children and then work," said Sister Jamison.

"Okay Sis Jamison, your children are grown and you have grandchildren now. Would you marry again if a man asked you?" Jillian asked putting her on the spot.

"Chile', I am too old, need some teeth and don't no man want no old woman who needs some new teeth." The ladies laughed on the phone at the thought.

"You can buy some teeth and there are some cute old widowed men with good pensions who need some TLC out there," said Jillian.

"Chile', go on we have gotten way off the subject. I am going to be your second mother right now and say it is past your bed time," said Sister Jamison.

"You say that because I am all up in your business," said Jillian.

"All up in my Kool-Aid and what is the flavor?" asked Sis. Jamison

"Grape," said Vernice.

"You girls can stay up all night talking. This old lady got to get some shut eye. Let's have a word of prayer before we go."

"That's great," said Jillian.

"Yes Ma'am," said Vernice.

"Father, we thank you for one more day. We thank you for these two young women who are working in your kingdom. God, continue to bless and protect them as they go about their daily lives, on their jobs and as they travel from day to day. Give them wisdom and knowledge in their every endeavor. Bless them with all provision, good husbands and families. Bless this conference. We bless you forever. In Jesus' name I pray and for your sake alone. Amen. Love you girls, goodnight," Sister Erma said sweetly.

"Love you Sis. Jamison," said Vernice.

"Talk with you Sis. Jamison and love you too," said Jillian.

"Good night," said Sis. Jamison.

"Sister Jamison, I will call you tomorrow," said Vernice.

"Okay. I will be here." Sister Jamison's phone went silent.

"Okay girl, we will talk later on this week," said Vernice.

"I know that's right. I look forward to hearing from you. Have a good night and a great week," said Jillian.

"Love you girl."

"Love you right back."

When Jillian hung up the phone she said thank you to God for good friends but more importantly, she thanked God for her family. Maybe somebody wonderful will show up at the conference for all of them. You never know what God has in store. God you know what we need. Bless us all, amen.

Chapter 2

It was another pleasant, cool day in Cincinnati. Today was Thursday and Jillian could tell that the season was about to change because there was a cool breeze coming through the office parking garage into the building this morning.

When she approached the lobby, Marvin was in his usual place and she knew that all was going to be right with the world.

On the elevator, Jillian suddenly started humming the song "Dream" by Shirley Murdock while checking out her reflection in the elevator. She had on her new black pantsuit, shoes and bag matching, ponytail hanging long and straight, thanks to her hairstylist. The suit was a little heavier than usual so it would warm and protect her from the cooling temperatures. The doors opened and Jillian saw Patricia pouring over some documents intently.

"Good morning, Patricia."

"Good morning Jillian," said Patricia, as she looked up ever so slightly with that dent in her forehead and frown around her mouth.

Jillian then stated, "Patricia, I can tell by that look on your face that something is wrong. Did Taylor & Edwards send back the contracts signed?" Jillian placed her belongings on Patricia's desk temporarily waiting for an answer.

"Yes, they were just messengered over right before you came in. They also attached a list of other services they are interested in us providing.

They want a separate cost quote immediately," Patricia said in a very dry tone.

"That's great! So what's the problem?" Jillian was ecstatic until she looked back at Patricia's face.

"Our computers have been running extremely slow lately and we need to determine what the issue is. Is the problem the computers, the server or the databases we are accessing? Since Taylor & Edwards has outsourced 90% of their information research services to us, our information managers need to turn things around in a timely manner. Otherwise, we could lose the contract," added a concerned Patricia.

"You are exactly right. I have been thinking about that, but I want to hold on to all of the money we have until the contracts are signed."

"Well now is not the time to wait on that. We need to think economically about what we purchase, but we must maximize the speed and dependability," said Patricia.

"I will check with the comptroller immediately to determine where we stand financially. You get on the phone and try to find out who we should get to analyze and solve our computer problems pronto. We need one with confidentiality clearance with Taylor & Edwards," Jillian said, while gathering her things.

"Wait Jillian, why don't we try to contact the computer services they use for their server maintenance and hopefully, we can get a good deal on the services we need. It will save time on confidentiality problems and compatibility issues with their servers." Patricia said.

"Great idea! Let's get on it right away. Patricia you are the best." With her things in her hands, Jillian turned and walked in her office thanking God she had a great assistant. Jillian knew that the key to any great organization was its people and not just the president, or visionary CEO. Fortunately, Jillian didn't have a problem acknowledging and celebrating the value and strengths of each team member.

By lunchtime, Jillian had received a report that indicated the amount of money they were able to spend for the equipment. Patricia made several phone calls and found the technology company that they needed. The company representatives were headed to Forrester at 3:00 p.m. to take a walk through and to discuss their needs and concerns.

Patricia walked into Jillian's office closed the door quickly and fell backward against the door. Her eyes were upward and her body language said that she was about to faint and slide to the floor "Okay boss indulge me just a minute."

"What going on? Besides you only call me boss when you could be in trouble or you're getting ready to hurt somebody." Jillian inquired

"Jillian, I'm about to put a hurting on somebody in a minute, but in a great way," Patricia said softly.

"What's up?" Jillian exclaimed.

"The representatives from Randolph Technologies are waiting to see you in the lobby. I have never seen three brothers look so good since my favorite group, 'Guy,' back in the day," Patricia closed her eyes and did a slight shake and shimmy from her shoulders to her waist.

"Okay, Patricia, your minute is up and the key to this company not going down the toilet is on the other side of that door. Girl, get a grip and show them in," said Jillian with a slight frown.

"Okay, are you ready?" Patricia straightened her clothes and mimicked putting her hair back in place.

"Yes, I am ready and show them in already," Jillian then gave Patricia a sharp look while putting the last papers in a folder and coming from behind her desk.

Patricia opened the door to the lobby and said to the visitors, "Gentleman, Ms. Forrester will see you now." Three very handsome gentleman entered Jillian's office.

Patricia continued, "Ms. Forrester, this is Mr. Byron and Myron Randolph, the CEO and President, respectively of Randolph Technologies and their associate, Mr. James Jones."

"Jillian, is that you?" asked Byron as he stopped dead in his tracks at the sight of her face. Byron took a long sweep over Jillian from head to toe. Letting his eyes thoroughly glance over every inch of her body. Jillian was checking Byron out right back and blushing greatly on the inside and out. Jillian was thanking God that her milk chocolate skin could hide how hot her cheeks were getting at Byron's glance. Jillian remembered that Byron was always the ladies' man of the two. She knew that she couldn't take what he said seriously because he could be saying it to about three other women too. His eyes were saying a lot and she was trying to believe the clear non-verbal communication. Byron and Myron were both classified as nerds, but Myron was the real nerd of the two. Besides loving technology, Byron and Myron were unique in that they were identical twins in size and height, but with different color complexion. Both men stood six feet three and weighed about 225 lbs. Byron had dark smooth chocolate skin while Myron had a lighter brown complexion like caramel candy. Studies had been done about the twins when they were younger. Their doctor wrote and published an article in a medical journal about their uniqueness.

"Jillian Forrester, look at you?" interrupted Myron who had been standing next to Byron watching them both and waiting his turn.

"Oh my goodness, yes, it's me. Byron and Myron Randolph? Look at you guys. I had no idea. I realize that this is unorthodox and not the way I normally start a business meeting, but can I have a hug?" They all laughed as Jillian embraced each twin, Myron first and then Byron. They smelled like Yves Saint

Laurent's latest cologne and dressed in similar clothing, but not matching tailored suits. The days of the twins wearing matching outfits had been abandoned by the time they reached their middle teens. Byron, being the mischievous one, took both her hands in his once the embrace ended and he slightly swayed them back and forth. He stood there holding and gently rubbing her hands in a slow circular motion that left Jillian quite uncomfortable. Byron knew he was wrong, but didn't want to let her hands go. He kept looking into her eyes to gage her reaction and to soak her all in.

Byron thought, 'Oh my goodness this is Jillian Forrester standing right in front of me.' Byron tried not to reveal with his eyes all of the rush of emotions that were going on in his head not to mention the fast beat of his heart at the sight of her. He thought, 'If she only knew how good it is to really see her. Get a grip and calm down boy.'

A look of confusion came on Jillian's face at how Byron was looking at her. She never dated or even had any thought that Byron even liked her other than a friend when they were younger. What is this? Jillian looked down at the floor quickly realizing that this was suddenly a very awkward and misunderstood moment. They both forgot they were in a corporate office and that there were other people in the room. Jillian had so many questions running through her brain. Byron, on the other hand, was continuing to take her all in. Jillian knew that she must somehow stop this scene from getting any worse or misreading the whole situation. She came back to herself from her thoughts in time to remember she was ignoring the third man in the room. She removed her hands from Byron's grasp and turned her attention to the other gentleman.

"I am so sorry your name is James right? I don't know you that well or I would hug you too." Everyone laughed as she shook his hand. James was much taller standing about six foot five and two hundred sixty five pounds. He looked like he could be a defensive end or tackle for the Cincinnati Bengals or some celebrity's body guard. This very large, gorgeous gentleman was standing there with an iPad, leather portfolio and iPhone. At five foot three, Jillian felt like a midget compared to these three men. Jillian enjoyed the sudden attention and affection, but knew they must get down to business.

"Well, shall we all have a seat?" Each man took a seat around Jillian's small conference table and Byron placed himself to her left, Myron was on her right and James was seated next to Myron.

Jillian began the meeting by stating, "Thank you gentlemen so much for coming on such short notice." She made sure that she looked at every man at table and not just Byron.

"You are quite welcome. We were already in Cincinnati when we got the call from our administrative team. We were told that you are a contractor for Taylor & Edwards so we knew that it was a priority and that your credibility was good. We just didn't know how well until now," said Byron looking at Jillian again with that intense look.

"Thanks so much. I consider that a great compliment," said Jillian.

"We have some idea of what you need, but need more details. With each client, we require a full diagnostic to be done on your technological and electrical infrastructure. Can you give us a little bit of history about your company that we can't find out easily searching Google™ about Forrester?" asked Myron.

"As you both know, but James does not, I have always been an avid reader and book worm. I have a Bachelor's degree in business administration, but needed a part-time job. So I got a job in a library in college. I loved libraries so I attended Michigan to get my Masters in Library Science. After graduation, I came back to Cincinnati to work for Taylor & Edwards working as an information manager. After five years on staff, they announced that they were going to outsource the information management portion of the company. I registered my company, wrote a proposal, put in a bid for the contract and won. They wanted to give the contract to someone that they knew and trusted, which is me. The reason why you have been called is that with the renewed Information Research contract for Taylor & Edwards, they have added more services to the initial contract. We have been experiencing computer problems of late and need to make sure that our systems can handle the new influx of service. The second reason we called you, is that you already have the IT Support contract with Taylor & Edwards. You have strict confidentiality agreements, security clearance, a long standing and established relationship." James and Myron were making quick notes on their iPads of all that Jillian had said. Byron on the other hand, just kept his eyes strictly on Jillian's face.

"How fast do you need the diagnostic work done?" Myron asked.

"Everything on your end needs to be done as soon as possible because our new contract begins in three weeks. We need to get our infrastructure in place with as few hiccups as possible," added Jillian.

"First, thanks so much for giving us a call. We both want to keep Taylor & Edwards happy. Secondly, we need to take a walk through and examine your systems. If it's possible, we need to do that today so we can get a better understanding of what we are working with. James is our senior project manager. Because we are working with you and Taylor & Edwards we will make sure that we give this assignment top priority and undivided attention," Byron said in a very professional voice, but his eyes were saying something else.

Jillian looked into Byron's eyes striving to remain calm, cool and collected. Inside, her stomach was doing flip flops.

Jillian could hear her sister saying in her head, 'stay cool and don't read more into this than it is. This is business.' Jillian repeated this phrase over and over in her head. Jillian dropped her eyes to look at her iPad quickly to avoid his gaze and to pretend to be looking at some notes. This is business, oh yes, this is business.

"Sure, we can take a walk through right now of our facilities." Everyone stood and proceeded out of office. Jillian stopped at Patricia's desk before moving forward and asked, "Patricia, we are going to take a walk through. Can you stay until we return or do you have to leave right away?"

"No, I can stay as long as you need me," Patricia looked at Jillian with a wink.

"Great, we'll be right back," Jillian looked back at Patricia and gave her that 'what's up with you?' look. Jillian didn't know what had come over Patricia, but she was going to ask her about it later. There is something about a fine and professional and hopefully, eligible gentlemen which makes some women do and say things totally out of their character.

Jillian escorted the three gentlemen through the various areas of the operation giving a general overview of the layout, work flow, current and future potential technological needs. Byron asked questions regarding the hardware and software needs and made suggestions or critiques when appropriate. Myron took into consideration the training needs for learning any new hardware or software that could be installed. James' role was taking notes, offering assistance, providing feedback and/or suggestions when necessary. Jillian was impressed with their skill and expertise. More than impressed, she was proud of them. She knew the Randolph twins personally and now professionally. Their tour brought them back to the front door of her office. When they entered her office, Jillian immediately wanted to know each of their thoughts. Jillian went to open the door to her office, but Byron was much quicker. He reached the door handle and let her go through first. "After you ma'am."

"Thank you, sir." Jillian replied.

Myron quickly looked at Byron and whispered, "Can you be a little less obvious? Slow your roll my brother."

Byron mouthed to Myron, 'What did I do?'

James said nothing. He rolled his eyes instead and shook his head at the exchange of the brothers. The three caught up to Jillian quickly and reassembled at her conference table.

"So what do you think?" Jillian was the first to break the silence.

"It's quite impressive," said Myron.

"You have done a wonderful job Jillian," added Byron. "There is always room for improvement and that is where we can assist."

They each sat down at the table and discussed thoroughly the various options for technical improvement of Forrester. Jillian was delighted by their attention to detail as well as an attempt to keep the budget low and affordable.

"Well, I don't have any more questions or concerns. What are our next steps?" Jillian asked.

"Since there is an immediate need, we will develop and email a proposal detailing the services we can provide, costs on the equipment and training needs as well as a turn-around time for project completion based on our notes today," added Myron.

"I will be the contact person to oversee proper installation and schedule any training with your employees once an agreement has been reached. I will be the one to make sure that we stay on target for the project completion date," stated James.

"Patricia will be your contact on this end for scheduling of installations and training, etc. with our various department heads. Here is my card for each of you, just in case, you have any questions for me," Jillian handed each man a business card. Byron looked at the front and back of the card quickly realizing that there was no cell number displayed only the office phone number.

"Jillian, just in case I have a question, is there another number that is best for after hours?" asked Byron.

"Sure, let me have the card and put my cell number on the back." replied Jillian. 'Lord, get this man out of my office so I can breathe,' thought Jillian. Byron never took his eyes off of Jillian as he handed her business card to her to place her number on the back. 'Lord, what's up with that?' Jillian asked herself. She knew already that doing business with the Randolph twins was going to be an adventure.

"There you are," Jillian replied.

"Thank you so much. We will be meeting in the morning and I will contact you as soon as the proposal is ready," replied Byron. Myron and James were preoccupied with their iPads and cell phones to notice the exchange between Byron and Jillian. To the untrained ear and eye, it looked like any other networking session with the transfer of business cards, but Byron knew that there could be the potential for something more. He saw no picture of a wedding or husband or child on the desk in her office so she probably wasn't married. Was there a boyfriend in the mix? Byron didn't know just yet, but he was going to find out more, much more. Jillian was afraid to even think about how much more contact Byron was going to have with her.

"Is there anything else you need from me? I don't want to keep you from the I-75 North traffic. I know how hectic that can be." Jillian asked.

"You are so right. I think I am fine with the information I have," stated Myron as he stood from his chair at the table, "I drove separately from Byron and I have another stop to make. So I am going to be on my way. Jillian, I look forward to doing business with you. It is great seeing you again and we shall be in touch soon." Myron extended and shook her hand before finally leaving.

"I have all of the information I need as well. I will stop by your assistance's desk to get her contact information," added James. "Good night Ms. Forrester, it was a pleasure meeting you and there is more to come." Both men headed out the door quickly which left only Jillian and Byron alone in her office.

"Thank you both so much. Have a great evening and safe travels."

Myron kept walking to the elevator but James stopped at Patricia's desk. Patricia was acting busy by surfing the web. When James approached her desk, Patricia looked up and said, "How can I help you, sir?"

"Ms. Forrester has stated that you will be the contact to coordinate the installations of equipment and setting up training sessions."

"Yes, that's me," a fully alert Patricia answered.

"I am going to need your contact information. Do you have a card?" James asked.

"Here's my card and my personal cell number is on the back," Patricia usually didn't place her number on the back of her professional card unless it was a gentleman that she wanted to get in touch with her.

"Thank you very much and we shall be in touch soon. Have a great day, Ms. Johnson," said James as he turned and headed toward the elevator. Patricia's eyes followed him all the way to the elevator until he stepped in and was out of sight.

Meanwhile back in Jillian's office, the office suddenly became private, quiet and intimate with the other two gentlemen gone.

"So, Byron, have we finished our business here or is there something else you need from me?"

"I have all I need business wise. Since I am hungry and I need to eat, would you have dinner with me tonight or do you have a previous engagement?"

"Uh, well, no," Jillian stammered trying to find the right words to say. She hadn't been asked out on a date in a very long time. She was suddenly very nervous. Her knees were shaking, her mouth became bone dry and her head was spinning with all types of questions.

Jillian finally found her voice and said, "My calendar is free, but let me check in with Patricia to make sure there have been no new developments."

Jillian knew there had been no new developments or Patricia would have mentioned it or interrupted her earlier after they returned from the tour. What she needed was a moment to get herself together. Jillian stood slowly so she could make steady her knees as she headed toward the door. Closing it behind her she mouthed to Patricia, 'Oh my God.'

"What? What?" said Patricia in a loud whisper anxious to know what was happening inside Jillian's office.

"He just asked me out for dinner. Why am I so nervous? I have known this guy since we were kids. Why does he make me nervous now?" Jillian asked under her breath.

"Girl, 'cuz he is no longer a little boy or a kid, he is a fully, grown gorgeous, financially secure man. Duh?"

"Girl, you better believe all that you just said, makes the difference. I need to calm down, it's just dinner right?

"Right," Patricia lowers her voice to a soft whisper, "tell me how it goes in the morning."

Jillian stated in her natural voice, just in case Byron was listening, "Patricia, are there any new developments since my meeting?"

"No Jillian, there are no new developments or anything that you have to take care of here." Patricia almost laughed trying to act natural and still carry on this farce of a conversation.

Patricia whispered, "What's the problem?"

Jillian whispered back, "He is so fine and an old friend. I usually mess up somewhere with these situations. I probably should go straight home and do this another time. I am being a chicken, right?"

Patricia mouthed again, "Oh good grief, a big chicken at that. You'll be fine. Go for it."

Walking back in the office, Jillian found Byron looking at the books on her shelf. Jillian stopped at the door and broke the silence and interrupted his browsing by saying, "find anything interesting to read?"

Byron turned at the sound of Jillian's voice and put the book back on the shelf where he had found it and replied, "Yes, you have some great books here. You know I have always hated reading."

"I remember," Jillian said calmly. "You always teased me that I would die with a book in my hand because I was always reading during our breaks at conference. I told you that you would die with some gadget in your hands because you were always trying to fix something," Jillian laughed.

Byron chuckled as he walked from the book shelf to stand right in front of her. He looked into her eyes and said, "You remembered that?"

Jillian looked away from his intense gaze and said, "Of course, I remember pretty much everything that happened at conference each year."

"That's good to know," Byron made a mental note.

Needing to suddenly move out of his personal space, Jillian moved to the comfort zone behind her desk. She looked down at an imaginary calendar and said, "Well it looks like everything is in order here and I can go to dinner with you. Do you have a place in mind where we should eat this evening?"

She knew she could have fun with Byron no matter where they ate. She also looked forward to a night of male companionship. It was also a nice change to be approached by a man that was flirting with some heat. Let the games begin.

Byron walked over to her desk and stated, "I've been so busy I haven't had a chance to visit *Pappadeaux's Seafood* since they have opened. How does that sound?"

"That sounds great. You have been really busy if you haven't gotten to *Pappadeaux's Seafood.* Let me get my things." Jillian picked up her purse, assembled her business bag and grabbed her jacket on the stand by her desk. Secretly Jillian wished she had worn a skirt or other girly clothes, but this was spur of the moment so Byron would have to take her as is. She stopped at the conference table to put on her jacket. Byron was close by so he said, "let me help you." He took the jacket from her and held it open while she put her arms through.

"Thank you."

"You are quite welcome. Do you want me to follow you or shall we ride together?" Byron asked.

"Well, I would love to change and I don't live too far? Why don't you follow me home? It will take about ten minutes and then we can leave from there. Is that alright?" asked Jillian as she turned to pick up her purse and bag from the table.

"Don't change on my account. You look fine. If changing clothes will make you more comfortable, what the lady wants the lady gets," Byron stated while facing her at the office door.

Jillian paused and blushed hot all over at the mere thought of getting whatever she wanted from Byron Randolph. Trying to keep it casual, Jillian went a little *sister girl* on him.

"Look at you being all accommodating. I must discover how you got all suave and debonair from the young man who used to boss everybody around. Walking around with the 'my way or the highway' attitude," teased Jillian.

"I was young then. I realize that pleasing someone else does not diminish your own pleasure, but heightens it. So, I aim to please," smiled Byron. Jillian wished for the professional Byron because this sexy man was making her say way too many prayers.

"Well, I walked right into that one. On that note, I must walk out of this office door," said Jillian.

Byron was raised a gentleman and since he was closest to the door he held it open while she passed through.

"Good night Patricia," said Jillian as she passed Patricia's desk.

"Good night Jillian. Good night Mr. Randolph."

"Good night Patricia," said Byron as he headed toward the elevator. At the elevator, he pushed the button and held the doors opened when it arrived. He offered to carry her things, but she declined. Jillian's mind was racing trying to make sure she didn't say or do the wrong thing.

Going down the elevator they were both quiet and deep in thoughts. When the doors opened on the first floor, Jillian exited and was met by Marvin, the security guard. "Marvin, this is Mr. Byron Randolph. Byron this is Marvin. Marvin I am headed out for the evening, take care of everything."

"Will do, Ms. Forrester. Have a great night."

Turning back to Marvin, she asked, "How is your baby doing?"

"Eating, sleeping, pooping, crying, playing and growing," laughed Marvin and he stared at the picture on his desk proudly.

"That's what I like to hear," laughed Jillian and Byron gave Marvin a slight smile.

"What, did he have a new baby or something?" Byron asked as they headed out of the door toward the elevator to the garage.

Jillian turned to face Byron and said, "Yes, his wife just had a baby about a month ago. He is so proud."

"Do you want babies Jillian?" inquired Byron while looking into her eyes for an answer.

"What a question to ask before we even get to the restaurant?" chuckled Jillian.

"That's not an answer," insisted Byron while waiting patiently.

"You just dive right in don't you?

"No time like the present," Byron pressed.

"Let me think about it and let you know," Jillian replied in a soft tone. She hadn't thought about it lately because she wasn't dating anyone. Babies were out of the question in Jillian's book unless you have a husband.

Switching the subject and continuing toward the garage, Jillian asked, "Where are you parked?"

"Second level. Where are you?"

"I'm right here."

"Yes, that's the benefit of being the boss."

"You are right. One day I am going to check out your parking space. You probably don't park your car in a garage at all. You just put your car into an elevator and you get out directly at a private entrance into your office. Right?"

"Something like that."

"For real? I can't wait to see that." Jillian knew that was the first real stupid thing she had said already. Strike one. She sounded like a fifteen year old seeing the circus for the first time. Jillian new she sounded goofy. Byron didn't seem to mind. He just smiled and was intent on hearing her every word.

"I want you to see that too." Those words came out of Byron's mouth like a command more than a desire.

Jillian willed her mouth to stay shut and her eyes to show no reaction to his statement. She swallowed hard, masked her astonishment and said, "I will wait for you here. I am in a copper car."

"What model?" Byron asked.

"An M-Class," Jillian said nonchalantly, but inside, feeling so much pride. She had wanted a new car after holding onto her Toyota Camry until Forrester was more financially stable. A Mercedes was her dream car and her father would have been so proud that she was able to purchase it on her own.

"I'll be in a red R-Class."

"Show off. You are still as competitive as always. You take everything to the next level," Jillian teased.

"Takes one to know one," replied Byron.

"I haven't heard that in a long time."

"We are definitely in our 40's."

"For sure, see you when you come down the ramp to this level."

"Go ahead, because I want to make sure that you get to your car safely."

"Okay," said Jillian. She realized that he was watching her walk away. She put a little feminine wiggle in her walk. Not too much, but just enough to let him know that she was all woman under this pant suit.

Jillian drove through Cincinnati looking in her rearview mirror to make sure that she didn't lose Byron at a stop light. She had a pet peeve about getting lost and people driving too fast when a car is following them.

She made a point to slow up and stop at all yellow lights. If the person in other car got caught by a red light, she would pull over and wait for them.

As she stopped at a yellow light, her cell phone rang.

"Hello."

"You can stop slowing down at the yellow lights, now. You are not going too fast. I am following close behind you and I won't get lost."

"Okay, I am sorry. I have a pet peeve about getting lost. Even more so, I don't like for others to get lost."

"Did you forget that you gave me your cell number?"

"I think I have a little ADD and forgot that. I'll drive a little faster and keep moving. Are you as hungry as I am?"

"I am famished."

"Great. I won't be long getting changed at the house. Bye." Jillian felt better about driving faster and really stupid all at the same time. Strike two. She had just given him her number. 'He must think I am a real nut,' Jillian thought. 'Maybe that is the reason why it has taken so long to even get a date? I am so absent minded about some things and end up being embarrassed. Lord, help me stop being so nervous, worrisome and awkward around men. Byron is somebody I should be comfortable with and able to be myself. Oh well, he hasn't decided against eating dinner with me so I will make the most of it.' With that thought in mind, she pulled into her garage and parking space. Each owner had his own parking space and a guest space right next to him. Byron pulled in next to Jillian and that made Jillian feel better already. Oh how she had longed for that space to be filled by someone at one time or another. Jillian got out of her car and walked to Byron's window. "Do you want to come upstairs?"

"Sure."

Gathering her things, they proceeded to the building entrance and passed security. "Good evening Ms. Forrester," said the guard on duty.

"Good evening, Bob."

"That must be great to have security on duty 24/7," Byron said. The elevator door opened and they entered.

"Yes, it is."

"What floor?" Byron asked as he looked at the panel of numbers indicating each floor.

"The twelfth floor. I have to put in my key to get to that floor," Byron stood back while Jillian put her key in the slot next to the number twelve.

"The security is great here. My parents were glad to know when I moved here that there were security guards on duty. My dad was always protective of his two girls. We always teased my dad that he was scary about everything. He could sometimes think of the worst case scenarios for every situation."

"How is your mom since your father passed away? I am sorry we didn't get to the funeral, but Myron and I were out of the country on an assignment. My mom and dad said that they came to the funeral," Byron said in an even, caring tone.

"My mom is doing fine. They were married 50 years and I think she thinks about him all the time. I know I do, especially during the holidays. He loved family. He protected and defended them whether they were right or wrong. You're right. I do remember seeing your parents at my father's funeral. That day is still a blur for me." Jillian finished that statement as they walked off the elevator with her key in her hand. She placed the key into her door lock and as she entered the living room, turned the lamp on. The nights were coming earlier since the time change. The living room was already dim with only a small shadow of light from the setting sun. Jillian loved to open her blinds and let in the sun and light of the new day. On the twelfth floor, Jillian had a great view.

"Have a seat I will be right out."

"This is a nice place," Byron called out to her.

"Thanks. Make yourself comfortable," Jillian called back out to him. She moved quickly into her bedroom and closed the door. Fortunately the bathroom was located in her master bedroom. She didn't have to worry about being covered as she was getting dressed. Her mother always said that women are fine in pants, but men still like to see women in dresses sometimes. She said it brought out the femininity of a woman and would attract a real man. Jillian didn't know all of the laws of attraction, but this new black knit dress felt good, looked good on her and made her look smaller in size. Hallelujah, success.

Byron was looking at her book collection when she returned.

"See anything you like?" inquired Jillian. She was standing in a knee length black knit dress, black hose, black shoes, cute black bag to match with a red wrap over her arm for the night air.

Byron looked up, "Yes, I like everything I see." Byron was looking directly at her and no longer interested in any book on the shelf. From the look on Byron's face, Jillian made the right choice in what to wear.

Suddenly blushing again and hoping he didn't take it the wrong way Jillian quickly added, "I'm sorry I was talking about the books."

"I know what you were talking about, but I also know what I saw on the shelf and who I am seeing across the room. As I said before, I do see something I like very much," he said with a slow and sly smile. "Are you ready to go?"

Jillian suddenly looked down to look away from Byron's gaze. She was trying to regain her composure because her keys were in her hand. She was somehow fumbling to check inside her purse. "I have my keys so yes, I am ready.

"Let's go," Byron said as he held the door open while Jillian turned out the lights. When the door closed, it was the beginning of an adventure for them both. Always the gentleman, Byron made sure that Jillian was safe, secure on and off of the elevator until they reached his car. Once they were both settled in the car with seat belts fastened, Jillian was the first to break the silence.

"I think that this is what you call a super tricked out car?"

"I guess so why?"

"I feel like I am in a car made for 'James Bond' with all of these controls on a console that look like they should be in a military vehicle."

"I can't tell you all of the details because they are classified. Randolph Tech does do experimental testing of a lot of products. We are testing some devices to see if they should how they could be added to all cars, but economically. So I agreed to test out some of the features on my car."

"Wow, look at you. I am going to have to be in careful in this car because I don't want to be ejected out of the seat like in the movies," Jillian and Bryon both laughed at that thought.

"That wouldn't be fun in that pretty dress," stated Byron.

"You got that right. What's this device here? It looks like an old beeper. I know you are too high tech for a beeper or does it do something else?" asked Jillian as she pointed to a device in the console.

"This device looks like a beeper, but in actuality, it is a prototype device to contact emergency help like the "on-star" services in your car, it can act as a phone, video camera and a television as well. With this device, you don't dial or tap, you just talk. Your voice is programmed and you just say cell, police, TV, video or just the word help."

"This is for the 'I've fallen and I can't get up' kind of help as well as a TV?" Jillian asked.

"Exactly. It's called the Randolph AT-100 for now."

"That sounds interesting and hopefully, profitable."

"I agree." Byron responded while watching her face.

"Do you realize that we have been sitting here in this car for ten minutes talking? You haven't started the car yet? I think I should stop talking so we can get going."

"You are fine. I enjoy talking to you. I always have. Even though we haven't spoken in years, Jillian, you have always been easy to talk to," Byron said.

"Thank you."

"I can see that you are still a geek just like me and Myron?"

"Exactly. My sister and I just didn't like to get dirty. We just loved to play games with you guys."

"You and your sister were always asking us how they worked."

"We didn't have brothers so we thought you guys were different and neat."

"Among other things other people called us."

"We didn't care what other people called you. You were our friends and protectors. We had a blast with you guys."

"Thanks." They both smiled at the memories.

The car was suddenly silent so Byron turned on the stereo that filled the car with Bose powered smooth jazz.

"That's a nice song," stated Jillian.

"Do you still sing?" asked Byron.

"Yes, every Sunday."

"My parents, Myron and I always talked about your singing when we would come home from the conferences. Even when you were a child, the crowd would be on their feet when you sang. The National Sunshine Choir always seemed to sing more times than was posted on the program so we could hear you sing again. I remember when you sang that time in Nashville. What was it?"

"The song was 'Weeping may endure for a night.'"

"That was it! It started out slow and then got fast at the end."

"You remembered," said Jillian.

"Of course, I remembered," said Byron, "Little do you know I pretty much remember every song you sang with the choir."

"Yea, everything except the title, but thank you anyway," giggled Jillian.

"Throw cold water on my compliment," Byron said.

"Oh my, he is sensitive. You know I was just teasing. Well, Lord, I was ten that night in Nashville and so scared that I thought I was going to throw up. I just held on to the microphone, closed my eyes and opened my mouth. I never once looked at the crowd or at the director just listened to the changes in the music by the musicians," chuckled Jillian.

"Myron kept on singing, but I don't think I sang a note just watching you," said Byron.

"You never told me that before," Jillian stated.

"There are a lot of things I have not told you, but one day I will," Byron informed Jillian.

"I look forward to it. Speaking of the conference, I am on the planning committee as usual and this year's conference is going to be here," Jillian said.

"Yeah, my mom told me. She also said that dad was going to be one of the speakers. Myron and I should probably attend that night."

"Yes you should. It will be like old times. Your dad is an excellent speaker. He gets to the point and sits down. Not like some other preachers I know who don't know how and when to sit down. My dad used to say, 'he just didn't know how and when to land that plane. He was finished after about fifteen minutes, but he wouldn't shut up and sit down,' Jillian laughed out loud at the memory.

"Believe you me as the pastor's children, we have had to sit and listen to too many of those boring, repetitious messages. Just saying over and over, 'can the church say amen?' 'Slap your neighbor and say such and such' or 'I wish I had a praying church.' I said amen the first twenty times you said it. I don't want to slap my neighbor again because my hand hurts and we have been praying for thirty minutes now so it's time for you to sit down," Byron and Jillian laughed in agreement.

Byron continued, "My brother and I called my dad the thirty minute preacher. My dad can introduce, deliver, hoop with the organ and sit down in thirty minutes. He tells his young preachers, if you can't get your message across in thirty minutes or less, you don't have a message, you are just mumbling a mess."

"Oh, poor dear. The life of a Preacher's Kid (PK) is just so hard. You get your pick of all of the girls in the church, the preferential treatment at every function and all of the 'first family' benefits. How would you like to be the Deacon's Kid? We get treated badly and other kids roll their eyes at us and it wasn't our fault. Usually their parents were mad at some decision made by the deacons as to whether their parent's auxiliary request was approved or denied. The life of being a deacon's kid is really the hard life," Jillian said sarcastically.

Just then, the GPS announced, 'your destination should be located on the right.'

"Well, we could go rounds on that point. I don't know about you, but I am ready to eat," Byron announced.

"Agreed," Jillian said.

Byron pulled into the nearest parking space in Pappadeaux's parking lot. "Wait here and don't get out. I am coming to open the door. My mom would fuss at me if she found out that you opened the door yourself."

"I won't tell if you don't tell," smiled Jillian.

"Nope. It is my intention to give you get the full Randolph treatment," continued Byron as he unbuckled his seat belt.

Jillian gently laid her hand on Byron's arm which stopped him, "Thanks for telling me. Just so you know, I am not one of those women. I am independent, but I enjoy the chivalry of a gentleman very much," said Jillian.

"Jillian you are truly different," said Byron.

"I hope you mean that in a good way," Jillian continued to look at Byron still seated in the car.

"No, I mean it in the best way," Byron said softly.

"Great, let's go in before they close," smiled Jillian. Byron finally got out of the car, opened her door and gently took her hand to help her out. They continued up the walk way side by side to the restaurant entrance. After a quick check of table availability, they were escorted to their table and took their seats. Byron and Jillian quickly placed their orders and then waited for their food to arrive.

"So are you going to tell me whether you want to have babies now or later? I haven't forgotten my original question," insisted Byron.

"You still want to know?" Jillian said.

"Yes I want to know. We are here at the restaurant now and we didn't order an appetizer, so I want to know," Byron pressed the issue.

"I must confess that in my twenties I would have said yes immediately. Now, in my forties, I say no. Do you want babies, Byron?" asked Jillian.

"Like you, I would have loved to have had children in my twenties. Now I am concentrating on finding a wonderful woman in which to share my love, life and business with," stated Byron.

"I am surprised that you aren't already married," inquired Jillian.

"I am kind of surprised too. I've dated a lot, but honesty, I am a one woman man. When I am dating a woman, she is it. I formally break-up with her before dating someone else. I don't play the field, juggle multiple women or lie or cheat. I wasn't raised that way and don't feel comfortable doing that as well. I respect women too much because of my mom.

Secondly, I dated a woman and she cheated on me. That heartbreak hurt me to the core," Byron stated.

"Wow, did your mom like her?" Jillian asked.

"No, she didn't like or trust her on sight. I should have listened to my mom," Byron said regrettably.

"I realize that when you are in a relationship with someone it is with that person and not their family, but other people do have a sixth sense sometimes about things that we can't see ourselves. We are so involved with the person and looking at the good side, but not seeing or even wanting to look for the bad side of the person," stated Jillian.

"You are right," Byron said. Just then, the drinks and salads were delivered to the table.

"Byron, would you pray over the food?" Byron took one of Jillian's hands in his and began the prayer over their food much to Jillian's delight.

"Love to. Father we thank you for the food we are about to receive. Help it to nourish our bodies that we may serve you in spirit and in truth, Amen."

"Amen." Jillian thought to herself, 'thank you God for a man who can pray out loud even if it is over the food.'

"I just thought of something. Do you remember when Bishop Bell prayed over the food at the conference in Denver? He prayed so long that the food actually got cold," Byron said. They both laughed recalling that scene.

"Lord, yes. People were asking if they could have their food microwaved. Hungry Christians is an ugly situation. That also had to be one of the coldest conferences ever even in March. I don't think that we have been back to Denver since."

"How about the time when Mother Brewer shouted so hard that her slip fell out from under her dress?"

"Oh no, she tripped over her slip and then fell, her dress flew up and she had no underwear on. We were just talking about that on the conference page on Facebook not too long ago. That was a conference to remember. We laughed about that for months later. The lead mother on the mother's board went to her and talked to her about it. We would have been famous if we had had a video of her shouting and falling down."

"She probably would have sued somebody too."

"You are probably right."

"I can't keep up with that stuff online. I have too much work to do."

"You know what they say about all work and no play makes Byron…."

"A nerd," said Byron.

"No, a tired nerd," laughed Jillian. Byron and Jillian continued with that same light conversation throughout the rest of their meal and even after they had shared a dessert. The house lights came on in the restaurant and they realized that it was the staff's final hint for them to leave. They had set up all of the tables, re-filled the salt and pepper shakers and the carpet sweepers were on and almost done.

"Well, I guess that's our cue." Byron had long paid for the check, but they kept sitting at the table enjoying each other's company.

"Yes, they can't get any more obvious than that. Soon they are going to lock us in here and turn the lights completely out on us," added Jillian.

"Would that be too bad? You, me and total darkness?"

"Still the bad boy I see."

"Did you expect me to change?"

"No and I am glad that you haven't."

"I will take that as a compliment."

"It is."

The staff was pleasant but it was evident that they were tired and ready to go home. Byron and Jillian strolled arm and arm to his car.

"Your chariot awaits, madam," Byron said as they approached the car.

"Thank you, kind sir," Jillian replied. Byron opened the door for Jillian and made sure she was safely inside before closing the door.

"Well, I guess we caught up on at least the last ten years since we've seen each other during that dinner alone," said Byron, once he was settled in the driver's seat.

"That means we have about ten more years to go," smiled Jillian.

"Yes, we do," agreed Byron. Smooth jazz played softly in the background as Byron navigated the car swiftly down the expressway to return Jillian home. It had been a long time since Jillian had had such a great time at dinner with a gentleman. Even though they were good friends, it felt really good to be with someone she felt comfortable. Jillian sat back, relaxed, enjoyed the ride home with the wonderful music and tried not to go to sleep. As a child, she remembered many nights falling asleep in the back seat of her parent's car on the way home from church. Well, it didn't work.

Byron had been watching her off and on fall asleep the past five miles of the drive to her building. Something inside Byron wanted to reach out, hold and protect her. Jillian was independent, smart, intelligent and beautiful. He was always attracted to women with curves or a fuller figure. Jillian was a real woman and not those anorexic sticks in the magazines with their bones showing. He was going to enjoy reconnecting with her whether she realized it or not. This was not all business.

"Jillian, wake up. You are home," whispered Byron as he nudged her left arm only so slightly.

"Oh, no. Did I fall asleep? No! That was the third strike. I can't believe I did that," Jillian asked as she put two hands on her face to make sure that there was no unsightly drool coming from her mouth.

"Yes, you fell asleep. Third strike? This is not baseball."

"Never mind. Was I snoring?"

"No you were not snoring. I think it is too late now if you were?" chuckled Byron. He thought, 'she hasn't changed a bit. Self-conscious about everything, sensible and sexy as all get out.'

"Well, yes, but thank goodness I was not. I am so embarrassed." Jillian was thankful that it was dark because she was sure her face was glowing from embarrassment.

"Sleep is inevitable and you are tired from a long day. By the way, you are beautiful when you sleep."

"Thank you. Well, I guess I'll be going now." Jillian forgot and started to open the door, but was immediately stopped by Byron's hand on her left arm again.

"Hold on. You don't think I stop being a gentleman right now do you? I am going to walk you to the door."

"Yes, sir." Jillian eased back into the seat.

As Byron came around to her side of the car, Jillian thought, 'Lord, I can't believe I fell asleep.' Byron didn't seem moved by her falling asleep at all.

"Here you go lady," as Byron helped her out of the car. "Do you have your keys?"

Jillian opened her purse and the keys were in the side pocket. "Yes, they are right here. Are you headed back to Dayton?"

"Yes, it is not far. I have to get back because we are meeting about your project in the morning."

"Yes, I remember," Jillian looked up into Byron's face and realized that he was watching her every move. His intense stare made her look away at her keys again. "Be careful on the drive home. Thanks for a lovely evening."

"It was my pleasure. I had a wonderful time with you, special lady. We shall talk soon. Good night."

"Good night." Jillian pressed the button for the elevator and it opened immediately. When Jillian turned and waved good bye. Byron turned to go to his car once the doors closed. Byron replayed every moment of their time together. The conversation, the way she smiled, how she treated the servers and how she interacted with him made him all the more anxious to see Jillian again. He had been alone too long. With running Randolph Technologies with his brother, there was little time for himself or a family. He had to attend business meetings, conferences, trade shows, networking events as well as develop new technology. Now, Byron wanted his own family. He wanted someone to come home to night after night. He wanted someone to build a life with who understood and could be included in his business, take on vacation, cherish and love. He wanted someone to talk to. No time like the present. He dialed her number again. With only two rings, Jillian picked up the phone.

"Hello."

"Are you in your condo yet?"

"Just walked in. Are you on the road yet?" Jillian double checked the door and headed to her bedroom to get ready for bed.

"Yep, just got onto I-75 and the road is stretched out in front of me. I don't know why I called. I guess I just wanted to talk to you again. I enjoy talking to you very much."

"No problem. I enjoyed talking to you too. Hold on a minute." Jillian took her clothes off quickly and grabbed a t-shirt and laid across her bed. Byron could only imagine what Jillian was doing because he couldn't hear the soft clothing placed on the chair.

"I'm back."

"What were you doing?"

"Getting ready for bed."

"Oh." Byron didn't need to hear that because it was bringing him a visual that could make it hard for him to sleep tonight. Jillian knew right then that was the wrong thing to say. It sounded too intimate and almost sexual. That was too much information for two very mature, single and lonely people. 'Lord, help us both.'

"By the way, thanks again for a wonderful evening and I am so sorry that I fell asleep. How fast are you driving?" Jillian asked quickly trying to change the subject.

"75, why?"

"Don't get a ticket."

"Thanks for the concern. What's your schedule like tomorrow?"

"I'm not very busy in the office on Friday. We are usually wrapping up the week and start preparing for the next week. I usually shut down the office around 4 on Friday unless an emergency arises. Why?"

"Just asking. Do you like football?"

"Love it."

"Do you go to many of the Bengals' games since you are so close to the stadium?" Byron asked.

"No, I don't get to the games much. You'd think I would since I can see the traffic from my house. I just stay at home, put on my jersey and watch the game on television. Where are you now?"

"Almost to Middletown."

"Oh okay, you're moving up the highway pretty quickly. Flying low as my father used to say." The conversation went back and forth for the next few minutes. Byron was trying to get as much information about Jillian's likes, dislikes, habits and pastime activities as he could. He hadn't seen her in more than 10 years and although she showed no hesitation in going out with him tonight, he had to know for future reference.

"Okay, Jillian I must ask you something before I get off of this phone. Are you seeing anyone?" Jillian was almost taken aback by the question and sat straight up in the bed.

"No I am not seeing anyone. I know we haven't seen each other in a while, but know this that if I am seeing someone, I am dedicated to them. I don't play the field. If I were seeing someone, you would know it. He probably would have met us at Pappadeaux's tonight or I would have called him and let you speak to him before we left my office. That's how old school I am. I wouldn't have needed his permission, but I just would have respected him that much. Does that answer all of your questions?"

"Yes and for your information, I am not seeing anyone either. Not even casually. I hope that answers your questions," Byron stated.

"Now that we have that cleared up. I have to work tomorrow and must get my beauty rest. Please text me when you get home." Jillian requested.

"I don't know about beauty rest because Jillian Forrester you are already incredibly beautiful. I know you do need your rest so on that note, good night madam."

"Good night kind sir." When Jillian hung up the phone, she turned off the light. Byron's statement made her blush which warmed her whole body. Jillian drifted off to sleep with a smile on her face and anticipation of their next time together. When Byron pressed end to his blue tooth, he smiled knowing that this could the beginning of something special. Quickly he rang another number.

"Do you know what time it is?" Myron instantly knew it was Byron by the ring tone. Sitting up in his bed and turning on the light, he wiped his eyes trying to get clarity before the conversation continued.

"Hello brother. It is not that late. It's just around midnight. I'm just about home from dropping off Jillian about thirty minutes ago."

"Don't tell me that you bored her that long after such a long day at work."

"Hey I am not boring. I am a great date."

"Yeah, right. So, how did it go?"

"It went great. We talked until they turned the lights up brighter from the normal dim at the restaurant. She is wonderful, intelligent, fun, genuine, Christian and very pretty as well. I like Jillian a lot. She felt comfortable enough with me that she fell asleep in the car. Before you ask, she doesn't snore."

"Yep, you bored her, she fell asleep. You must like her a lot or you wouldn't be calling me at midnight waking me up. This reminds me when you were crazy about that girl Jamie in high school who wouldn't go with you to the junior prom."

"Whatever. Why did you bring her up? Who knows where that girl is now? Jillian, unlike Jamie, agreed to go out with me. I also found out that she is not dating anyone. So that's even better."

"Good for you."

"Yes, great for me. It looks like my car will be heading down 75 south for more than just business. Believe you me, I plan on making Jillian Forrester my business. I think I am going to send her some flowers in the morning."

"That sounds nice. Do what you do, my brother. It looks like from my handy tracking system on my phone that you are about 2 miles from home."

"Yep I will be pulling in the driveway shortly."

"Well, I am going to let you return to your happy thoughts about Jillian while I return to my happy dream. Be careful and bye brother."

"See you in the morning." Byron smiled as he thought about how grateful he was to have a brother who understood him perfectly. The twins had been competitive since birth. Byron knew that no matter what, his brother wanted him to be happy and successful. He turned into his driveway, the garage door raised and he entered a spacious six bedroom, five bathroom, tri-level framed on thirty five hundred square feet house. It was beautifully decorated house filled with modern, minimalist furniture. There was a sixty seven inch flat screen television with surround sound and all of the latest technology set in front of a comfortable arrangement of a Lazy Boy sectional couch. The furniture arrangement was set up for watching any of the NFL, NBA or NCAA line-up of games. The kitchen was complete with all of the latest appliances. Each bedroom was decorated with its own color scheme with matching wall color and linens. There was a weekly housekeeper and butler on staff. The something missing amongst all of this lavishness was someone that who would love Byron unconditionally. Byron prayed to God for direction to obtain that love. If Jillian was the one, let him know and show him how to love her like she deserved to be loved. In the meantime, he was excited about what he was beginning with Jillian and the new possibilities. He turned on his computer, ordered her an arrangement of flowers and texted Jillian, 'I'm home and good night.' He threw back the covers on his California King bed, smiled at the thought of Jillian and fell asleep as soon as his head hit the pillow.

Chapter 3

It was promptly 9:00 a.m. when Jillian exited the elevator. She was wearing a red knit pant suit with gold accessories, matching shoes and bag, her signature ponytail and a smile on her face with a purposeful stride in her step. She woke up this morning with that same smile on her face after the wonderful evening she had with Byron. It had been about three years since she enjoyed the company of a fine gentleman who wasn't related to technology or church business. Jillian didn't know where this relationship was headed, but it felt good to have someone who seemed to be attracted to her again. It was Friday. She had no big plans for the weekend, but planned work a short day so her weekend could begin.

As she entered the door to the reception area, she was immediately greeted by Patricia, "Good morning and how did it go last night? You don't really have to tell me because by that smile I can tell that things went well."

"It went great. I had a wonderful time." Jillian paused and placed her belongings on Patricia's desk.

"Are there any juicy details?" Patricia asked with great anticipation.

"Look at you. What do you call juicy details? The juicy anything is that it was a very nice dinner, wonderful conversation in a relaxing, comfortable atmosphere. That's all Ms. Lady," Jillian picked up her things from Patricia's desk and entered her office. When the door opened, she was greeted with the fragrance of one dozen yellow roses in a clear vase sitting on her desk.

"Who are the flowers from?" asked Jillian.

Patricia came to the doorway and replied, "From someone who apparently also had a great time last night. Check out the card."

Jillian opened the card and it read, 'Thank you for a wonderful time. These are beautiful flowers for a beautiful lady. See you soon. Have a great day, Byron.

The card made her smile all over again. She didn't think she said or did anything special. Whatever she did do or say, the card said that Byron enjoyed it. 'Oh my goodness,' thought Jillian, 'he thinks I'm beautiful.' She cried quietly with slow hot tears on her face. Given Jillian's history she was still taken aback every time a man said she was pretty or beautiful. Jillian wasn't gullible, but never thought she was beautiful.

Jillian wiped her eyes and told Patricia, "That's nice of Byron to send me flowers and this card. Thanks for putting them in water Patricia."

Jillian hadn't received flowers from a gentleman after a dinner date in years. This was special and no matter how corny it may sound, she liked and felt like she deserved the attention. Jillian was ready for whatever happened next.

Patricia liked the smile on Jillian's face as she watched her read the card. Patricia knew that it had been a long time since Jillian had a guy approach her and secretly, she wanted her to find happiness, no matter what.

"I didn't put them in water. They were delivered in that beautiful vase." Patricia smiled as she went back to her desk leaving the door slightly opened to hear Jillian's further instructions.

"Oh, okay. Are we ready for the Friday Forrester meeting?"

"I am ready when you are," Patricia came back into the office, closed the door and sat down across from Jillian's desk. With her iPad handy, Patricia was ready for her weekly Friday morning meeting with Jillian. These meetings were to wrap up the week's activities, develop a plan for the next week and determine goals for moving the business forward profitably. At the conclusion of their meeting, Jillian met with team leaders of the information and field research departments which ended around lunch time.

The phone in Jillian's office suddenly rang.

"I wonder who could be calling?" Jillian asked.

Patricia explained the call, "I told the switch board to hold all calls and only forward a call in here if it was an emergency.

"Forrester Information Management, this is Patricia how can I help you?" Patricia paused for a brief moment and then she smiled at Jillian. "Uh, Yes, Mr.

Randolph. I'll see if she is available." Jillian looked up from her notes and Patricia noticed the sudden interest in her face.

Patricia mouthed to Jillian, "Do you want to talk to him?"

Jillian put her hand up to her ear to mimic a phone and mouthed, 'I will call him back.'

Patricia nodded okay and drew her attention back to the phone.

"Mr. Randolph, Ms. Forrester is in today and currently in a meeting. Can she call you back? Great, I'll give her the message and she will call you as soon as she is finished," Patricia hung up the phone and said, "Before you ask, he didn't say what he was calling about. So before you panic, it could be about their meeting this morning. Or, he could want to hear your voice or want to take you out again. Let's finish so you can find out for real what he wanted and not sit here distracted by trying to guess."

Jillian bowed her head and chuckled ever so slightly, "Am I that predictable? Patricia, you know me too well. I would be sitting here trying to figure it out. We need to finish up anyway. The thing I love and hate about relationships is the emotional roller coaster ride."

"I know, but I love roller coasters. Sit back and enjoy the ride," said Patricia.

"I'll try, but it is a bad habit of mine. I get so anxious. I wish I could just be cool like my sister. So I think we left off talking about the trade show in the Bahamas?"

"Yes ma'am, right there."

Jillian and Patricia wrapped up their discussion and concluded the agenda items right around 11:30 a.m. Patricia closed the door to Jillian's office to give her privacy to make her calls or conduct other business. Jillian picked up her cell phone and dialed the number for Byron that was now in her call history. After the third ring, Jillian thought she was going to have to leave a message, but she suddenly heard, "Hello."

"Byron? This is Jillian."

"Hey lady, how are you doing?" Byron's voice was low and soft.

"I am fine just wrapping up some business for the week. Sorry I couldn't take your call earlier. Are you busy?"

"Not right now especially if I can hear your voice."

"It is good to hear from you as well. By the way, thank you so much for the flowers. They are simply beautiful."

"I am glad that you like them. You are a beautiful lady that deserves beautiful things and to be appreciated in beautiful ways."

"I am glad that we are on the phone and not in person."

"Why? Are you blushing again?"

"I am not going to admit that to you," Jillian chuckled under her breath.

"That laugh lets me know all I need to know right now." Byron was thrilled to know that he could make Jillian laugh. Knowing that he could make her blush on the phone was even better.

"So, what's up?" Jillian attempted to change the subject before she got them both off track.

"Well, two things. We met this morning and have a proposal for you regarding your technology issues. Secondly, I am coming to Cincinnati and wanted to stop by and go over the proposal with you around 3. Is that alright?"

"That sounds good to me. I want to finish for the day at 4. So I will see you at 3."

"See you then." When Jillian hung up the phone she picked up her scratch note pad and fanned herself ever so slightly. Byron could have easily sent the proposal by messenger. His coming to meet her in person was nice and it wasn't unusual, but gave her an inkling that he wanted to see her again.

"I saw your light go out, so what's up?" asked Patricia as she swung open Jillian's office door.

"Do you watch my light often?"

"Yes, what did he say?"

"He is coming here with the proposal at 3."

"Do you have an amount that you can spend for the technology he is proposing yet?" Patricia asked.

"No, I need to call accounting and get an amount." Jillian stated.

"Yes you do. After Mr. Randolph shows you the proposal, you will agree to it and then he will want to take you out again tonight to celebrate," Patricia teased.

"We shall see about all of that celebration. For now, I am going to take his coming here at 3:00 p.m. to mean that he is bringing the proposal to me in person instead of by messenger. That is all," Jillian said as she smiled.

"Jillian's got a boyfriend. Jillian's got a boyfriend," Patricia sang over and over in the voice of a 4 year old.

"I don't know about a boyfriend, but he is interested. He sure is cute too. Okay, let's get back to business," Jillian chuckled at Patricia's teasing.

"Okay, I'll stop. Make the call to accounting before you get distracted again. Then you are all set to day dream until your boyfriend comes," said Patricia and she exited Jillian's office.

"Stop it right now," Jillian called after Patricia as she dialed the accountant's number and Patricia closed the door. Jillian thought to herself, 'this is kind of nice.'

Patricia saw Jillian's light go out again and she gently knocked on the door. "It's about 12:30, are you going out for lunch or should I bring you back something?" asked Patricia.

"Bring me back a cup of soup and a half sandwich from the shop around the corner. Whatever is the special of the day," Jillian said.

"Cool," Patricia said.

"Thank you." Jillian continued working until Patricia brought her lunch. Upon its arrival, Jillian continued to eat and pour over her plans, respond to emails, check on any help she needed to give her researchers, other notes and any project tasks until around 3:00. Jillian knew that once Byron arrived the rest of her day would be over. She had plans to clean on Saturday, Sunday church and the game on TV. Simple. Jillian thought, 'that was before Mr. Byron. We shall see.'

Just then, Patricia called and announced that Byron Randolph had arrived.

"Send him in, Patricia." Jillian braced herself for seeing Byron again so soon. She knew he was going to look good. Well, to Jillian's surprise and delight Byron walked in looking like a million dollars in a navy blue suit that was tailor made for him. He wore no tie, but his shirt was opened collar with his initials on each cuff. He was carrying a matching portfolio and his iPad.

Byron moved closer to the desk and said only, "Hello lady."

"Hello sir, how are you?" Jillian asked.

"Fine now that I've seen you," Byron said looking directly into her eyes. Jillian's stomach turned a double back somersault.

"I know that you don't say that to all of your clients," Jillian said.

"No, I don't because I wouldn't be in business very long. My brother and parents would disown me," Byron gave a big smile and stood waiting on her instructions.

Jillian got lost in that smile and forgot to tell him to have seat at the conference table. "Oh I'm sorry, where is my mind. Let's sit at the table."

"Sure."

"So, what do the numbers look like?"

"Well, we have taken a look at all of your equipment needs and you will need hardware upgrades more than just additional software. The hardware is not able to support the software needs and that is why your machines are slowing down and locking up on you. You will also need a server. Now, we have worked up numbers that reflect a new, upgraded server or an additional server to what you already have."

"That sounds like patch work to me."

"Yes, since we don't know your budgetary constraints or flexibility, we gave you several options."

"Thank you so much, but Taylor & Edwards is too large of a client to be patching. I have seen people lose large amounts of business and become very non-productive because they didn't have the infrastructure in place to accommodate the demand on the hardware and software. How long is the guarantee on this equipment?" Jillian inquired.

"As you know, hardware is not guaranteed more than five years. Your accountants can do the depreciation numbers, but that is about all you can get. You also know that technology advances at a rapid rate so in five years the technology will be outdated as well. You are right. You need to make sure that your infrastructure can handle any future upgrades." Byron replied.

"In technology, change is constant." Jillian stated.

"Now training can be handled one of three ways, on-site, bring your people to us or remote."

"The best way is always in person, but the easiest is remote. I have the numbers on all three options so let me run it by my comptroller. I am going to try to catch him before he leaves. Do you have the time?" Jillian asked.

"You are my last appointment for the week. I will be happy to wait," Byron watched Jillian walk away and smiled to himself. 'I am not going anywhere and you are going out with me tonight. You just don't know it yet.'

"Thanks, I will be right back," Jillian left to run the numbers by her accountant. She didn't have time to waste or delay on this project. With less than 3 weeks until the new contract took effect, this was crucial. She found her accountant and they were able to work out the numbers without dipping into her reserve fund to pay Randolph Technologies for this contract.

When Jillian returned, Byron was busy on his iPad, but stopped immediately to give her his full attention.

"Byron, we have a deal, but I need to know what we need to do to get started."

"We need the equipment costs first so we can place the order immediately. James can place that order online tonight if necessary. Most deliveries are made overnight. If the inventory is in stock, you should have the equipment next week, installed within two days and we begin training the next Monday or Tuesday."

"Okay, let me call down and get you a check cut so you will have it before you leave."

"You get the check and I will call James to get the order in."

"Don't you want to wait on the check before he orders?"

"No, I know that you are good for the money and a woman of your word. Time is money. You do your thing and I will do mine."

Jillian smiled as she moved to her desk to make the call. In her mind, she realized that Byron believed in her and her company. She appreciated that in a man. It was refreshing working with someone who wanted to make sure that her business was successful. Randolph Technologies was the right company and Byron Randolph was the man for the job.

"Steve, I realize that you are trying to leave, but we need the check for the equipment amount cut before you go. I left you a copy of the proposal and it is just the equipment amount only for right now. I am in my office if you could bring it to me on your way out. Thanks so much." After Jillian hung up with her accountant, she heard Byron finalizing his call with his assistant James. She remained seated at her desk and just watched Byron in action. Jillian thought, 'There is nothing like a man that can handle his business, smart, loves God and good looking to boot. Lord help us here today.'

"Go ahead and place the order for the equipment. You can use our account for now. I will have the check for the equipment in a few minutes. Make arrangements with Ms. Forrester's assistant for projected training dates in two weeks. I am not coming back to Dayton tonight. I am staying in town to take care of some things this weekend. If you need me, you can call me. I will be back in the office on

Monday morning. Cool. Thanks man. Have a great weekend," Byron ended his call, but appeared to be lost in thought.

"Byron, are you okay?" Jillian asked as she stood up from her desk and came over near Byron at the conference table.

"No, I'm fine just thinking. How are things on your end?" Byron asked.

"Fine on my end. Steve is on his way up with the check in just a few minutes and then we should be fine to sign contracts. How are things on your end? Anything you need from us?"

"No, we are fine on our end. James is placing the order now and he will call your assistant Patricia with options for the schedule for training. It's about 4:00. What time are you shutting down for the day?" Byron asked hopefully.

"As soon as we sign these contracts, I am done for the day."

"Great. You know what I was thinking?" Byron looked at Jillian as he asked.

"What?"

"We work well together." Byron stated.

"Yes we do." Jillian agreed.

"So, we should celebrate that great working relationship. Any plans for tonight?" asked Byron with a pearly white smile on his face.

"What if I said yes?"

"I would do everything in my power to convince you to change them."

"That's a good answer. Why do you ask?"

"Because, I have two tickets to see *Angie Stone, KEM, Ledisi and Anthony Hamilton* at the Aronoff tonight and wondered whether you would join me," Byron brought them out of his jacket pocket and gently waved them in front of Jillian.

"How did you get those tickets? I thought that concert was sold out weeks ago?" Jillian asked getting excited just looking at the tickets.

"It was sold out, but I got my tickets as soon as they were available. Now, before you let that beautiful mind of yours start racing, I always buy two tickets. I never go to a concert alone even if I have to go with my brother. And no, I wasn't dating someone else and going to take her instead of you. I haven't been dating anyone in months. So there."

"Okay, I didn't say anything."

"But, you were thinking it."

"So you are now a mind reader in addition to being a geek?"

"Yes, I have special powers."

Jillian chuckled, "I bet you do. Well, I can't go like this so I had better go home and change."

"Are you hungry for dinner now or can you wait until after the concert?"

"I can wait. I had a late lunch so I am good until later."

Just then, there was a gentle knock on the door.

"Come in," called out Jillian.

In walked Steve with the check for the equipment costs. Jillian quickly introduced Steve Barnes to Byron and she signed the requisition form. "Thanks Steve and have a good weekend."

"You too, Ms. Forrester."

"Okay, here are the contracts to be signed. I have provided duplicate copies so just sign here, here and there." Byron opened his portfolio and provided her a pen. Byron was standing so close to Jillian that his cologne still smelled heavenly even though it was the end of the day.

"You have already signed the contracts. Were you that sure?"

"Of course I was sure. If there was any hesitation, I am the go to guy that hashes out the deal and makes it happen."

"Alright then. Here is your pen back." Jillian handed the second signed contract back to Byron who placed it in his portfolio and looked up at Jillian who asked, "So what's the plan from here?"

"I am staying in town tonight. So I am going to go to check into the hotel and pick you up at your place around 7:00. The concert starts at 8:00. I don't know about you, but I like to get to my seats early and people watch."

"So do I. See you at 7:00 p.m."

"Are you ready to go now? May I walk you out?"

"No, I need to straighten up my desk and check in with Patricia before I go. Thanks so much for making this equipment process easy. I feel so much better about this upgrade and know that I am in good hands with Randolph Technologies." Jillian resisted the urge to walk out with him right then. She wasn't doing a very good job of playing hard to get going out with him two nights in a week, but had to do something.

"It was my pleasure and yes, you are in great hands with Randolph Technologies and Byron Randolph." Byron reached out to shake Jillian's hand all the while keeping his eyes fixed on hers.

"Thank you sir." Jillian said, dropped her gaze and thought, 'don't look at his hands, don't look at his hands.' Too late she looked at his hands.

"Well, I will give you your space so you can handle your business. See you at 7."

"Great. Thanks Byron."

Byron headed toward the door and said, "You are welcome."

Jillian sat in her desk chair with a thud trying to catch her breath. The door was ajar and Jillian heard Byron ask Patricia, "Excuse me, Patricia isn't it?" Byron asked.

"Yes it is," Patricia said softly.

"Good night Patricia." Byron said as he continued to the elevator. Patricia watched Byron until she heard the elevator bell ding and the door close.

Patricia headed back into Jillian's office and said, "So boss lady, do we have a deal and a date?"

"We do, we do," Jillian smiled and stood straighten her desk to leave. "I need to get home to prepare. So, first, here are the contracts signed. Second, you should be hearing from James Jones, Randolph Technologies' assistant, by Monday or Tuesday about possible training dates. I would like for the training to take place here because the staff needs to be trained on the exact equipment that they will be using. Finally, go home and enjoy your weekend."

"Yes, I will and you have a great weekend yourself."

"Thanks. We shall see what happens." Patricia closed the door behind and Jillian began thinking about everything that has happened in the last two days. 'Alright Lord, two dates in one week, what's up with that? If I didn't know any better, I would think that this man doesn't want me out of his sight and really likes me. Lord, I want to tell you thank you that's all. Look at the time. I better get out of here.'

Jillian wrapped up her business at the office quickly and with the bouquet of roses in her arms, got to her car and sped to her condo to change for her second date with Byron Randolph. Jillian couldn't believe that she was actually going to attend the concert that she gave up hope of attending a week ago. 'Wow, is all that she could say to herself and kept driving.'

A few blocks away, Byron was placing his key in the lock of his hotel room while on the phone with his brother, Myron.

"Myron, I am going out with her again."

"Great Byron. Where are you taking her?"

"To the concert tonight."

"I thought I was going to that concert with you?"

"No, man not when I can spend it with a beautiful woman. We can go to another concert some other time. If this keeps up, you'll have to get your own tickets and your own date."

"Thanks a lot. Good thing because I got tied up here with work and couldn't have met you any way."

"What's got you tied up?"

"Well, a company wants a demonstration of our alert system Randolph AT100. I am putting the final touches on the prototype so we will be ready on Monday. I think that it has the potential to do well."

"Go for it brother, you are the R & D department. I am about to shower and change for my big date with Jillian."

"You really like her don't you."

"I always have."

"Always have? How long have you had a thing for Jillian?"

"All of my life."

"So why have you been wasting time with all of these others girls all these years?"

"I don't know. I never wanted to approach her until I had everything of mine intact. My business, house and finances had to be in order first. We worked so hard in college and worked so hard to build the company. I didn't want to put any woman through that struggle. Mom told me that Jillian was engaged and going to marry that other guy from Chicago. You know the one, Roger. I never ever trusted him. He was always bad even in the Sunshine choir at conference. When mom told me that he broke her heart and got another woman pregnant, then, I knew it was too soon and she wasn't ready. Then mom told me that she started a business. I knew that would take some time and I wanted to give her some space. She is real independent, which is one of the many things that I really like about Jillian. So I got busy and now here it is ten years later. God has brought us together through our businesses."

"I can hear the violins playing in the background."

"Oh shut up, you know what I mean."

"Yep, I know what you mean. You love her."

"Yep, I think I love her."

"All those poor girls who thought they had a chance with you. You were wasting their time with dates and movies. Your heart was always with Jillian."

"You got that right. Now, in a couple of hours, my body is going to be where my heart has always been. Move over Shakespeare, I am a poet."

"Corny, you. I am happy for you and hopefully, I will have the same thing soon. Don't keep the lady waiting any longer. Give her the full Randolph treatment. Shut-up, get ready and have a good time."

"Thanks. You will find the same thing one day too. Good night."

"I hope so. Good night to you too."

Jillian arrived home around 5:00 tired and invigorated all at the same time. She had a date on a Friday night. She could hardly believe it. She reminded herself, 'No falling asleep like you did last night.' She went straight to her bedroom dumping everything on the bed. 'What to wear?' She quickly dialed her sister, Monica.

"Hello."

"Monica, how are you?"

"I am fine what's up? You never call unless you need me to decorate, design, style you or cook something. Which is it?"

"I need you to style me."

"You have a date?"

"Yes, I have a date."

"Who is it girl?"

"Please don't tell me that is some nerd from the church."

"Well, kind of. You are right on the nerd part and he does attend church."

"Who?"

"Byron Randolph."

"One of the twins?"

"Yes, one of the gorgeous twins."

"How did you hook up with him?"

"Long story short. He is doing some work at Forrester. He and his twin Myron have a technology company and they are helping with an upgrade of our hardware and software for the Taylor & Edwards' contract."

"Okay, that is great. So where are we going?"

"He is taking me to the Angie Stone, KEM, Ledisi and Anthony Hamilton concert."

"Girl, that concert was sold out ages ago. I know he was supposed to take somebody else, but chose you after he had already broke up with her, right?"

"No, he told me that he always buys two tickets and he hadn't dated anyone in months. I have no reason to doubt him yet. He is coming at 7:00 and I haven't showered or nothing. Here are my choices. Jean, jeans and more jeans. I am normally not a jeans wearer, but it's cool and tonight seems like the best time. What do you think?"

"Is everything black and a little snug to show off your shape?"

"Yes it fits and I'm wearing the new jewelry from the Shepherd collection."

"Go girl and knock him dead. Call me tomorrow and tell me how it goes. I finished my clients up early so I'm staying in tonight with my husband, by a cozy fire and my daughter is at college. Hallelujah!"

"Don't rub it in because that sounds wonderful. I will let you know how it goes. Good night, Sis."

"Listen, have a good time and more importantly, just be yourself. If he can't handle it, he's not the one."

"Thanks I'll remember that. Bye."

"Bye."

Well, wardrobe is one thing that we can check off our list. Now it's off to the shower I go. Jillian lit a vanilla candle to create a great aroma and headed off to the shower singing Anita Wilson's arrangement of

"Shower the People" by James Taylor. By the time Jillian was dressed and ready, the entire condo smelled like vanilla and "Hypnotic Poison" by Dior. What a combination and it was sure to leave a lasting impression for anyone.

At 6:45 p.m., there was a call from downstairs asking Jillian if they should let up a Mr. Byron Randolph.

"Yes, let Mr. Randolph up please. Thanks so much and have a great night." Jillian thought, 'he's early.'

"Sure will Ms. Forrester. Good night to you too."

Jillian gathered her purse and scarf and took one last quick look in the mirror. Looking in the mirror at herself she smiled at her reflection, winked and blew herself a kiss.

Suddenly the doorbell rang and Jillian knew that it was Byron, but her parents taught her to always ask first since she moved away from home years ago.

"Byron?"

"Yes, it's me." Byron replied.

Jillian swung open the door with a smile on her face trying to look sexy and casual. Down inside she was glad they weren't eating until later because her food would have been doing somersaults along with her stomach.

"Hello, sir." Jillian said in a very low tone while she took Byron all in and he stood there doing the same. He was wearing black jeans, a cashmere sweater with a matching black leather jacket. What a combination.

"Hello, yourself. You look scrumptious and seeing you twice in one day is making me have an excellent week," Byron said.

"Thank you very much. You are truly something else. You know exactly what to say don't you? I am sorry I am being rude keeping you in the hall. Come on in." Jillian took two steps backward to allow Byron into the condo and gently closed the door behind him.

"Look at us, great minds think alike. We must have the same stylist," said Jillian.

"You are right," said Byron while keeping his eyes on Jillian the whole time.

"Let me get my purse and scarf."

"Jillian, you smell intoxicating, what is the fragrance?"

"*Hypnotic Poison by Dior*," Jillian said as she turned to gather her belongings from the couch.

"I like it very much."

"Thank you," Jillian said, as she turned back toward the door. Byron was leaning against the door with his arms folded across his chest admiring her every move. He had watched her walk from the door, to the couch and now headed back in his direction. This staring he was doing with his eyes was going to be a problem. His eyes were so penetrating that it reminded Jillian of a lion stalking his prey. It startled her at first and then made her very self-conscious. As a child, Jillian was sort of clumsy so when she turned to find him staring at her, she almost lost her balance.

"I'm sorry, I didn't mean to startle you." Byron stood up straight from the door and quickly moved closer just in case she lost her balance. He put his hands gently on her elbows to steady her. His nearness made it even more overwhelming. She was several inches shorter than Byron, but with her heels, a slight head tilt would have taken little effort for Byron to swoop in for a kiss. 'Too soon' thought Jillian, but she was ready whenever.

"I wasn't expecting you to be looking at me so intently. I keep thinking that there is something wrong and I want to immediately start checking myself," Jillian said with a nervous smile.

"There is no need for double checking. You look delicious. Just so you know, you are so incredibly beautiful I have a hard time taking my eyes off of you. Second, I am enjoying every minute of our time together. I am watching so intently to record every moment with my brain camera to recall later. Someone once told me that 'a woman is a complex creature and to best learn how to please, protect and provide for her you will have to study her.'"

Jillian tilted her head up slightly to look directly in the eyes of Byron and said, "Well, first thank you. Second, you really know how to make a girl feel special and it sounds like you are taking the advice from someone who is a very wise man."

"Yes, he is very wise because he's my dad. That's the reason why he has been married forty plus years to my mom."

"I knew I always liked Bishop Randolph, but now I have one more reason to add to my list."

"Are you ready?"

"Ready when you are."

"Let's go."

Byron held the door for Jillian as they walked in silence to the elevator and garage with their conversation still on their mind. Byron treated Jillian like a very expensive, precious and cherished heirloom. The full Randolph Treatment. Once settled in the car, Byron asked Jillian as he put the car in drive heading out of the parking lot, "Do you want to select the music we listen to on the way."

"Why? Are you afraid that I will fall asleep before we get to the concert which is only about 5-7 minutes away?" Jillian said.

"Yep." Byron replied smugly. Jillian laughed out loud.

"Okay, how about some upbeat R & B to get us in the mood for the concert."

"Oh my, Sister Jillian you listen to that worldly music?" Byron teased.

"Alright Mother Williams I have you to know that I listen to all types of music."

"Oh my goodness, is she still alive?" Byron asked as he changed the channels on the Satellite Radio station.

"Yes Lord, she is alive and still as feisty as ever. She is still on the conference planning team which I am on and driving us all nuts. She is a wealth of information, but my mom says 'she drove the team nuts for years.' I see how because she gets on my nerves. She gets an A plus for consistency." Jillian relayed. Byron chuckled again as he listened to Jillian.

The beauty of living in downtown Cincinnati is that it wasn't very far to the Aronoff Center for the Arts on Walnut Street. Jillian hated getting lost so when Byron took a different route to the Aronoff Jillian thought she had to ask, "Which way are you going?"

"Don't worry about it. Just sit back and let Randolph transportation get you there safe and sound."

"Okay. I just have a pet peeve about getting lost anywhere I go."

"Well, as close as you live, we could have walked, but I don't want to walk because the temperatures are supposed to dip down into the 40's tonight. You are my precious cargo and I will get you there don't worry."

"Well, I will shut up, enjoy the music and the chauffeur."

"Thank you."

Jillian didn't want to relax too much because she knew a smooth car ride could rock her straight to sleep. Suddenly, Jillian realized that they were in the back of the Aronoff at the loading docks. There were trucks on the landing and in each of the driveways that had 'Randolph Technologies' written on the side. Jillian thought, 'oh my, we are going back stage.' Byron pulled up right behind one of the large trucks and put the car in park.

"I am not trying to be fresh, but I need to get in the glove compartment for a second, excuse me." Byron reached across Jillian to open the glove compartment and retrieved two 'all access passes' to the concert. Jillian couldn't help but notice that he smelled exquisite a mixture of fresh air, rain water, woods and linen.

"No problem, you are fine. I see that the trucks say 'Randolph Technologies' so you have supplied the equipment for this event?"

"Yes ma'am. Now, put this on and let's get inside." Jillian quickly put the all access pass around her neck, unhooked the seat belt and had her purse in hand when Byron came around to open the passenger door. He took her hand in his to help her out of the car and guide her through the maze of trucks, people, equipment and doorways inside the theatre. Jillian always thought holding hands and being led by her date in a crowd was incredibly sexy. They were greeted by people moving about like busy ants. Byron walked through checking on everybody and everything to make sure that all was ready to go and there were no problems. Byron introduced her to his key people and he was reassured that everything was fine. They entered the *Procter & Gamble* Hall from the stage to their 2 front row seats. An attendant stopped by their seats and asked, "Mr. Randolph, would you like something to drink?"

"Just water for me. Jillian would you like some water as well?"

"Sure, thank you." The attendant quickly returned with two glasses of water remaining until they were finished and removed the glasses promptly before the concert started.

Jillian truly felt like Cinderella at the ball. She had been at the Aronoff many times for events and even sang on stage with various gospel artists, but this was different. She was rarely speechless, but tonight she was at a loss for words. The lights began to blink so the concert was about to start.

"Here we go." Byron leaned in as he whispered it in her ear. Jillian thought 'good thing I put perfume there. Thank you to my mama for good home training.' She smiled and got ready to get lost in the performances of some of her favorite artists.

Well, the artists didn't disappoint they held back nothing as they gave it their all. Each performance was over the top. Jillian felt like she had been in a music dream. Byron took her backstage and she was able to meet and have her pictures taken with each artist and compliment them on an awesome job. There were photographers, singers, musicians, promoters, agents everywhere which added to the excitement of the evening.

Byron gently pulled Jillian close from the hustle of backstage and asked her if she was as hungry as he was. She readily agreed and they made their way to the car. Once they were both settled in the car and moving through the streets to the highway, Byron turned to ask, "Well, what did you think?"

"I am clearly speechless and that is very hard for me. I will truly have a hard time sleeping tonight. I thank you for inviting me."

"You are welcome. Let's get some food before you faint on me. How about the Cheesecake Factory?"

"Perfect," said Jillian. Byron drove the car to I-71 North toward Montgomery Road. In Jillian's mind, she didn't care where they ate as long as there was food and it was in his company. Business was never far away from Jillian's mind so she finally had to ask, "So how long has Randolph Technologies been taking care of concerts in addition to doing stuff for companies?"

"We started doing concerts from the beginning. We don't sing as we did when we were little, but we love music and really started providing equipment for events at home in Indianapolis. When we expanded to Ohio and landed the Taylor & Edwards' contract, business progressed from there. We've had the contract at the Aronoff for about four years now. The previous contractor's owner died and he didn't have family to keep the business going so, we landed the contract. I usually get tickets to each event," Byron explained.

"Yes, now I know why you have tickets to each event. It's like having season tickets. You have a seat no matter what," Jillian said.

"Something like that. You're truly a football fan?" Byron asked.

"Football is my favorite sport," Jillian declared.

"Who's your favorite team besides the Bengals?"

"I don't really have a favorite team, but love the sport. I admire the quarterback position. I was a Terry Bradshaw, Roger Stauback, Reggie Cunningham fan from way back. I support the new guys in the position as well, Michael Vick, RGIII, Teddy Bridgewater and Cam Newton. I like watching the leadership styles and how they can move a team to victory at any cost."

"I never heard of anybody with that approach to watching sports before?"

"I am different. I get inspired from many totally different situations. Inside and outside my industry, but my goal is to be a better boss and leader."

"You are the real deal Jillian Forrester."

"I try to be if that's what you mean."

"It still surprises me that you don't have season tickets. You miss all of the excitement of the traffic, people, smells and touchdowns?" Byron inquired.

Jillian chuckled as she said, "I know, I know, I am missing out. Lately I have had meetings after church on Sundays for conference planning and after singing two services, I'm tired, grab a meal and I just go home for a quiet evening."

"Do you prefer quiet evenings home alone?" Byron looked at Jillian quickly and then back to the road to gage her reaction. Jillian took a long deep breath and admitted, "Yes and No. Yes, I like quiet evenings at home, but no, I don't prefer to be alone. I just choose to be alone rather than with the wrong person or group of people."

"That's a fair answer. I also don't prefer to be alone either, but I also choose to be alone until the right person makes me not want to be alone anymore." After that, thankfully, Byron exited right off of I-71 and onto the Montgomery Road exit and then into the Kenwood Towne Center. Jillian didn't have a comeback after that statement. Byron didn't valet park. He parked far enough from the mall, but close enough to walk to the door. Byron wanted any excuse to hold Jillian's hand anywhere.

The hostess seated them in a nice cozy booth. *The Cheesecake Factory* menu is a book so they needed a few minutes to look over the menu. Once the server took their order, Byron was the first to start the conversation, "So have you ever thought about being an artist up on a stage like that in concert?"

"Sure, I believe everyone that sings fantasizes about it. When I was younger, I spent hours practicing with records in the basement. I put the records on repeat and they played over and over again. That's how I learned to direct a choir listening to "*The Hawkins*

Family" or *Andre Crouch* records. I loved their music then and still do today." Jillian's eyes lit up and smile brightened at the thought of those days of fantasy.

"You should have seen your face just then when you were telling me about that. You sure you don't really want to have that life right now? It's possible."

"I guess anything is possible. My dad kind of squashed those hopes when he said that I would be broke if I did music as a major in college. I did minor in music, but I pursued the more practical business degree instead. I still get my love of music out in church each Sunday."

"I just want you to know that you can still do it if you want to. There is nothing that can stop you when you make up your mind."

"I know. I give that same speech to young people all over Cincinnati."

"It's true and I'm not just a saying it because of who you are. You can do it, if you want to. Let me know if you change your mind, I do happen to know a few people," Byron ended with a shining white tooth smile that should have been on an upcoming Crest commercial.

"Thanks mister motivational speaker, I'll let you know if I change my mind." The server arrived with their food and they both told the server 'thank you.' Byron reached for Jillian's hand to pray over the food as he had last night and at his amen, they both started eating like polite ravenous wolves.

"Is it good?" asked Byron.

"Yes, it is really good and hot. Is your food good?" replied Jillian.

"Yes, very. You really don't know how hungry you are until you start eating."

"Exactly. One thing about Cheesecake Factory's food it is consistently really good. I don't think I have been to one across the country that I haven't enjoyed."

"Same here."

Byron and Jillian continued to make small talk throughout the meal. They discussed their likes, dislikes, college years and other topics that would fill in the gap. Secretly, Byron loved to hear Jillian talk. It was refreshing to be with someone that was insightful, intelligent and beautiful. Her mouth, her eyes, her hands and her voice literally mesmerized Byron. He was attracted to her inside and out. Byron had dated a lot, but his heart was always in Cincinnati with Jillian. Jillian was easy going and didn't seem too demanding. Jillian did have a high standard in the way she worked, lived, presented and represented herself to others. The added bonus to beauty and brains was her ability to use and be fascinated with technology. Jillian was a geek like him. He knew that he had hit the jackpot. Byron was making detailed notes for future reference of every detail of the things she said and didn't say. He planned to use the information to benefit the both of them.

"Are you up for dessert?"

"Sure, only if we share a piece of cheesecake. I am really trying to watch my weight."

"Why don't you let me be the judge of that? From where I am sitting, I like everything I see, just like it is." There was that stare again that made Jillian happy, overwhelmed and scared to be too hopeful all at the same time.

"Okay, what would you like? You choose."

"Thank you for the compliment and I choose turtle cheesecake." Byron motioned for the server and placed the order for the dessert. A very large piece of caramel, pecan turtle cheesecake arrived on a plate with two forks."

"A lady after my own heart, all of my four favorites, caramel, nuts, chocolate and cheesecake. Yes, real men eat cheesecake."

"I know that's right. I'm sorry, but I should have asked if you are allergic to nuts."

"Nope, I am not allergic to nuts. My friends say that I am nuts at times." Jillian giggled like a five year old. She covered her mouth so she wouldn't spit out anything. She was having a great time with Byron. 'Lord, this is great' was in both of their thoughts.

Byron asked about how the next steps for conference planning were going.

"Well, I was supposed to contact Vernice tonight, but it appears that my schedule was wonderfully rearranged thanks to you. I will find out on tomorrow where we are on the National level. Pamela sent Vernice a list of questions that we had for the national planning team. I envision that the conference is going to go well. Our intentions are good, we are putting in the work and good response is coming in from churches around the country so we are making good progress."

"That's great. I'm glad I could steal you away from business for a while. You sound like you are giving an update to the White House media."

"It did sound like that. Sometimes I don't know how to relax." Jillian realized.

"Well, we'll have to change that," Byron said with a naughty grin and eyebrows raise. "So, how is Vernice?"

"She's fine."

"Is she still married or divorced?"

"She's been divorced for years now. Her son's father just left her and her son one day. She is a wonderful girl too."

"You sound like you have firsthand knowledge about people being unfaithful."

"More than you want to know, but I don't want to talk about that tonight."

"Okay, you know Myron always had a crush on Vernice. He was a little hurt when she married and moved away."

"Really? I didn't know that and I am sure that she didn't know that either. Mm, wouldn't that be interesting?"

"Don't you tell her either." Byron teased as he pointed his index finger directly in Jillian's face. "Promise? I don't have a knife to have you make a blood promise. Myron would kill me if he knew I revealed his secret crush. Pinky swear." Byron put out his pinky for Jillian to grab a hold and promise.

Jillian put her pinky in his and said, "Okay, I promise I won't tell her. By the way, these are butter knives and not sharp enough to draw blood. By the way, who was your crush, Byron, so many years ago?

"You."

"Me?"

"Yes, it was always you."

"Where have you been? I had no idea about how you felt."

Byron leaned in with his answer, "I needed to be ready, mind, body and soul for you. I wanted to come correct. When I walked in your office two days ago, I believe that I was finally given my chance."

Jillian was shocked and speechless again. "Wow, you have made me speechless twice in one night."

"I didn't mean to, but I want to always be honest."

"Thank you for your honesty. I am just surprised, pleasantly, but surprised." Jillian sat back in her seat to take it all in, thinking, 'I have my answer. He is coming for me for real.'

Byron brought Jillian out of her trance, "Well, I believe that we did a great hurting on that cheesecake and our meal. I am officially full."

"Yes, I am stuffed. Thank you for everything and I do mean everything tonight."

"You are quite welcome."

Byron took care of the check and they headed toward the door. When they were walking outside, Jillian felt Byron's hand find hers and they walked hand and hand to his car. Even though the Cincinnati night air was crisp and cold Jillian felt warm inside from just enjoying the moment. When safely in the car, Byron asked as he started the car, "What are you doing tomorrow?"

"First, I am sleeping late."

"What do you call, sleeping late?"

"Eight o'clock."

"Eight o'clock! I thought you were going to say at least ten." Jillian laughed at Byron's dramatic expression.

"No, I can't sleep that late. I am an early riser and always have been since I was a baby. If I sleep past eight o'clock, I am probably sick or fell asleep watching television. How late can you sleep?"

"Sleep, what is that? I have come to the conclusion that I will probably get my best sleep in heaven. I don't really sleep much. About 4-5 hours is all I can get in every night. I get that from my mother. Myron, on the other hand can sleep until noon with no problem. Mom said she moved my crib far away from Myron's because I would reach in and wake him up on purpose. After she moved the cribs, I would cry or make noise until he woke up. I have always been a little mischievous and downright bad at times."

"A little mischievous? I am sure having twins was a hard and busy job. You didn't help matters by waking your brother up early and making the job harder. Shame on you!" Jillian teased.

"Yep, that's me, waking people up early. The life of a real bad boy," Byron said as Jillian laughed.

"I agree, that's you. Remember when we were at convention and you used to run through the halls yelling in the classrooms and then running to hide."

"I still have the marks on my behind from those whippings."

"You deserved it."

"I don't know what I was thinking about."

"I don't know either. It's like something turned off in your brain and you forgot that everybody was going to recognize you. They used to say, 'that one twin is bad. Which one? The dark one.'

"Yes, that was me, the dark one."

"One of my mom's friends said, 'I hope Jillian doesn't pick up any bad habits hanging around those twins.' My mom defended you guys and said, 'she won't.' Jillian doesn't like whippings." Jillian laughed at the thought of all of the times that the twins got in trouble especially Byron. She continued, "But look at you now, all grown up, responsible and successful."

"What about you? I could say the same about you."

"Thank you." They both went silent and only the music played in the background. The streets were relatively empty so Byron was able to move the car smoothly down the highway to Jillian's building. He wanted to talk to Jillian all night asking her all of the hard questions. He knew that he had shocked her enough tonight by telling her that she was his childhood crush.

He would stop now because he knew she was the one. He had no intentions of giving her anything less than the attention, appreciation and one day, the love that she so rightfully deserved. They quickly arrived at the building door.

"Well, we are here."

"Yes, we are. Thank you again for an incredible evening."

"You are welcome. I'll walk you in."

"Okay." Byron came around to her side of the car and helped her out of the car. Still holding her hand, he closed her door with the other hand. He continued holding her hand until she was safely in the lobby and standing at the elevator. Byron turned to push the button on the elevator and desperately wanted to kiss her luscious lips, but bent and kissed her hand instead.

"Good night."

"Good night to you as well." The elevator door opened and once she stepped inside, Byron watched her until the doors closed.

When Byron passed the security desk, the officer said, "Excuse me sir, I don't know you, but Ms. Jillian is one of kind. I have worked here for more than ten years. She is probably one of the nicest people I know. She treats everyone kind and decent. She doesn't treat you like you are something under her feet like the others. If you really care about her, don't let her get away."

"I don't intend to. Thanks man, good night."

"Good night sir."

As Jillian rode up the elevator, she said to herself, 'this must be a dream. I have got to pinch myself. Byron just kissed my hand. That is so romantic.' When she put the key in the door, her cell phone rang.

"Hello?"

"Hey, are you in your condo?" Byron asked.

"Yes, I just walked in the door. Your timing is perfect. Where are you?" Jillian said while dropping her keys at the door and heading down the hallway to her bedroom.

"I'm sitting here waiting at the stoplight about 4 blocks away from the hotel. I just had to call and make sure that you were safely in your condo before I would be able to sleep tonight."

"Thank you. I am so glad to know that chivalry is not only 'not dead' but thriving inside a Randolph man." Jillian placed her purse in the chair and fell gently on the bed to talk to Byron in the dark.

"You are quite welcome. Listen, you never finished telling me what else you were doing tomorrow besides sleeping until 8."

"No, I didn't because I forgot the initial question," Jillian paused only a second and then continued. "Well, this is not my week for getting my hair done so I will probably have a late breakfast around 10 and then go to the stores at the mall to look shopping."

"What is look shopping?"

"When I go to the stores to look, but end up shopping." Jillian let out a low sexy laugh that made Byron laugh as well to hide the real groan that was going on deep inside him. Byron was having some very unholy thoughts of what it would be like to be in Jillian's bed and not having to talk to her on the phone.

"Oh, I get it. The lady likes to shop, but tries to trick herself into thinking that she is only looking."

"Right. At least, I have a limit to the amount I can afford to spend. When I get to that amount, I stop and go home."

"Oh, okay. What's your favorite color?"

"Green really because it is my birthstone. I am a Gemini."

"That's why your logo is green?

"My logo is green for Forrester, like the Forest. Get it?"

"I get it. My favorite color is blue."

"It looks good on you too."

"Thank you ma'am." Byron stayed on the phone with Jillian well into the morning asking the question that would give him her personal preferences in his 'Jillian database' just to please her. He wanted to please her more because she wasn't trying to manipulate Byron into getting her anything. She was already providing for herself. Byron knew that Jillian was saving herself for the right guy. In his mind, he officially off the market and appointed himself as that right guy. The one woman for him was on the other end of his phone line, Jillian Ann Forrester.

"Wow, it is 4:00 a.m. and my phone is hot," Jillian looked at the time on her cell phone.

"It is our first all-nighter." Byron said.

"That sounded dirty." Jillian added.

"Where did your mind just go?" Byron asked with a laugh that was filled with innuendo and mischief at the same time.

"Don't try to play innocent, you know what I mean."

"Yep, I know what you mean. I confess I did mean for it to sound dirty."

"I'm speechless again."

"I'm doing my job then."

"Good night Byron."

"Good night Jillian."

Jillian groaned as she pressed end on her phone. A few blocks away, Byron groaned even louder. If tonight was any indication, Jillian knew that would be seeing him soon. She was hopeful about their relationship. She got under the covers and fell to sleep with a smile on her face. Byron knew he was going to see Jillian and it wasn't going to be soon enough for him. Byron's hotel room suddenly got darker and lonelier. He hadn't noticed it before because her voice in his ears warmed his heart. The warmth in his heart suddenly spread to his body and he took that body into the bathroom for a cold shower.

Chapter 4

The next morning at eight o'clock on the dot, the phone rang. "Hello?" Jillian's voice was hoarse and scratchy from only 4 hours of sleep.

"You are not up yet? That's a good sign. You are usually up watching TV, washing clothes or working by now. Your voice sounds like you had a late night. So, how did it go?" The very happy Monica said on the other end of the line.

"Great. I am so sleepy."

"What time did you get in?"

"I got in around midnight, but we talked until 4:00 a.m."

"Fantastic! That means he is very interested in you and enjoys talking to you. When are you seeing him again?"

"I don't know, but this going out on Friday night is something else. I am not used to it."

"You will get adjusted. You are not used to dating on any night, Friday, Saturday or Sunday through Thursday, what are you talking about girl. You are so rusty and out of practice it is not funny."

"Thanks so much for reminding me. I am thrilled, but tired at the same time. Just when I settled into being alone with my 'total quiet eating at home by myself routine' boom, here comes Mr. Byron."

"I told you that would happen as soon as you stopped worrying about it and start working on something else, somebody would come in your life. Who knew it would be someone that you already knew and let alone, one of the twins."

"Who knew," Jillian's voice trailed off and just then a beep was on the line indicating someone else was trying to call. "Hold on, Monica, it's mama." Jillian clicked over, "Hey Mama, let me call you back I have Monica on the other line." Jillian hung up on her mother and called her back and was now on a three-way call.

"Mama?"

"I'm here."

"Monica you still there?"

"Yep, I am here. Hey mama what's up? Jillian has something to tell you."

"Monica... Why you put me out on Front Street like that?"

"What's up Jillian?" Jillian's mother asked.

"Well, I have been out with Byron Randolph, one of Bishop Randolph's twin sons, twice this week."

"Which one was Byron, the dark one or the light one?"

"The dark one," Jillian and Monica said at the same time.

"Oh Lord, is he serious or just playing? You know them little boys back then were terrorizing everybody."

"I think that he is serious. Mama, he is all grown up now. We are just beginning to hang out. It started with doing business together. He and his brother have a company that sells and works with setting up computers and other technology. I met with their company on Tuesday about what my company needed. We went to dinner on Tuesday and then we signed the contracts on yesterday. He invited me to go to a concert and dinner last night after work to celebrate."

"That sounds nice. Just be careful. I want you to be very happy. I don't want you to be hurt again."

"I know mama."

"When are you supposed to see him again?"

"I don't know, but we talked until 4 this morning. That is the reason why I was still sleep when Monica called."

"Well, it sounds fine for now. What do you think Monica?"

"I say she should have fun, be herself and if he can't handle it, dump him." Monica said easily.

"You always were the one who could easily dump somebody. You know Jillian loves hard and gets hurt easy. She is not as strong as you are to bounce back from a hurt," Jillian's mom said.

"I know, but hopefully, she learned from that last guy. She's got to be tougher and move forward if it doesn't work out," Monica added.

"You are right. I hope so," her mom added.

"Hello! I am still here on the phone," Jillian interrupted.

"Sorry." Mama and Monica both apologized for overlooking Jillian. Jillian was the oldest, but they still treated her like a baby. When it came to business, Jillian was independent and fine by herself. With regard to relationships, they always protected her like a small child trying to cross the street.

"I realize that I haven't been really successful in relationships, but I am hopeful. More importantly, I am going to enjoy it, whatever this 'it' is. Well, I have one more thing to tell you. He said that I was his childhood crush."

"For real Jill? Wow."

"Monica, you haven't called me Jill in ages."

"I know. I couldn't help it."

"Mama what do you think?"

"That was a lot of talking on the first or was it second date?"

"Second." Jillian and Monica said simultaneously.

"Well, at least, he is not holding back nothing," her mama said emphatically.

"Right," Monica agreed.

Mama and Monica both agreed with Jillian for her to just enjoy it while it lasts and don't get her hopes up too high or feelings in the relationship too deep.

"Well, since I am up already and it is about 9 a.m., I should get some things done. I didn't get home until late and kind of behind schedule. I love you both and will let you know if anything else progresses."

"Okay, goodbye and talk to you soon. Love you both." Mama said and Monica agreed, "Good bye Sis." When they both hung up the phone, Jillian was left in silence on her bed making a mental 'to do' list. Her housekeeper came once a week which was included in her owner association package. As she looked around her room, there was little cleaning to be done because Jillian cleaned up after herself. She knew that she should contact Vernice later this afternoon about the conference agenda. She thought she might run to the outlets just to look at what was new for fall and winter. She wasn't starving, but a warm bowl of 'cream of wheat' sounded good this time of year. She had just finished her list when the phone rang again for the third time this morning. Without looking at who was calling, Jillian just answered the phone.

"Hello."

"Good morning beautiful. How are you?" It was Byron. This was turning into a habit. A good habit that Jillian didn't want to break.

"Fine. How are you?"

"Hungry. You up for some breakfast."

"Sure. What time?"

"I will give you 30 minutes. Be sure and dress comfortable."

"Where are we going?"

"Just dress comfortable and no high heels."

"Okay, but where are we going?"

"I will tell you over breakfast."

"You won't give me a little hint of where we are going?"

"No and stop asking questions and get in the shower."

"How did you know I wasn't dressed?"

"Lucky guess, but you just confirmed it."

"Aw man, nerdy girl just walked into that one. The hazards of not having a brother growing up or I would not have fallen for that one so easy."

"Yes, brothers do help with that sometimes. While I am thinking about it, tell me, pajamas or no pajamas?"

"Wouldn't you like to know? See you in thirty minutes, bye." Jillian said with a little laugh and hung up the phone. Jillian ran to the shower to make sure that she was ready on time.

Twenty eight minutes later, there was another call from security. "Ms. Forrester, Mr. Byron Randolph is here. Send him up?"

"Yes, send him up."

Jillian heard the elevator bell sound. Her heart wanted to swing the door open before Byron knocked on it, but she didn't want to seem too anxious or 'thirsty' as the young people said. There was a knock on her door, she counted to five and then opened the door. A little trick her baby sister Monica taught her.

After she counted to five, she opened the door. "Hello."

"Good morning lady. Are you ready?"

"Yes, let me get my bag. Where are we going again?"

"Look at you trying to be slick. I never told you before so there is no 'going again.' You don't get to know until breakfast. Be patient. Is the *Pancake House* okay with you?"

"Sure, I haven't been there in a long time."

"Did you get enough sleep?"

"Yes, I don't sleep a lot. Five hours is about all I need. Even if someone kept me talking until 4 and then my sister woke me up at 8."

"That means you only slept four hours, so you are missing one hour of sleep right? Okay, I will give you one hour in the car to sleep to make up for it." Byron said looking at Jillian and smiling.

"You weren't supposed to bring that up again. If it happens today, it really is your fault," Jillian said with a laugh and gently slapped Byron on the arm as they descended on the elevator toward the car. Their conversation flowed easily until they got to the circular entrance outside of the condo lobby.

Jillian suddenly stopped, "Where is your car?"

"I left it at the hotel. I rented this for the rest of the weekend."

"It's nice."

"Thanks." Byron opened the door to a sleek, black Ford Expedition. "Do you need my shoulder in addition to the step?"

"No, I think I can make it. You know I'm height challenged." Jillian giggled as she stepped inside the truck with the assistance of Byron's hand and her flat shoes.

"Don't worry gorgeous I got you."

"Thanks again. I can be clumsy."

"Just fall into my arms. I'll catch you."

Jillian almost slipped at those words. Once in the car, Jillian changed the subject quickly by continuing to probe and prod Byron for the plan for the day, but to no avail. She gave up, sat back in the seat, watched the sights and just relaxed. Smooth jazz was playing in the background and although she was sleepy, sleep didn't come.

After breakfast and the server was clearing the table, Jillian asked, "Okay, I have laughed until my side hurts, I am full of breakfast and the company is so wonderful, but where are we going?"

"Shopping."

"Shopping? Shopping for what?" Jillian added.

"Well, I have an idea, but don't know what we'll find. That's the reason why I got the truck because I just wanted to be prepared just in case, I saw something great that would fit and take it with me. So, we will both find out soon enough. Are you up for an adventure?" Byron asked.

"Sure. I know I am in for an adventure with you." Jillian said with a smile.

Byron smiled back. He took care of the check, took her hand and led Jillian out of the restaurant to the car to go to the mystery destination.

As they rode Byron asked, "Okay, so how did you pick out your office facility and furnishings?"

"Well, I knew that I wanted to be downtown, so I just started driving around one day with Patricia until we found several locations. We called and then secured the current location. I had been working out of my house for years. We outgrew the small space and so it was time to move. I had a decent deposit saved and with my new contract, I would be able to afford something relatively nice. This building had been vacant for a while and the price had been lowered so I was able to get a great deal. My sister Monica furnished everything. I gave her the money and she decorated everything. I don't have that gift. Why?"

"Just curious. Myron and I are thinking of expanding into Cincinnati. I want your opinion on a building that has been zoned to double as an office space on one floor and living quarters on the other. My house in Dayton is paid for and I will probably keep it or rent it, I haven't decided yet. I am getting tired of staying in hotels when I stay in town as well as the drive back and forth. As you know, the Taylor & Edwards contract is going to be increasingly demanding and being available immediately is a must. Driving one hour with the traffic can potentially make arriving on time difficult. You feel me?"

"I feel you. That is the reason why I live down town. It costs more, but I have to be near my business. I am excited for you both I can't wait to see it. Is it East or West area from the towers?"

"Forrester is on the West of the towers and I am looking at the East side of the towers."

"Wow, if you purchase this space, Forrester and Randolph would have Taylor & Edwards on lock like an Oreo cookie."

"You've got that right," Byron said. Jillian's phone rang and she recognized the number of her friend Vernice.

"Hello Vernice. What's up?"

"Hey girl. What are you doing, having your cream of wheat?"

"Well, not quite. I am out and about already. What's going on?"

"Nothing much. I was just touching base with you about these questions from your meeting this week. Do you have a minute?"

"No, not really because I am not home."

"Hey Vernice!" Byron shouted in the background. Jillian looked at Byron in horror and mouthed, 'no!' and rolled her eyes at him.

"Who is that in the background? Sounded like a man? Girl are you on a date?"

"Well, I will just tell you that the person who let his presence be known is somebody you know and wanted to say hello. Outside of that, I have no more to say. So, I am going to put you on speaker phone. Ready? Go ahead Vernice."

"Hello, Vernice this is Byron Randolph."

"Byron Randolph? Lord, a blast from the past. How is your brother and parents?" Vernice asked.

"My brother and my parents are doing well. How are you doing?" Byron asked.

"I am doing fine, but curious why are you with Jillian right now?" Vernice asked.

"Well, I was in town and we are hanging out working on some projects together," Byron said.

"Oh, okay. I am sure that there is more to this story, but we will leave it at that," Vernice stated.

"Yes, please stop right there," Jillian added.

"Jillian, we have to talk soon."

"Yes, ma'am we do. Let me touch base with everybody on tomorrow at church and then give you a call later on Sunday evening. Are you going to be home late?"

"Give me a call anytime. I will let you get back to your hanging out. Bye Byron, love you Jillian."

"Good bye Vernice," Byron sounded off.

"Love you too. Bye Vernice," Jillian hung up the phone and hit Byron again.

"Girl, you hit hard. I am glad that I'm not light skinned or you would leave a bruise," Byron said laughing.

"Sorry for hitting you so hard, but now I know why you got so many whippings as a child. Doing and saying stuff you shouldn't have."

"What? What did I do?"

"Lord, you know that you weren't supposed to say anything. Just sit over there, drive and be quiet. I am glad that Vernice is not a part of the convention gossip hotline. You know how church folk are. Help us Father today."

"No, Vernice is not that way. Why are you panicking? Are you embarrassed to be with me? Byron said with a laugh.

"No, I am not embarrassed to be with you. I have been all over town with you these past few days. I just want my space until…"

"Until you know whether this is for real or am I playing with your emotions or taking advantage of you, right?"

"Well, can you blame me? I am having a great time with your crazy self."

"No, I can't blame you. I am having a great time with you as well with your gorgeous self. Let's just keep having a great time. Okay?" Byron wanted Jillian to relax and just enjoy herself. He knew exactly where this was headed and this was the next step, getting her opinion on the new office and his living space.

"That's fine with me," Jillian was relieved to know that she could speak freely. On the other hand, it was great to know that he wasn't trying to hide the fact that he was hanging out with Jillian. She was torn on her own feelings about other people knowing about them besides her immediate family. Oh well, the cat is kind of out of that proverbial bag.

"So, here we are," Byron said as he put the truck in park. Jillian realized that they stopped in front a two story building. Jillian and Byron got out and walked around the building first. The building needed much repair, but she could see the potential. "My first question is are you going to do any production here or is it strictly a meeting place for clients and production staff?"

"This is for meeting with Cincinnati based clients, a gathering place for production staff while here in town and living quarters for me. Myron wants to stay close to the Research and Development, Production and Manufacturing departments in Dayton. We have a small staff that remains in Indianapolis which was officially our headquarters and starting place. We are just expanding to Cincinnati. This tri-city area is our base of our operation. We will be expanding hopefully, to Louisville, Nashville, St. Louis and Dallas." Byron explained their plans, but kept his eyes focused on Jillian.

"Wow, it sounds aggressive. Can we go inside or is someone meeting us here?"

"No, I have the keys." Byron reached into his pocket for the keys and Jillian continued to inquire about the building.

"Have you already bought it or are you still looking to buy it?"

"We are still looking to buy it. A contract is not signed, but the realtor trusts me."

Byron and Jillian spent at least two hours walking through the facility. Byron relayed his vision for the facility and got her input. He valued her opinion greatly. She was impressed with his vision and bought into it immediately.

"Do you have time to go out to Ikea with me to look at some furniture?" Byron asked.

"Sure. I am no expert, but I know what I like when I see it."

"That is all that matters. Give me your honest opinion."

Byron and Jillian spent the afternoon looking at furniture, comparing other office space in the North side of town with what they had seen downtown. They truly worked well together. Their camaraderie was great, their tastes were very similar and the attraction was there physically and mentally. Byron and Jillian had gone from store after store, mall after mall looking comparing and giving their opinions on every kind of furniture, electronics and furnishings that they saw. It was approximately 5:00 p.m. and getting dark because of daylight saving time. They hadn't stopped to eat lunch and it was now time for dinner. Jillian realized that she had spent the day with this man. She hadn't gotten anything done on her 'to do list' and it didn't even matter because she was having a ball. Byron loved spending the day with Jillian as well, if he had his way, he would be spending the rest of his days and nights with Jillian.

"Are you hungry?" asked Byron as they drew nearer to the car.

"Starving. What did you have in mind?" asked Jillian.

"First, why are you so accommodating? Do you have a preference or choice of where you would like to eat?"

"No, I don't have a preference. Where ever we go I am sure to find something to eat. I like to eat, as you can tell, but I don't have a preference." Jillian bent her head to look slightly down at herself as she stated this fact. "You have asked my opinion on stuff all day. You know I have a preference on some things and other things like where to eat, really doesn't matter. I don't have food allergies so I can find something to eat on any menu."

Byron walked right up close to Jillian and looked her in the eye and said, "Young lady, never again put down the way you look or your size in my presence again. Is that understood?"

"I don't think I was putting myself down, just stating a fact."

"I love the way you look on the outside. More importantly, I love everything about you, both inside and outside. Is that understood?" Byron took his hand and gently cupped her face to make sure that she understood how much he meant his last statement. He almost gave in to the temptation to kiss her right there in the parking lot. He allowed his left thumb the luxury to caress her left cheek. Jillian closed her eyes and enjoyed his touch.

She covered his hand with hers and leaned her head back slightly to look in Byron's face as she said, "Yes, I understand you perfectly, but some habits die hard. After years of this battle, I won. I am now finally comfortable in my own skin. I love myself and my life. It was simply a subconscious thing to say about myself."

Byron took his hand from her face and grasped her hand instead to place a kiss in her palm. "Okay, I'll let you slide this time. No more of that. Let's go." They had only taken two steps when suddenly a car backed out of a parking space three spaces from where Byron's car. With Jillian's hand still in his, he grabbed her by her hand to keep her from being hit.

"What?!" Jillian cried out not seeing the car but only feeling the tug of Byron's hand.

"Get back baby!" Byron said as he pulled her to him. The car came to a screeching halt. Byron's arms were firmly around Jillian's waist and her head landed in his chest. "Are you alright? Did he hit you?" Byron asked with the words warmly in her ear. He continued to hold her while he turned her toward him to assess any damage.

"No, I didn't get hit. Thank you. I wasn't paying attention. I didn't see the car moving." Jillian said breathlessly. His arms felt wonderful. He was so strong and comforting. She never wanted him to let go. Byron waved his hand at the car to pull out of the parking space and head to the exit while never letting her go. Jillian looked up to see genuine concern in Byron's eyes and it intrigued her.

Byron was protective and wanted to kiss her right then but continued to hold her instead saying calmly, "I saw his tail lights and I'm sorry if I grabbed you too hard, but I didn't want you to get hit. You sure you are okay?"

"You're fine, I'm mean I'm fine." Jillian said as she blinked her eyes to correct her stammering because she was a bit taken back by the incident.

"Yes, you are fine and so precious to me. Every day I want you to know it." Byron released her body, but held onto her hand as they walked the few steps to his car. At the car, he didn't release her hand while he found his keys in his left pocket and pressed the button to unlock the door. Byron opened the passenger door and made sure that Jillian was safely inside.

After Byron was securely in the car, he turned to Jillian and asked one final time, "You sure you are okay?"

"I'm fine and thank you." Jillian replied. Jillian was deeply touched by this man and she wanted him to know it. She leaned in to kiss him on the cheek, but Byron turned his head slightly, and it landed on his lips. Just a brief contact at first. She had opened that door and Byron was determined to walk right in. He cupped her face with his hands and kissed her thoroughly. He was eager to explore each contour of her mouth. Her tongue, her lips and breath fueled a hunger deep inside of him that would not be denied. She was as eager to respond to the gentle and passionate visitor. She touched his face while branding him with her own tongue in like manner. This wasn't his plan or on his agenda to act like a teenager in a parking lot. Byron didn't care and neither did Jillian. They kept kissing until they had their fill.

Byron finally released Jillian when he heard a sudden growling noise. "Baby, I think that was your stomach growling."

"Yes, I think it was too." Jillian giggled.

"I know that you are hungry for me, but I need to get you some food first."

"Wow, you are something else." Jillian smile.

"Yes I am and you are gorgeous, but I digress. Let me call for reservations." Byron planted another quick kiss on her lips and then reached for his phone. He knew that he wanted a restaurant quiet, scenic, delicious food and with live music. He decided on the *Montgomery Inn* on the river. There was no wait and they arrived in thirty minutes. Tonight, there was a jazz trio playing two shows. They were seated at a roomy circular booth just close enough to hear the band. They were far enough so they could talk without yelling. There was a small area to dance and Byron asked Jillian, "Do you dance?"

"Not since high school. I do have rhythm, but I don't know if my feet got the memo. I can sing, clap, sway and play a tambourine in church at the same time, but when I add my feet, my body doesn't want to cooperate. I will give it a try if I have a good and patient teacher."

"I think I am a good teacher especially with a willing student."

"You've got a deal." The server returned with their drinks and they placed their order. The band started playing "Get Here" by Oleta Adams. Byron stood up and asked Jillian to dance. Byron turned to face Jillian and she asked, "Okay teacher, what do I do first?"

"You are a bossy student aren't you? Give me your hands and I will place them where they should go. You have to step in a little closer, follow my lead and move with me to the music. Just relax. It will be fine," Byron whispered in her ear.

"Okay."

Byron brought Jillian's hands to his chest because she wasn't tall enough to reach his neck. Jillian stood five foot three and Byron was easily over six feet tall. Jillian hated that she didn't have her heels on at that moment. His arms were long and his hands just made it to her waist. Jillian was afraid that he would have to bend in half to get that low. She started off looking down at her feet to make sure that she didn't step on Byron's toes. His chest felt like a well sculptured rock under her hands and scented with the most heavenly, intoxicating aroma. The smell took Jillian's attention away from her feet, feeling of inadequacy or the rest of the people in the room. She concentrated on flowing with and following Byron's lead. Byron was gentle and strong all at the same time moving them in a slow motion in one corner of the small dance floor space. They were joined by three other couples on the floor which made the dance floor smaller and their dancing even closer.

"Not too bad for your first time out on the dance floor. I think you've danced before, but didn't have a good teacher," When Byron began speaking, Jillian realized that she was going to have to look up to see his face.

She lifted her head slowly and said, "I don't know about the teacher, but this student is just hanging on for dear life. Thank you for taking the awkwardness out of this. I won't be wearing flat shoes around you very often. Flats make me too short."

"It doesn't matter about your height as long as you are in my arms." With that said, Byron took her on one more turn on the dance floor and when he turned back to the table, realized that the food had arrived. "I see that the food has arrived, let's sit down." Byron took Jillian's hand and led her back to the table for a scrumptious meal and conversation. Byron loved to tease Jillian to see her smile and she would hit him back just as an excuse to touch him. The band came back to the stage with a fast set of songs. Byron and Jillian joined the others on the dance floor again. When they returned to the table, Byron said, "Jillian, you don't move too badly."

"I have one move, side to side, back and forth, snap your fingers, that's it. Thank God the music is good and ole' school or I would be floundering like a fish out of water," Jillian giggled and smiled that beautiful smile. Byron had looked at her lips each time she smiled with longing. He wanted to taste them over and over again. They sat for a while longer listening to the music and watching the water. The band played the Teddy Pendergrass hit, "Turn off the lights" and Byron said, "Come on, I need one more dance before we go."

The dance floor was crowded with as many people as possible for the final slow song of the night. Byron would use any excuse to bring Jillian as close to him as possible. He didn't care. Unbeknownst to him, Jillian didn't mind either. She just was trying not to embarrass herself. She felt protected and cherished in his arms. She felt that nothing would hurt her in his arms. This was a great feeling. Her dad always said, 'Jillian, you need a knight in shining armor to protect you.' Could Byron be that knight in shining armor that she had been longing for? She told herself, 'I hope so.' After that dance, the lights came on and the restaurant staff was preparing to close. Even though the song ended, Byron's contact with her hand never seemed to end. Byron bent to Jillian's ear and said, "Well, they are kicking us out of another restaurant this week."

"Yep, we are such terrible customers." Jillian giggled.

"Exactly. Let me get the check and let's go," Byron paid for the check and they headed to the car. Byron opened her door and as she stepped on the side board to get in the car, he softly said her name, "Jillian." She turned and looked down in his face. Because she stepped up, she realized her face was directly across from his. Byron placed both hands on the car door frame and leaned in for what he had wanted to experience again today, was her lips on his. The first contact was open mouthed, greedy and wet. They had both just enjoyed a wonderful meal, but food wasn't what Byron was hungry for. He already knew that one kiss would never, ever be enough. He continued with a second, third and fourth kiss placing them softly and slowly on various parts of her mouth. It was left up to Jillian to determine the next move. He was going to take his cue from her. Overwhelmed by the shear hunger in kiss, Jillian almost fell inside into her seat by the electricity of only their mouths touching. By the fourth kiss, Jillian knew Byron was waiting on her and she couldn't help it. She gave into her desire to be back in his arms. In an instant her arms were around his neck and his hands were around her waist pulling her tight to his chest. Her feet were still planted on the side board to give her balance. Their mouths were open and tongues were doing a mating dance as old as time. The world around them was no more except the satisfaction of being in each other's arms and the gratification of the pleasure coming from their mouths. To the outsider, they sounded hungry like they hadn't eaten for days. The receipt in Byron's pocket was proof positive that they had just eaten. What Montgomery Inn was serving wasn't what Byron and Jillian were hungry for. Not another deal, project or contract signed could satisfy this need. They were so caught up in their kiss that they didn't realize that there was a gentleman who needed to get in the driver's seat of his car. He had been waiting outside his door after securing his wife on the passenger side.

He couldn't wait any longer so he said, "Excuse me man, I just need to get in my car." Byron and Jillian turned their heads simultaneously at the sound of his voice. They broke their embrace quickly while Byron secured Jillian in the car and closed the door. He turned to the gentleman and said, "Sorry man, you know how it is?"

"I used to know how it is. Enjoy yourself."

Jillian was in the car straightening her jacket, catching her breath and multiple questions where running through her mind, 'What was that? Woo girl? That was incredible.'

When Byron settled in his seat, he turned to Jillian, placing his hand on her left cheek and said, "Before your mind starts racing with a multitude of questions, you are incredible. I loved every minute of it and I hope to be kissing you like..." Jillian stopped him in mid-sentence by turning in the seat on her knees to place her body across the console and her hands on either side of his face to resume the kiss. She surprised herself. Back in the day, they would say, 'making out.' The windows were getting steamed, breathing became choppy and the dance of tongues kept their own time. Jillian hoped that the kiss would state for her how much he meant to her and that she wanted him in her life for a long time.

"Well, church lady it is good to know that there is some fire down in them bones and it not just holy ghost fire," Byron said as he broke away from her embrace and leaning heavily back against the head rest.

Jillian couldn't help but laugh and rest her forehead on his adding softly, "Don't tease me, but I have to say, church boy, you bring it out of me. You are what the church mothers were warning all of us about." Byron and Jillian both chuckled again. Jillian was glad that it was dark because she knew that she was blushing.

Byron lowered his voice to a deep baritone and said, "I don't know about all of that, but you are a great kisser." Byron kept his arms securely around Jillian to keep her near him. He felt that she wanted to return to her side of the car, but he wasn't quite ready to let her go. He added, "Before you so wonderfully interrupted me, I was saying, I hope to be kissing you like this a very long time."

"Aw, that's so sweet and thank you." Jillian said quietly.

Byron continued to look into Jillian's eyes while she remained in his arms and bent his head just slightly for one more kiss which turned into five more but who was counting.

When they finally stopped, Byron said, "I need to get you home to get some rest before your big day tomorrow. Don't blame me if you are sleepy and when you sing some of your notes are cracking."

"I will blame you for getting me out of my routine," Jillian smiled.

"Your routine may be off, but I have had the week of my life. So, get over there on your side of the car young lady and keep your hands to yourself. The console is the dividing line and don't you come across it again." Byron positioned his hand like an imaginary knife up and down the console to emphasize the dividing line. Byron and Jillian both laughed at that statement.

"Ha, you started it," Jillian said quietly as she looked down at her hands and then back to Byron's face.

"Yes, I started it and I didn't realize what Pandora's Box I was opening when I kissed you. Help me Lord, with this woman right here," Byron continued to tease while looking up at the ceiling.

"Aw man. You've got your nerve," Jillian said with a smile. Byron started the truck, put it in reverse, proceeded to exit the parking lot and onto the adjacent street. Byron reached for her hand that was lying in her lap. Jillian pulled back her hand quickly.

"I thought we were keeping our hands to ourselves?" Jillian teased.

"No, this is my truck for the weekend. I can put my hands where I want to put my hands. Girl, give me your hand." Jillian laughed again while extending her hand. Byron took her hand in his, looked into her eyes and smiled that devilish smile that she was coming to love. He kissed her hand so softly and held it until they pulled into her building drive way. Byron's heart was completely filled with love, desire and care for this woman. He knew it. He could feel it. It was unlike anything that he had ever experienced before. He knew that he would fight anybody who stood between him and winning her love for him.

Byron stopped the car and got out to open her door. Jillian was not helpless, but Byron would find any excuse to touch her. He reached for her hand one more time to help her down out of the truck for a final time this evening. She was his precious passenger. You handle all cherished things with the ultimate care. They slowly walked to the elevator door. The security officer was at his desk, but only observed them briefly when they entered. Byron wanted to relish this last few moments before Jillian got on the elevator. His walking pace was extremely slow. Jillian turned to Byron with her back to the elevator.

"Well, here we are," she said with a touch of sadness. 'Why do I have to have such high standards,' Jillian thought to herself. "I had a wonderful day and thank you for everything," were the words that Jillian finally said.

"You are welcome, beautiful. Call me when you get upstairs so that I know that you are in alright. I would love to come up, but I don't think that is a good idea tonight. I can't be held responsible for what I want and would love to do with and to you."

"I think that is best considering one, I am a good girl and two, I might stop being a good girl and let you."

"My goodness, I will be up half of the night trying to get to sleep after hearing that," Byron bent his body in half to get one last kiss before going to his very lonely hotel room. He took his left arm around her waist and his right arm encircled her neck to bring her in close. Their eyes instinctively closed on contact and the minutes ticked by as neither wanted the kiss to end. Finally, Jillian was the brave one and withdrew her mouth from his and encircled his waist with her arms in an embrace that said, 'we've got to stop this or soon we won't be able to.' Jillian released Byron, pressed the elevator button and stepped inside. When she turned she could see that Byron was still breathless, lips were swollen and eyes were filled with longing while she placed the key card in the slot next to the number twelve. Byron didn't move until the doors closed. He stood there for a moment hoping that she would return. He watched the numbers above that elevator door keep going higher and higher away from him. He turned and walked quickly to his car. He had only driven to the end of the block and was sitting at the light just in time to receive her call.

"Hey beautiful, are you in okay?"

"I am in. Thanks again for everything. I had a wonderful time," Jillian had secured her front door and was making her way down the hallway to her bedroom. She turned on the light and flopped down on her bed after taking off her shoes. She leaned back on her mountain of pillows.

"You are quite welcome. What's wrong? There is a sad tone to your voice?" Byron asked.

"Nothing, just a little tired and need to go to sleep," Jillian was screaming, down inside 'everything is wrong! My body is screaming for you right now.' Jillian knew that it wasn't the right time so she made up an excuse. She also knew that she was overreacting and would sound like a silly third grade girl if she passed him a note that said, 'do you like me enough to marry me, check yes or no.'

"Because it has been a long day, I will let you get away with it this time. On another day, it is not happening young lady. Understood?"

"Yes, sir."

"Good night, lady."

"Good night to you too Byron," Jillian slowly hung up the phone. She wanted to continue the conversation, but that would be another time. She knew that going forward in this relationship with Byron on whatever level, she would have to be honest with him. At forty, she should be able to express her feelings. It appeared that Byron was being honest with her. She could see in his eyes that he was very attracted to her and his kiss promised volumes. Why did she hold back? She knew exactly what it was, she didn't want to scare him off. She had spent her life thinking that every failed relationship had been her fault. In her experience, she usually fell hard for the guy hoping that he would return her feelings. In the end, the guy was just using her. She had repeated this cycle so many times it was hard to try again. She had just gotten the pieces of her heart put back together after the last incident.

A few blocks away, Byron was getting into bed reliving the day and wondering what was really bothering Jillian? He wanted to call his brother and ask him about it, but resisted. Myron was probably in the lab somewhere working on their latest invention. Good for him. He turned out the light instead and while lying on his back, questions soon rushed to his mind. 'It's apparent, there is no one else? If there is someone else, it is not serious. No one called, texted her and she called no one all day.' Byron had seemingly kidnapped her for the entire day and night for that matter. He felt like she wanted to say something more, but hesitated. He would relish one more chance to be with Jillian on tomorrow. He didn't need to ask what her plans were for Sunday. He knew better. Church is where he would find Jillian Forrester on Sunday. Fortunately, he was fine with waiting until after church to spend more time with her. Byron told himself, 'To church I will go. I want to be where she is.'

Chapter 5

The alarm clock went off at 6:30 a.m. and normally, Jillian arose quickly. Today, the early riser was moving rather slowly this morning. She had two hours to get her voice and body together to sing at the 8:30 and 11:00 a.m. services. As an experienced singer, Jillian had some tricks up her sleeve. She had tried all of the remedies from a cap full of oil, hot showers, hot tea, decaf tea, lemons, peppermint and gum to keep her voice in shape. Today, it was going to take them all and God to give her the voice to get through these two services. She ran to the kitchen knowing that she had better start her tea kettle prior to stepping in the shower. Jillian moved quickly back to her bedroom to get quickly dressed.

Since it was fall headed to winter, the closet was filled with dark colors so a nice black pant suit, comfortable heels, pearls, unwrap my ponytail sounds like the order of the day. Because Jillian sang a lot, her clothes were classic and conservative. Her mother had the skirt not too tight and sit down not too short test as well as the raise your arms and the sleeve is long enough test. Fortunately, this pant suit came with a long jacket which should have everything 'covered up' to everyone's liking except probably Byron Randolph. Where did that come from? Jillian smiled to herself at that thought. She caught Byron staring at her from head to toe too many times this weekend. The mothers would be scolding her now by saying, 'get your mind off of that boy and keep your mind on Jesus.' She chuckled to herself as she turned on the water to the shower.

A few blocks away, Byron woke up early thinking about Jillian as he turned on the TV. He wondered what time her church services started so he reached for his iPad for the church's website. He was tempted to text her to say hi and ask about service times, but didn't want to spoil his surprise. The time was 7:15 a.m. which was way too early for Byron on Sunday morning. He grabbed the room service menu to order breakfast. He would eat and get dressed slowly to prepare himself for the big surprise.

Meanwhile, Jillian pulled into the church parking lot and it was nearly full. At 8:25, she was running from the parking lot to get into position prior to service starting. She had missed group prayer so she removed her coat, her purse from her shoulder and kneeled down at her seat to say a quick prayer on her own. She was young, but still old school. The lights were dimmed for corporate prayer so Jillian was able to slip in next to Pamela in the soprano section as the media department was handing out microphones. Pamela and Linda were standing there with bowed heads.

Pamela leaned over and whispered, "Girl, where have you been? Everything alright?"

"Yes, I am fine, but moving slow this morning" Jillian confessed.

"You have a hot date last night or what?" Linda said with a smile waiting for Jillian to give her an answer.

Jillian gave Linda a side glance and said, "who me a hot what?"

Pamela replied, "A hot date. It could happen?" Jillian knew she was wrong and repented immediately. 'Forgive me Lord' that really wasn't a lie or was it? I didn't say I had a date or didn't have a date. I just asked a question. Jillian knew she had had a wonderful date and she could still remember the kisses to prove it was a date. She wasn't ready to admit to anyone except her sister and mother about going out with Byron just yet. It was too new, too personal.

The early service went well and there were approximately 10 minutes between services. Linda and Pamela cornered Jillian quickly and said in unison, "What happened?"

"I was moving slowly this morning that's all," Jillian was a terrible liar and they both knew it. "Can't I be late to church once in my life and not get the tenth degree?" Jillian added.

"No!" they both answered staring her in the face.

"Given the concern of you both, forgive me for being late this once. Secondly, I thank God that my girls have got my back. Third, I pray that this will be my first and hopefully, last time late on Sunday morning," Jillian gave a quick chuckle to hopefully, throw them off. She knew that they were still going to inquire, but for now, that would have to do.

Jillian's friends kept up the inquisitive stare, grunting and smacking their mouths together in that way only friends and mothers can when looking at something or someone suspicious.

Pamela nor Linda was convinced, but they decided to let her get a pass this one time. Linda spoke up and said, "Okay, we will let you slide this time, but if it happens again. We are coming after you. Got it?"

"I got it?"

Pamela asked, "What are you doing after church?"

"Going home to take a long nap."

"Ah ha! So you did go out last night and that proves it!" Pamela exclaimed.

"You usually go out with us or go home and eat alone. You are going straight to sleep? Who is he and what is his name?" Linda pried.

Just then James poked his head in the choir room and said, "Ladies we are about to get started for next service."

"Okay," Jillian called back. Thanking God all the time that she didn't have to continue with the scrutiny of her friends and moved quickly toward the door.

"She is not getting away that easy. We will find out one way or another," Pamela whispered to Linda as they entered the sanctuary.

The minister of worship opened the 11:30 service with a prayer and scripture. The band tuned up for a high praise song and the service was well under way. The church was rocking and rolling. The people were clapping their hands, the praise team was swaying back and forth, fans were waving and Hallelujahs were heard all over the building. Hands were lifted in the air and several eyes were closed. Jillian was always watching throughout the entire service even during prayers or solemn worship times. Jillian's first pastor always said for you to continue to concentrate on God, but keep your eyes open. Jillian adhered to that philosophy and today it was more important than ever. The chorus of "*Our God is an Awesome God*" was ringing out clear when Mr. Byron Randolph came in the sanctuary door. He looked like a runway model making his entrance onto the stage. He was impeccably dressed with a black suit tailored to perfection with a light grey shirt, grey handkerchief, but no tie. Byron stopped at the back door and did a sweep of the sanctuary. Unfortunately for Jillian, he selected her side of the church. The usher immediately recognized Byron and had no problem smiling in his face, switching her behind in front of him while she ushered him down to the third row.

Jillian knew she was jealous as soon as she got upset about how the usher greeted Byron. What did the usher have to do with anything she was just bringing the man to a seat? Of course, she greeted him warmly. If a single, straight, good looking and educated brother comes into church, wouldn't you want to put your bid in first? What girl wouldn't? Jillian felt ashamed at her immediate jealously. It wasn't like Byron was her boyfriend, her man or husband. She had no right, but last night's kisses sure did give her a reason. As soon as he sat down, he was sweeping the choir stand trying to get Jillian's attention. Jillian ignored him by pretending she didn't see him. She closed her eyes quickly and then started looking up toward the filled balcony at no one. Jillian thought, 'Why was she having so much trouble looking his way? Nobody knew they had been out together but her mom and sister. What was the big idea?'

Jillian knew that it was only a matter of time that her friends would put them together and she wasn't ready for that yet. Jillian also knew that as good as Byron looked today she would lose all focus on the service just by taking one glance at him. 'Help me Jesus' Jillian prayed silently.

Since most of the congregation had their eyes closed they didn't notice Byron when he came into the sanctuary. Once the usher seated Byron she quickly went to the pulpit and whispered to the minister who normally welcomed the visitors. Jillian suspected that Byron Randolph's name was being added to the list of special guests. The minister quickly ended the prayer by saying, "For these and all other blessings we ask, thank you and praise you In Jesus' precious name. Amen."

The church responded with a loud chorus, 'Amen.' There was no way to completely avoid Byron now. Next up in the service was the acknowledgement and greeting of all visitors. The business owners call it pass your business card and the single sisters call it pass him your number. The minister said, "Good morning and Praise the Lord to everyone. We have come to one of favorite times in our service where we greet our visitors. Whether you are here for the first time or haven't been here in a long time, please stand."

The congregation applauded, smiled and greeted the visitors nearby. Jillian thought, 'stop being stupid. Look in Byron's direction. It's not like you haven't known this man all of your life.'

As soon as she looked in Byron's direction, he gave her a long stare and a quick nod of his head. Jillian smiled and nodded her head back. Just then the minister continued, "We are so happy to have one of our own as a special guest today, Bro. Byron Randolph. For those of you who are new to us, Byron Randolph is one of the sons of Bishop John and First Lady Linda Randolph from Indianapolis, IN. Bro. Byron grew up with most of us in the Christian Church World Fellowship Conference. We are happy that you joined us today. Be sure and greet Bro. Byron as well as all of our guests as we sing this song."

The band began to play the church welcome song and the praise team chimed in with the lyrics. Jillian was singing so there was no need for her to leave the pulpit area. She did notice that Byron was immediately greeted by several people from within and outside of his seated section. He shook hands, was hugged and at times, kissed on the cheek by many. Some of the real fresh, hungry and 'wanting a man real bad' sisters lingered and touched him a little too much in Jillian's opinion. That jealousy spirit was creeping back on her. Fortunately, the welcome song ended and the service continued. After the last choir song, Jillian moved from the front row to the back row of the choir loft and got out her cell phone to check for text messages. Thank you Lord, she had gotten three. The first one text was from her mother that said, 'hey I see that your boyfriend Byron is here. Do you guys have plans after church?'

Jillian replied, 'He is not my boyfriend and no we don't have plans, but I would like for us to have plans. Lol.'

The second one was from Jillian's sister, Monica, 'girl, the dates must have gone great he is at church. You will have to give me the details later. Lol.'

Jillian replied, 'I hope much later. Lol.'

The third text was from Byron himself, 'hey beautiful. You look and sound wonderful.'

Jillian replied, 'thanks. Glad that you are here.'

Jillian quickly placed the phone back in her purse and she tried to keep her mind on the sermon. Byron's intense looks in her direction, despite her being on the back row of the choir stand were quite disconcerting. Once when Jillian was looking Byron's direction she noticed that the usher had passed him a piece of paper. The single girls strike again to bid to be 'Mrs. Byron Randolph.' Jillian felt a wave of hot, unholy anger come over her. Who was she angry at really? Maybe she was angry at herself for liking him so much and at the same time, fearful of getting hurt again. Jillian told herself that 'at least, he has been pursuing me and I haven't been chasing after him. He came into my office, asked me out and spent money on me.' Jillian wondered if she would feel better if he wasn't so attractive, educated and financially stable.

When the choir members started standing, instinctively Jillian stood as well. Jillian didn't have a clue what the sermon was about or why she was really even standing. She snapped out of it long enough to look one more time at Byron. He was still looking her way and she realized that he was the reason why she hadn't heard any part of the sermon. 'Lord forgive me,' is all that Jillian could quickly pray. While the pastor prayed the dismissal, Jillian wondered what was going to happen next or who was going to approach whom. She then remembered that she needed her coat from the back. When the pastor said, "Amen," Jillian quickly moved to the door of the choir room. At the same time, the women in the audience quickly moved toward Byron. Several shook his hand, asked about his parents and eagerly wanted to know what brought him to church today. He wanted to get to Jillian to speak and then take her to lunch, but was literally mobbed by people. They blocked him in the pew and wouldn't let him out. Jillian spoke to a few members in the choir room and when she came out, saw the large group surrounding Byron. What to do next? She knew it was wrong to leave without speaking, but didn't want to approach him. Their chemistry might give something away. So she did the unthinkable. She left.

Just as she got to her car the phone rang.

"So, are you guys meeting later or what?" Her sister Monica said excitedly on the phone.

"Hello to you too," Jillian said slowly and quietly.

"Why do you sound so down? What happened?"

"I didn't speak to Byron and I left church."

"What do you mean left church? You are in your car talking to me right now instead of in church talking to Byron? Why?"

"Well, when I came out of the choir room, he was surrounded by people and especially the hungry, single and female kind. I just chickened out."

"Chickened out. This is not eighth grade. Have you lost your mind? Is this the same guy that you practically spent the week with?

"Yes."

"This is the same guy that came to church today looking like he should have been on the cover of GQ magazine and by the look in his eyes, only came to see you. I sure don't remember him really noticing anybody else in the choir stand or pew next to him. His eyes were on you. You left him with the church chicks and clean up women. Jillian, you didn't give them a chance to steal him, you gave him away. I know you are not stupid in business, but you are acting really stupid right now."

"I know, I know. It sounded better in my head when I did it. As soon as I got in the car and drove off, I knew that it was a bad idea. I wanted to keep what we shared this week to ourselves. I knew if I went up to him just to speak other people might know."

"Why does that matter what other people think? If you keep seeing him, other people are going to eventually know. Men like that pursue until they get what they are pursuing. It is apparent no matter how much self-doubt you have, that he is attracted to you and came on your turf to prove it. He could have stayed where ever and hooked up with you later. He may have pretended to want to worship with us, but he came primarily see you. Doesn't that count for something? I don't get it. To the trained eye, it was probably more obvious that you didn't speak to him. You have known the guy all of your life. You didn't do anything, but run around getting into trouble with

Byron and Myron all of time. Make me understand. What is the problem?" Monica asked.

"I am just trying not to mess anything up. I don't know."

"Let me calm down and see it from your point of view. Your experience is limited and has not been the greatest. Think about it, what is he going to think when he can't find you in the church after he is finished speaking to other people?" Monica inquired.

"I know. I should have texted him and said, 'I'm leaving and talk to you later or something.' I sent him a text during service. His was the third text I received after you and mama's text. I am hoping that I haven't acted too silly and he calls or texts me or something."

"Well, I hope and pray he does call. No matter what, you have got to master that fear of rejection and realize that Byron hasn't rejected you. Furthermore, you have got to stop thinking that every guy you meet is trying to hurt you. Until he does, you can't assume that he will. I know it is hard. I was there for all of the other break ups, devastations and failures, but let's hope that this is not one of them."

"I know, I know."

"Where are you now?"

"I am on Interstate 75 headed home."

"Well, call me later and hopefully, with some good news."

"Okay. Thanks for everything. I must do better."

"No problem big sister."

"Bye."

"Bye."

Several minutes later, Byron looked around and realized that the choir was gone and the ushers were picking up trash in the back few pews. Byron thought, 'Where is Jillian?' He didn't want to be rude to Mother Williams who clearly had known him since before he and his brother were born. She was still talking about things that happened in the 1970's and going one decade at a time. It would be Monday before she finished. He had to get away from her. He said, "Mother Williams, I really do want to hear the end, but I didn't get to speak to one of my oldest friends, Jillian Forrester. Let me see if she is still here if you don't mind."

"No problem baby. You will be at the convention?" Mother Williams asked.

"Yes, ma'am. God bless you and have a great day."

"Alright, see you then." Mother Williams continued to watch Byron quickly walk away. She thought, 'he looks the way my Harold looked about fifty years ago. He's smart, young, handsome and 'sho 'nuff a man on a mission. He could be just a man in love. Watch out Jillian Forrester. I am going to have to put her on my prayer list.'

Byron hurried to the choir room. It was empty except the musician and the choir director were talking.

"Excuse me. Have you seen Jillian Forrester?"

"No, she's gone. She left a long time ago," the musician replied.

"Thanks." Byron went out the back door of the church and quickly dialed Jillian's number. Jillian saw the number on her phone and realized it was Byron. She steadied her voice and herself for the inevitable.

"Hello," Jillian said calmly.

"That was rude. You didn't even come and speak to the special guest visitor at your church?" Byron asked with irritation, a bit of sarcasm in his voice, but trying to sound teasing at the same time.

"When I came back out, you were surrounded by people. You had your back to me and didn't see me. I didn't want to interrupt so I left."

"You just left! You didn't send a text or call. I came to church to see you, take you to lunch and you just left. Where are you?"

"Home."

"Home already? Don't move, I am coming right over."

"But, Byron?"

"But Byron nothing. Sit your beautiful butt on that couch. Answer the buzzer and let me up to your condo. Do you hear me?"

"Yes, sir."

"Don't you yes, sir me. I am... Never mind, we will talk when I see you."

Jillian had never been around the grown up mad Byron Randolph, but she was about to see it in full affect. Byron sped down the highway toward her condo muttering to himself. 'Why did she leave the church? We could have been eating a wonderful dinner right now at a cozy restaurant. I could be looking into her eyes with some soft music playing in the background looking out at the Ohio River getting a kiss or two. What I am going to do with this girl? I know she knows I like her? How could she not know how much she means to me? She's smart, intelligent, beautiful, spiritual and sexy. Lord help me, she is sexy. I love everything about her. Did I just say love? Oh my, it is worse than I thought. I think I do love her. I can't tell her right now, it is too soon.' Byron arrived at her condo in record time given it was Sunday with little traffic and the fuel from his anger was making the car go even faster. He parked his truck in the front of the building because he didn't intend to be long or come out alone. He walked very intently toward the elevator. The security guard said, "good afternoon, sir, can I help you."

"Yes, I am Byron Randolph to see, Jillian Forrester in Condo 1201."

"I will buzz her and give you access on the elevator." Clifton, the security guard on the weekend, buzzed condo 1201 and Jillian answered.

"Thank you."

"Ms. Forrester, there is a Byron Randolph to see you."

"Yes, Clifton, let him up."

Jillian heard the elevator when it reached her floor. The carpet on the floor masked how intently Byron was walking to her door. It didn't stop as Byron pressed hard and rapidly on her door bell.

Jillian opened the door and was immediately greeted with two hands cupping her face and his mouth quickly on hers. No hello, no yelling or no words, just his hands and mouth. Her eyes opened wide and was clearly unable to speak because it was otherwise engaged by Byron's mouth. She almost fell backward from the force of his kiss. Byron quickly released his left hand, gently wrapping his left arm around her waist, pulling her closer to him. His right hand remained on her face. He caressed her right cheek to reassure himself that she was really there and hopefully, to let her know how glad he was to see her. Jillian was dumbfounded, excited, glad, happy and embarrassed all at the same time. When Byron released her mouth, he leaned his forehead on hers and said, "Please don't do that again."

Breathlessly and in a whisper, Jillian responded, "I won't."

"Why?"

"I panicked."

"Why?"

"I thought people would see it."

"See what?"

"How much I love being with you."

"Wow," was all that Byron could say.

"I wanted to keep it to myself for just a few minutes. I realize that it was stupid, but sometimes when I'm scared, I do stupid things. Before you correct me, I know I am not stupid I just do stupid things sometimes when I panic."

"Okay, I think I got it, but let's sit down so you can explain it to me." Byron and Jillian sat down and slightly turned to face each other on the couch.

"Okay, can I be real honest."

"Please."

"I have been pinching myself all week. You are really out of my league. I looked at the other women and was jealous. I overlooked all of the genuine well-wishers and older, married members and saw all of those hungry, single church women standing around you. I saw the note passed to you in church today. It made me panic, want to protect myself, angry and jealous all at the same time."

"It did?" Byron smiled a little.

"Don't tease me, Byron Randolph. I am trying to be open and honest with you."

"Sorry. I am listening." Byron immediately wiped the grin off of his face. He had to admit down inside, he was happy that she was angry and jealous. She cared about him just as much as he cared about her.

"Thank you. As much fun as we have had this week, I am looking for the shoe to fall or a big problem to arise or something bad to happen. I am just trying to guard my heart. It has been broken so many times, I can't count. It is one thing when someone breaks up with you face to face, man to woman. But, when you have to find out your man's cheating and got somebody else pregnant, it is hard. Not to mention that she was a fellow choir member in your same church."

"Really?"

"Really. It is a wonder I can sing in the choir at all. I love God more than I love anything else. I love Him with everything in me. I want to serve Him until I die. Whenever, where ever and with whatever my hands and gifts find to do for Him."

"I love that about you, but I'm confused. Why did you leave church? Why did you run out like that without saying anything?" Byron looked puzzled and clearly wanted a straight answer from Jillian.

"There is no problem, that's the problem. You are single and do everything that I've wanted from a man and it scares me. I see the potential with us. It is apparent that we are attracted to each other and it is bordering on sin. I am starting to feel things inside that I don't want to feel things and don't want to unless you are serious. I love the way you treat me when we are together. I love it all, but I need to be sure."

"Let me spell it out to you. I want to be in a relationship with you in every way. Given what happened in the past, I know that I have to earn it. You are too special to think I will automatically receive it. I want to date, court and spoil you rotten. I want you to miss me, be able to smell my scent anywhere, long for me and call me every day just to hear my voice."

"Well, I apologize. I confess that I love the way you look at me. You couldn't have been more obvious unless you had placed an ad in the Sunday bulletin."

"Well, about ten people didn't notice me looking at you, because they gave me their number." Just then Byron pulled out a bundle of papers and handed them to Jillian. "You keep them, I don't need them. I have what I want right here."

"Are you sure?" Jillian looked directly into Byron eyes for a straight answer. Byron moved in closer and looked directly into Jillian's eyes very calmly and without reservation.

"I want to see you as much as possible. My heart almost skips a beat when I think about you, see you, talk to you and touch you. My house in Dayton is cold, lonely and empty this weekend because after seeing you in your office, I didn't want to go back to it without you. I stayed in Cincinnati in a cold, lonely and empty hotel room rather than go home just to be nearer to you. I want to kiss you right now and every day of my life. I am very sure of those things. I am also sure that you are hungry and need some dinner since it is after 2:00 p.m. and you sang two services." Jillian chuckled and Byron smiled.

"Have I made myself clear?"

"Yes, you have. So you like me a lot huh?"

"If you only knew," Byron's voice trailed off. He didn't just like her or simply desire her, but he wanted it all, her heart, body and love.

"Well, I guess if we are going to dinner, I should change out of this jersey and leggings." Jillian stood quickly and was stopped by Byron's words.

"No, you don't have to change, just get some shoes, your bag, a jacket on and let's go."

"Where?" Jillian asked wrinkling her face in the most curious way.

"Don't you worry about where. I have it all planned. I need to go by the hotel and change into some jeans and we can go from there."

"Okay." Jillian walked back to the couch and leaned down put both of her hands on his face to plant a sweet, sexy and thorough kiss on his lips. "Thank you for everything."

"You are welcome." She found the remote, turned on the TV and then handed him the remote. She could see through the glare on the screen that he was not watching the TV, but watching her walk away to her bedroom to change. Thank God he respects me or I don't know whether I would have the strength to say no to whatever his eyes are asking for. She almost bumped into the table that her purse was sitting on. 'I hate being so clumsy.' Jillian thought to herself. 'Help me Lord.'

With her purse in tow, she walked down the short hall to her bedroom. She could hear the voice of her mom and her sister, Monica saying, 'girl, look your best and shine when you are with him, every time.' She didn't trust the just put on jeans part of his speech. There is no telling where Byron is taking me. I better use my brain and change clothes. Jillian opened her purse, found her cell phone and sent a short text to her sister. 'He's here and I am changing clothes so we can head out to dinner and whatever else.'

Monica replied quickly, 'Yippee!'

Jillian took off her jersey and leggings and put on a light weight black turtle neck sweater, nice black jeans with a comfortable heeled shoe, her new *Michael Kors* bag and an orange leather jacket. Even though she was going out she was still showing her support to the Cincinnati Bengals.

When Jillian returned, she paused to watch Byron on the coach. Byron had his coat off, one arm up over his head and leaning back on the coach comfortably. Jillian thought, 'Lord, he looks good on my couch. I got to get him and his gorgeous self out of my house.'

"Okay, I am ready." Byron stood up from the coach, found the remote and turned off the TV. He smiled at the very sight of her. He could look at her all day and every day. He thought, 'I am one lucky man.'

"Wow, you look gorgeous, but you didn't have to change out of your jersey."

"Well, my mama always told me to be dressed and ready for anything."

"Anything?" Byron smiled that smile that only one side of his mouth was turned upward and his one eye was cocked to the side. Jillian remembered the book cover of the three little pigs. The wolf looked exactly like Byron looked just then. He looked ready to huff, puff and blow her house and all of her inhibitions down with it. She was playing with fire.

"Yes, anything. Well, almost anything, I guess," Jillian said with a smile looking up at his very tempting face. Byron laughed.

"Never mind. Be careful what you say. Let's get out of here," Byron picked up his coat from the couch. Jillian found her keys on the entrance table and turned a small lamp light on for when she came home later.

Byron held the door for Jillian to leave, but stood close while she secured the door. At the elevator, Byron leaned in close just to breathe in her scent. "You smell divine."

"Thank you." Jillian turned her head only slightly.

"I must warn you that from this point on I might just want to do this a lot."

"Smell me?" Jillian turned her whole body toward Byron this time.

"No, this." Byron placed a soft kiss on her lips.

"Well, I must warn you that I may like that a lot," Jillian replied with a smile and the elevator doors opened.

Once inside the truck, Byron asked, "Do you like Mexican food?"

"Love it," replied Jillian.

"Have you been to the View Cucina yet?"

"No, not yet."

"Good, then we will start there and see where the night takes us. I hope that we can listen to some wonderful music later," Byron said hopeful.

"Sounds great," Jillian replied.

Byron pulled out of the drive onto the street and took her hand in his. They rode to the sounds of smooth jazz on Sirius XM Radio.

When they pulled up to the hotel, Byron told the door man that he wasn't staying long and could he leave his car outside. Upon being offered a large tip, the truck remained and they both entered the hotel. Byron was staying on the concierge floor in a minisuite. The room was complete with an area for working. There was separate bedroom and a small living room. When Jillian walked in the room, she could tell that Byron was neat and organized. His laptop was open along with a few papers on the table. Byron was the perfect host and found the remote, turned on the TV and said, "Make yourself comfortable. I'll be right out." He then sealed it with a kiss.

Jillian made herself comfortable on the couch and heard the water running in bathroom for the shower. She turned on *ESPN*. The announcer said that the Sunday night football was a late one at 8:30 p.m. and that *Cincinnati Bengals* were playing. In a few minutes, Byron came out of the bedroom looking like a casual wear model. He was wearing black jeans, a mock turtleneck and lightweight leather jacket with loafers to match. Jillian thought, 'Lord, have mercy, he is simply delicious.' She realized that Byron asked her was she ready to go, but she said nothing. Brought out of her trance Jillian said, "I'm sorry, yes, I am ready to go." Jillian finally found her tongue.

Byron smiled that sly fox smile and said, "Great." Thinking to himself, 'She's all mine. Hallelujah.'

When they arrived at *View Cucina*, the music was loud and so were the people. There was a live band out on the veranda with a small dance floor.

"Let's go inside to eat, then go outside to enjoy the band later."

Byron helped Jillian down from the truck, with her hand in his walked to the entrance. The hostess promptly seated them in a cozy booth. Menus accompanied by salsa and chips were brought to the table immediately.

"Let's see. Do you like faquitas?" Byron asked while looking over the menu.

"Love faquitas," Jillian responded.

"We will just get enough for two and share."

The server took the order and they sat at the table for a minute with only the music in the background. Byron was seated on the same side of the booth as Jillian. He had decided that he didn't want to be across the table, but wanted to sit close.

"Okay, so I will start. What did you think of service today?" Jillian asked.

"I thought it was good, but hard to concentrate."

"Why is that?"

"Because you were there distracting me."

"Distracting you how?"

"Just sitting there, being you. You've been distracting me for years."

"Where have you been all my life?"

"Waiting for the right time."

"Is now the right time?" Jillian asked.

"The right time and way past time all at the same time," Byron whispered in her ear.

"By the way, did you know that it was my company and office that you were coming to that day?"

"No, I really didn't know it was you. I knew that the company was Forrester, but not you specifically. The thing that has amazed me is our chemistry," Byron said.

"Yes, I know. I know that adjustments and compromises have to be made in any relationship, but the core of the relationship should be love, mutual respect and enjoying each other," Jillian added.

"I agree. Let's kiss on that," Byron stated.

"Any excuse will do," they both laughed out loud and sealed it with a kiss. Just then the server came with their food and drinks and he coughed slightly. "Excuse me, but your food is served."

They laughed again, said thank you, prayed and began to eat. The sizzle of seasoned beef, chicken, shrimp and vegetables over a very hot plate filled the air. The tortillas were hot, the salsa was diced and mixed to perfection along with rice, soft enough to melt in your mouth. The small talk continued with much laughter in between bites of faquita and rhythmic Spanish beats in the background.

"Okay, I have a question for you. How long has it been since you've actually gone to a game?"

"Years. The games are outside in the cold. If I had my way, I would love for Cincinnati to have an inside stadium like the Colts."

"Well, have I got a surprise for you."

"What?"

"I have an executive suite for every home game of the Bengals."

"Wow," Jillian said quietly.

"Wow? Try to contain yourself girl," Byron said sarcastically, "we are going to the game!"

"For real!" Jillian added with a big cheesy smile. "I wasn't supposed to grin that big or say it that loud. I am excited!"

Byron laughed and said, "I am glad." Byron took care of the bill and they headed to the door. "I didn't want to tell you earlier because I really wanted to surprise you. I could tell by the jersey and leggings that you had plans to watch the game."

"Yes, I did. Thank you so much for the surprise. I love good surprises," Jillian said grinning like a kid on Christmas.

"My brother and I share the suite during the season," Jillian wondered in her mind how many other women Byron took to the games. She reminded herself that she had already done and said something stupid today. She didn't want to make the same mistake twice especially in the same day.

"That's great."

Byron was always the gentleman. He opened the door for Jillian and once they were settled in the truck, Byron reached for Jillian's hand once again. Jillian warmed all over again at his touch. When they arrived at the stadium, Byron reached over Jillian and retrieved his VIP parking pass and season tickets. The parking attendant opened the gate and greeted him with, 'Hello, Mr. Randolph. There is a space on the tenth row. Enjoy the game.'

"Thank you." Byron replied and parked the truck and came around to open Jillian's door. That was now his custom. Jillian let out a breath and prepared herself for another adventure with Byron. Byron took Jillian's hand and they headed to the gate of the stadium. Once at the gate, Byron handed the attendant their tickets and they were let into the door leading to the elevator to the executive and private suites. They walked down the corridor to the executive suite door. Byron opened the door to plush seats, a mini-bar, a sliding glass window opening onto the field and two female assistants who were serving drinks and finger foods. Byron pointed out that the bathroom was down the hall if she needed it and that the game should be starting in about an hour or so. They sat down in the center two seats.

"Excuse me, Mr. Randolph, will Mr. Myron Randolph be joining us tonight?"

"No, he will not. Just myself and Ms. Forrester."

"So glad your family member could join us this evening. Would you like something to drink?" One of the servers asked.

"Water for now. Jillian, you want something to drink?" Byron asked Jillian.

"Water is fine," Jillian answered.

"Make that two waters for me and my date," Byron said as he looked the server right in the eye.

"I'm sorry ma'am. Yes, sir," replied the server unenthusiastically. Byron led Jillian over to their seats. He opened the sliding glass window and showed Jillian the football field from their seats. There were screens in the room to give a close up view of the field and the game.

"Where did he find her?" the one server whispered under her breath to the other one.

"I don't know, but she is sho 'nuff different than the last one." The two servers were eyeing Jillian, unbeknownst to her. The women knew that they should keep their opinions quiet because they liked the perks of working on the executive suite level of the stadium.

"Shhh be quiet. It is none of our business, but he is so fine. He could do better. She must be doing something that other girls won't do."

"A man that fine, what wouldn't you do?" the two teased.

The attitude of the server changed when she delivered the waters to Byron and Jillian. "Here we are," she said sweetly and added before she walked away, "Is there anything else I can get for you?" The young woman's back was clearly to Jillian and her words were only directed at Byron. Jillian was too excited to notice or care that she was being ignored and demeaned.

"No, thank you," Byron said and turned his attention back to Jillian. It delighted him that Jillian loved football.

"I am so glad that you like football." Byron said.

"I don't like football, I love it. I can't believe that I am finally at a game instead of watching it on TV. Thank you so much for inviting me."

"You are so welcome. I love seeing you smile and excited about something that I do for and with you."

"It's so easy when you are spoiling me like this," Jillian added.

While Byron and Jillian exchanged pleasantries, the two disgruntled servers continued watching them both.

The first quarter of the game was well under way. The Bengals had scored a touchdown and the other team hadn't scored.

"Byron, I'll be right back." Jillian touched his arm as she excused herself to the ladies room with her purse in tow. The ladies restroom was relatively empty because the game was in full swing. While she was taking care of business in the stall, the two women entered the restroom. Their voices were very loud and sounded much like the young women who had been serving them earlier.

"Girl, can you believe that fine Mr. Randolph showed up to the game with that woman? Lord have mercy. I have seen him with different women before, but nothing like her."

"I know he likes peanut butter because he don't bring no white women up in here."

"Yeah, but I didn't know he liked chunky peanut butter." Both women let out another round of laughter that seemed to get louder with the echo in the bathroom. Good singing sounds good with the echo in the bathroom, but being laughed at or made fun of wasn't quite so pleasant.

"That was cold."

"Cold and true. She's kind of thick."

"She's classy. Did you see that beautiful Michael Kors she was carrying?"

"Yep, chunky or skinny, he don't date trash."

"You right girl."

Jillian thought, 'they are talking about me? I may be larger than both of them, but not by that much. Okay, do I sit in this stall and hide or do I say something? Say something.'

Just then Jillian exited the stall. "Excuse me ladies. Do you like working in the executive suites or do you want to go back downstairs on the party suite level or God forbid, on the general concession stand level? If you like it up here, I suggest that you first, be wise enough to check the stalls before talking about anyone and/or their date on this level. Second, remember that no matter whether Mr. Randolph has brought 1,000 women to these games before me and 1,000 more women after me, I am here as his special guest tonight. Understood? Excuse me again while I wash my hands and take my fine chunky peanut butter behind back in that executive suite with my date."

Neither woman said anything. They moved to let Jillian pass to the sink to wash her hands and exit the bathroom.

In the hallway, Jillian marked a one in the air and said, "That's one for the big, pretty girl and zero for the haters," Jillian knew that she had made a vast U-turn from her behavior at church this morning. She realized that women would always be criticizing her relationships whether in the church or in the street. Furthermore, those two women were dangerous. She was now going to have to watch her drink and food. In the end, she made herself clear, didn't run like a scared, hurt chick, but acted like a grown woman handling her business.

"Are you okay?" Byron said when Jillian returned to her seat.

"I am fine. What's the score?" Jillian said quickly.

"It is still Bengals, seven to nothing. Lions are on the Bengals' 40 yard line trying to score." They both were looking at the field when Jillian put her purse down.

"Well, with that interception, they won't be scoring right now. Go!" Jillian yelled.

"Yes!" Byron yelled in the air and he thought, 'I am in heaven. She likes two of my favorite things, football and technology. It can't get any better than this.'

With that interception score, half time began and Byron was approached by one of the servers again. "Excuse me Mr. Randolph. We have on the steam table hot wings and chips with spinach dip. There is a fruit tray and miniature cupcakes for dessert. What can I get you?"

Jillian stood up immediately, turned and looked the young woman in the face, "is it okay if we serve ourselves?"

The young woman frowned tightly and said, "Well, I guess that is alright. Is that fine with you Mr. Randolph?"

"Sure, that is fine with me." Byron said. "We will just serve ourselves."

"Well, if you need anything, call the concierge desk at extension 1000."

"Thank you so much." Jillian smiled a very big smile as the two exited. Jillian walked toward the table and saw the array of drinks and desserts arranged so nicely. It was half time. "Do you want anything Byron?"

"I may grab a cupcake when I come back. I am going to the men's room. By the way, since you conveniently dismissed those two from the suite, I am going to get a little taste of my sweet right now." He planted a soft kiss on her lips.

"I just wanted to serve you and myself. Is that okay?"

"That's okay, but I just want you to let somebody else serve you for a change." Byron said as he planted one more kiss on her lips before he walked away.

"No problem. Another day I will." Jillian wondered what he would say if he knew that she had just told off his two prompt little servers. Oh well. She fixed each of them a plate of fruit, wings, chips and cupcakes.

Just as Byron headed back down the hall from the bathroom, he overheard voices. "Who does she think she is dismissing us from Mr. Randolph's suite? How are we supposed to get a tip if we don't serve?"

"Well, would you trust us to serve after what you said about her in the bathroom?"

"It was all in fun. I didn't call her fat just chunky peanut butter. You know Mr. Randolph can do better than a sister that size. He has brought better looking women in here before."

"What does it matter to you what woman I bring to the game?" The two young women turned quickly at the sound of Byron's voice. They knew that their mouths had finally gotten them into some real trouble.

"The last time I checked I was a full grown man able to pick who I will and will not date, no matter the color or size. Secondly, my parents are in Indianapolis and my twin brother is not here tonight. On earth, those are the only people I answer to about my relationships. Finally, I would appreciate it if the two of you would march back into that suite, apologize to my date and take the last look around the executive suite level because you will not be serving me or anybody else on this level once I speak to Human Resources. Is that understood?" Byron asked.

"Yes, sir."

The two women turned and slowly went into his suite and apologized. Byron stopped and called the concierge desk.

"Apology accepted," was all Jillian would say to their insincere apology. The Concierge manager appeared and apologized for the employee's behavior as well. When they all left the suite, Jillian replied, "wow."

"I see why you asked if we could serve ourselves. Those two must be out of their minds to think that they are going to talk about you or anybody else with me and then serve us. I think not. That is totally unprofessional." Byron was so angry he was muttering. He knew it now. He loved Jillian. When he loved, he loved hard. No matter what public opinion said, he was going to fight for what was his. He walked from the suite door and plopped down hard on the soft cushioned chair. Jillian sat down beside him and placed her right hand to his face. At her touch, Byron turned to face her.

Jillian brought her face in close and said, "You are right. They were very wrong for what they said. I thank you for defending me. I have been talked about before and will be talked about again. Most of my life, no one has apologized for the hurtful things that have been said to me. It comes with the territory. It is just life. I am finally comfortable in my own skin."

"I am very territorial. If I can help it, I won't tolerate you being disrespected. To me, you are gorgeous, beautiful, and intelligent. I am thankful that you are in my life."

"Thank you. I must confess that I said something to them in the restroom already."

"You weren't going to say anything to me?"

"No, I was trying to put my big girl panties on and handle the situation since I didn't handle myself too well earlier today. Who wants to be the snitch?"

"Jillian, sometimes you have to stand up to the bully. Even after you said something, they still were talking about you and I caught them." Jillian gave Byron another sweet kiss that meant thank you even more than her words.

When Byron released her, he looked her straight in the face and said, "Jillian, I feel like you are my precious gift that I've had another chance of cherishing. I don't mishandle my gifts. I don't tolerate disrespect. If I know about it, I will handle it."

"I appreciate that more than you know." Jillian was thankful that he wasn't treating her like she was helpless, but treating her with the highest regard and care. Jillian loved that in Byron more than she was willing to say right now. Jillian thought, 'Lord, I am caring about this man more and more." With the roar of the crowd, they both realized the second half of the game was starting.

"Come on we are not going to let anything ruin this game for us." Jillian looked into his eyes, kissed him again and grabbed his hand to head back to the other seats.

"Cool." Byron said as he winked at Jillian.

"Go Bengals!" They both shouted as the game was underway.

Despite all of the drama with the servers, Byron and Jillian had a wonderful time during the entire second half of the game. They served themselves of the food prepared until they were full. Jillian surprised Byron with her knowledge of the game. The Bengals won the game 14 to 7.

Byron decided that he didn't want to let her go just yet. A room with slow, smooth jazz, low lights and this woman in his arms would cap his night off nicely. Once they were settled in the car, he turned to Jillian and said, "I want to stop by this jazz spot for just a few minutes. Is that okay?"

"That's fine." Jillian couldn't believe that she said that, but she knew that she could sleep anytime. Tonight was wonderful and she didn't want it to end just yet.

"I am going to be busy this week and won't be able to kidnap you like I did last week. I need one last chance before the hustle and bustle of the week."

"If I fall asleep in your arms, please wake me."

"Don't worry, I know exactly how to wake you up."

That made Jillian blush all over and she turned her face to the door to hide her real reaction. She was simply mush about now.

Byron backed the truck out of the parking space and reached for Jillian's hand. Just then her phone rang and she retrieved it from the side of her purse.

"Yes?"

"Are you still with Byron? Your sister told me that things had worked out and you guys were out together tonight."

"Yes, ma'am I am."

"Hallelujah! Thank you Jesus!! I am praying that this is the one! Okay, I will get off of the phone and let you get back to him." Her mom was loud, all giggles, prayers and laughter.

"I will try to call you later if it is not too late. Bye."

"Bye baby." Jillian hung up the phone smiling.

"Guess who that was?" Jillian turned to Byron as she put her phone away.

"Your mom I take it."

"You are right."

"Checking up on you?"

"Yep. Nothing like a mother's love."

"Believe you me I know it." The traffic was bad coming from the stadium. The Club wasn't far so it didn't take long.

Byron pulled up about a block away from the *Bluzz Wisp Jazz Club* on Race Street. It was crowded on the street after the game and people were coming in and out of the club. There was a special jazz quartet playing tonight. Most of the people were seated at the tables. There were only a few people dancing. Crowded meant close and that was all Byron wanted was to be close to Jillian. They found a table and Jillian put her bag across her body and placed her jacket on a chair nearby. The jacket was so orange it could be seen even in the dim light.

"The band is wonderful. Do you want to dance?" Byron asked. He noticed that Jillian turned her head slightly and let out a low moan. Byron took her hand gently in his and gave it a slight tug to encourage her not to hesitate.

"Sure, I'll try," Jillian fixed her eyes directly on Byron letting him know that he was the reason that she was willing and nothing else.

Byron took an even firmer grasp on her hand as they walked to the dance floor.

"I got you," Byron said.

"I hope so because I don't have a clue what I am doing."

"Just follow my lead and relax in my arms."

"I think I can do that." Byron was left handed so he held onto her right hand, eased his right arm around her waist and her head landed where it should, on his chest. The group played Teddy Pendergrass' *Turn Out the Lights*.

"Do you know how special and rare you really are?" Byron whispered in her ear.

"Um, no, how rare am I?" Jillian looked up from Byron's chest into his eyes.

"You forgot special."

"Oh sorry, how special and rare am I?" Jillian laughed slightly.

"You are so special and rare because you can go from a church choir, to the football game and now you are slow dancing with a date all in the same day. That is truly special and rare."

Jillian laughed at the thought. "No, I am just versatile," responded Jillian.

"She got jokes."

"Yes, I try out the humor every once in a while," Jillian was smiling, but Byron wasn't. His eyes were so focused on every trace and etch of her face because he didn't want to miss anything. Byron wanted her in his human database to get him through the week.

"Jokes and beautiful too?" He couldn't resist. His mouth placed a gentle kiss on her forehead, then her eyes, nose, each cheek and then finally her lips. Jillian thought she would melt right there on the dance floor. Byron was holding Jillian tight because she feared she would lose her balance. She was suddenly light-headed. The room was literally spinning from the intoxication of the music, smells of food and drink, crowd and finally, the pull and consumption of his lips. 'This guy must practice or I am out of practice,' Jillian thought. 'He just can't be that good.' He was that good and he wanted Jillian to remember it all week long. He had neglected a lot of work to be with her this week and it was all worth it. His brother, administrative team and housekeeper wondered whether he was moving to Cincinnati this week. In Byron's mind, he wanted to stay and never leave.

When the song ended, they were still in a tight embrace. The song, the beat and the lighting completely changed and they still hadn't stopped kissing. Yep, it happened again. It was Montgomery Inn all over again. Nobody and nothing else mattered. They were oblivious of their surroundings, but this person, this kiss, right now. Jillian thought, 'this can't be happening. Is this it?' Jillian hoped so because she didn't know how she would get Byron out of her system, if he wasn't the one.

Byron didn't care about who was watching or what was going on around them. Everything in his body wanted this woman, right here, right now in his arms all night and every night. He knew he should stop, but he didn't want to. He was a grown man with a grown woman doing what grown people want to do, enjoying each other in a warm embrace and a hot passionate kiss. 'Lord, help me,' went through Byron's mind as he tried to end the kiss, gain his composure and then figure out where they were on the dance floor in reference to the table that was holding Jillian's coat. Fortunately, other people had joined them on the dance floor so he was able to guide Jillian back to her coat without bumping into anyone else. It was a feat not easily done. Byron helped Jillian put on her jacket. He then clasped her hand, kissed it and hand in hand they left the club.

Byron drove slowly back to Jillian's condo. Once he stopped the truck in the driveway, he finally broke the silence, "I don't want to scare you and I hadn't planned to say this, but I love you. I want to hold, love and spend every day of my life with you. If we didn't have obligations the next several weeks, I would buy two tickets and leave tonight for somewhere. I want you every day, in every way. I am not expecting an answer or response, but I just wanted to let you know how I am feel.

Jillian was shocked, excited and overwhelmed all at the same time. When Byron finished, Jillian had tears in her eyes. As she turned toward him, they fell slowly down her cheeks. Byron reached for his stash of tissues in his console and said nothing while he slowly wiped her eyes. Jillian didn't wear much make up which made her all the more beautiful. There was no blush to smear, no mascara to run or no eye lashes to protect. Her natural beauty made Byron want her even more. Compared to the rest, Jillian was the most gorgeous woman in the whole wide world.

"I know that you aren't expecting an answer or response from me, but I feel that I should give you one. I feel the same way and was hoping that I wasn't having these feelings all by myself. That is what the tears are about. There is nothing like having feelings for someone and they reciprocate them. It is quite overwhelming," Jillian said as she was composing herself. She reached for more tissues so she wouldn't look a total mess.

"I know that you have been through a lot. When people have been through a lot, they don't have time for or want to play games. I also realize that the 'cool, pretty girl code' is not to ask the guy, but wait until he tells you. So, I wanted you to know," Byron said.

"I greatly appreciate it. My sister Monica follows the 'pretty girl code' very strictly. She's got a list a mile long. I can't keep up with it. I just try not to break the rules that I know," they both laughed. Jillian continued, "I am about to break one of those rules by telling you that I would love to continue talking to you all night, but I will be asleep in a minute, if I don't go inside," Jillian laughed again.

Byron said, "I totally understand."

Byron walked Jillian to the elevator for one last time this weekend. He would rather be taking Jillian home to their house, showering together, slipping under the covers and making love until the early morning. He knew in his heart that that would be their life one day soon.

"Well, this is it," Jillian said softly.

"Yep, this is it. Give me a call when you get upstairs."

"Okay," was the only word Jillian could speak before Byron's hands came around Jillian's waist to draw her closer? She was getting used to Byron's tall frame and as he bent down for what he wanted, her arms went easily around his neck. The kiss was hungry, moist and lasted a long time. Byron wanted to place an undeniable impression on her to remember him all week long.

"Good night," was all he could say as he released her to walk onto the elevator.

Jillian said nothing because she was trying to make sure that she didn't faint as she got on the elevator. When the doors closed, she leaned slightly against the left wall of the elevator with a low moan. 'Lord, what have I gotten myself into? I'm in love,' went through Jillian's mind. As soon as she walked in the door, secured the lock and headed to her bedroom, the phone rang.

"Hello, I was just about to call you?" Thinking that it was Byron.

"So where have you been?"

"Who is this?"

"Your long lost friend, Jeremy. I have been thinking about you and wanted to give you a call."

"Jeremy, you have the nerve to call me at one o'clock in the morning on a Sunday night? Have you lost your mind?"

"Yes, I think I have, but I know that you are about to help me find it."

"Hold on." Jillian clicked over to take the other line, hoping that it was Byron this time. "Byron?"

"Everything alright?"

"Yep, I just got a call on the other line and I will call you back."

"Call me back when you are done."

"Okay." Loving it that Byron could hear the slightest change in her voice, but annoyed that Jeremy was on the line. Jillian thought as she switched over to the other line, 'What does Jeremy want? He didn't call me this late when we dated.'

"I'm back. What's up?"

"Well, hold on. I am not trying to upset you. I'm just calling to see how you are doing."

"I am doing fine. What do you want?"

"Well, I was wondering if I could see you sometime."

"First of all, I haven't heard from you in more than five years and secondly, you're in Dallas and I am in Cincinnati. I don't believe that we will be seeing each other soon."

"Oh, I beg to differ. I now live in Louisville, KY."

"Louisville? What are you doing in Louisville?" Jillian realized that she was asking too many questions. She was sounding interested. She wasn't interested in Jeremy who was a controlling, budgeting, nerd with about as much personality as a wet paper towel. Her mom had thought that he would be so stable, secure and sensible for her to date and marry. Back then he was just boring. Jillian was interested in smooth, sexy and strong Byron Randolph. What was she thinking even staying on the phone with Jeremy Garrett?

"New job, more money and a new city. I see that congratulations are in order on your little company. What's it called?"

"Forrester Information Management Company," Jillian said dry and with the enthusiasm of a cold wet sack.

'Little company?' Jillian thought, 'who does he think he is?' Jeremy already knew the name of her company, the location and the profit earnings per year. He thought that with time he could convince

Jillian to marry him. Their two portfolios combined could make a nice retirement package someday. He would love to get his hands on the income that could be generated from her company's monthly receipts or potentially a sale to another company.

"Wow that is great. Well, I am free every weekend so I thought I could come down one weekend and we could hang out. What about this weekend?" Jeremy sounded about as excited as someone about to sand paper a room prior to painting. Jillian had only to remember a few minutes ago she was loving a very heated kiss in the lobby and the lingering embrace on the dance floor. Byron saying 'I want to spend every day in every way with you' brought her back to her senses. Jeremy could just stay in Louisville for all she cared.

Jillian thought, 'This weekend! I don't want to see you any weekend!' Jillian realized that Jeremy was assuming that she was free and not involved with someone.

"Jeremy, thanks for calling and congratulations on your new job, but I am currently in a relationship." Jillian thought that her relationship with Byron was a relationship. He said that he loved her. She had thought that before, but this was different.

"Oh, I am sorry. I guess I should have asked that first before offering to come see you."

"Yes, you should. Listen Jeremy, it's late and I have a long week ahead. I am going to have to cut this short and say goodnight. Thanks again and good night."

"Oh okay, good night." Jeremy knew that he must keep his eye on the prize if he wanted to profit from his little project.

Jillian couldn't believe that Jeremy had called. What did he really want? All she wanted was to get in bed and talk to Byron one more time. She showered, put on pajamas and up under some soft sheets with a firm mattress. She almost fell asleep until she remembered that she needed to call Byron. When she picked up the phone, she realized that he had already called.

"Hey, baby, I was getting worried. I called back and you didn't answer." Jillian blushed from head to toe. Now, this is what I am talking about.

"I took a hot shower and must have missed your call."

"Just the thought of you in a hot shower is making me feel some sort of way. By the way, you are forgiven and I will be awake another hour."

Jillian giggled like a teenager at his words. "Sorry and thanks again for everything."

"Everything alright on the phone call?"

"Yes, it was nothing. It was just an old friend from too long ago."

"A woman I hope."

"Do I hear a touch of jealousy Mr. Randolph?"

"Not a touch, but a ton of jealousy where you are concerned."

"Can I be honest?"

"Please."

"It was a guy that I haven't heard from him in five years. I really don't know why he called," Jillian inquired.

"I know why he called. He realized what he left and wants it back," Byron sat up on the side of the bed and continued talking with quite an attitude. "What's his name? Do I need to come over there and keep an eye on you? You know I told you before, I protect what's mine."

"Oh yeah?" Jillian said sweetly.

"Oh, yeah." Jillian's sweet 'oh yeah' melted Byron right down to a 'Barry White' low bass level.

"I like the sound of that. Right there may keep me awake for about 5 minutes because I will sleep very soundly knowing you care about me that much."

"Take it to the bank baby."

"I will. I just wanted to be honest with you. I don't like deceit of any kind. Agreed?"

"Agreed."

"As for his name, it doesn't matter because I don't plan on seeing or talking to him again."

"That doesn't mean he won't be trying to see or talk to you again. The mere fact that he called late at night states what his intentions are, I know."

"I know you do. Now, as much as I love talking to you, it is now about 2 a.m. and I will be a walking zombie in the morning when I wake at 7:30."

"I know, me too, so good night beautiful."

"Good night to you too." Jillian immediately turned out the light and was probably sleep within seconds because she didn't remember anything past taking off her glasses, pulling up the covers and turning over. Oh yeah, she did remember that hot dream with Byron in it though.

On the other side of town, Byron wasn't getting to sleep quite so easily. He called his sounding board, Myron.

"What's going on Byron?"

"A lot. I'm in love."

"I know that. What else is going on?" Myron asked.

"Some other dude called her after five years."

"And?"

"She told him she was seeing someone."

"That's good so what's wrong?"

"I'm jealous and I think this guy is trying to win Jillian back."

"That's good that you are jealous, but how can he win her when you've been with her all week?"

"Yes, I had a great time too. I didn't want to leave her tonight, but I am uneasy about this old/new guy trying something."

"Well, first, you know how you feel about her. Tell her. Don't blow it. Tell her. Don't be like me who is attracted to the wrong women, gets dumped and still can't get over them. Brother, I don't know how many times I have to tell you. Jillian is perfect. Go for it. Don't let her get away or you'll regret it."

"I told her I loved her. I sounded about 13 years old saying it. She says she thinks she loves me too."

"Don't worry about that. We all make a fool of ourselves at times. She just needs to know you meant it."

"I promise I won't let her get away. I don't like this other guy after her. I feel like I have to protect her from something. What that is, I don't know."

"That's what Randolph men do. We love, protect and cherish what is ours. Handle your business. Give her the Randolph treatment. Love on overload."

"Thanks brother. You are right. I am tired and not really ready for this week. I am so behind it is not funny."

"I got your back and everything is going good. We have kept you abreast of everything. When are you getting in town, in the morning?"

"I should be there first thing. I think I am going to take Jillian home to mom and dad's this weekend. What do you think?"

"Mom and dad are going to love it. I am staying here. I have some things that I am working on and there is a tech conference in Phoenix that I'm headed to and need to prepare for. Be with your woman, spoil her and make her fall in love with you head over heels."

"Thanks. I will see you in the morning. Good night."

"Good night."

Chapter 6

Byron put his love project into overdrive on Monday. The first text came at 6:00 a.m. before Jillian even woke up to just tell her that she was on his mind. The phone call to Jillian was at 7:00 a.m. and they talked until 8:00 a.m. and almost made her late. The flowers arrived by 9:00 a.m. right before she walked in the door. Roses to be exact, long stemmed, in a glass vase and bright red to make the message clear. When Patricia saw Jillian's face, she followed her in her office and demanded to hear how the weekend went. She enjoyed the entire tale of the events of the weekend and realized her boss was madly in love. It showed all over her face. In between calls and other interruptions, Jillian hadn't told Patricia about Jeremy yet. Around 11:30 a.m., she had to explain a delivery. Some cheap carnation arrangement arrived via *Nanz & Kraftz* florists in Louisville, KY. Jillian and Patricia read the note, laughed and called to have a runner deliver them to the security station to brighten the lobby. Jeremy was clearly out of his mind to think that she would consider even a dinner with him based on those tired flowers.

At 4:30 p.m., Patricia delivered a note to Jillian. It stated, 'go home, put on a dress and be ready by 7:30 p.m. I've got to see you, signed Byron.' Jillian tried not to be excited, but she was. Patricia laughed at her and told her to leave now so she would have plenty of time to get ready. At 5:00 p.m., Jillian walked out of

Forrester and headed home. Jillian took a quick shower and got dressed by 6:30 p.m. Her sister reminded her that black was always in fashion and appropriate. There was still time to check email, mailbox and check in with the news until Byron arrived. To her surprise, security called her condo at 7:25 stating that a car was waiting for her downstairs. When Jillian arrived downstairs, there was a very large Lincoln town car and a handsome driver.

"Ms. Forrester?"

"Yes?"

"Mr. Randolph would like for me to drive you to a private location."

"Thank you." The driver opened the door, put her in the back seat and they sped down I-75. Her phone rang.

"Hello."

"Hey beautiful, are you on your way?"

"Yes, I have been officially kidnapped in a lovely Lincoln town car I think by your request."

"Guilty. I had to see you tonight so I brought you to me."

"Where am I going?"

"Sit back, relax and enjoy the ride. See you in about an hour."

"Okay." When Byron hung up the phone, her phone rang again. It was Sis. Erma.

"Hello, Sis. Erma."

"Chile', are you alright? I haven't heard from you in more than two weeks. What is going on? I believe the Holy Spirit is telling me that it must be a man."

"Yes, ma'am the Holy Spirit is telling you right. It is a man, a wonderful man. As a matter of fact, this very wonderful man has had a car pick me up and I am being transported to an unknown location to meet him. I got a call last night from an ex and it seems that he is trying to make a play for me. But I am not going to let that happen!"

"Whoever the second man is, if you let it, it is the devil himself trying to stop what God is trying to bless you with."

"I believe that you are right Sis. Erma."

"I know I am right, chile'. Stay on course with what God wants for you and don't get distracted by what the devil is trying. You know where the devil lives." Jillian laughed out loud at that statement. There was nothing like the statements from Sis. Erma. She loved this lady and always enjoyed their time together whether on the phone or at conventions. "Okay, I have delivered my soul, now about the convention planning."

The two continued to discuss conference business and how they would have another conference call to tie up loose ends.

"You young girls have everything all planned and organized. I love you like my daughter so I must ask.

Is this young man a church boy or a heathen?" Sis. Erma asked. Jillian laughed.

"No ma'am, he is a church boy, very much a church boy. I can tell you because I trust you. He is Byron Randolph, one of the twins of Bishop and Sis. Randolph. Jillian said.

"Hallelujah! He's a Levite, a pastor's boy, educated, good looking, smart, saved and one of ours. Chile', you are not going no place from the Fellowship. Hallelujah! I'm about to do my dance right here in my living room." Jillian laugh again.

"Until tomorrow, Sis. Erma, be blessed and I love you."

"I love you too chile'. Good night and enjoy."

"Good night to you too."

Sis. Erma was so happy she could scream again. There was nothing like the good church girls getting with those heathen worldly boys who knew nothing about God, church or respect for the commitment of the girl, herself. It could lead you down the wrong path and she knew all too well.

Jillian was so happy with herself and smiled as the ride took her further and further up I-75 North toward Dayton. She checked her email one more time and saw that there was nothing pressing so she sat back and did what Byron ordered, relax with a smile. Just like she did as a child in the car, she fell asleep. Fortunately, she was not too far into sleep that she didn't realize that the car had stopped. When Jillian woke up, she checked her mouth for fresh breath and began checking her dress. The driver opened the door to a lovely, large, modern house which sat on a very plush and green property. There were literally no next door neighbors to this home. Jillian did a full three hundred and sixty degree turn to take in all of the surroundings. She hadn't visited Dayton much so it was totally unfamiliar. The front door suddenly opened and there stood Byron. He walked toward the car with purposeful strides. He looked good enough for the cover of a magazine, eat on a plate and take home to her mama. He had on jeans and a light, mint green cashmere sweater. Mint and chocolate always go together perfectly and a smile that showed his beautiful white teeth. He was glad to see Jillian to say the least.

He reached into the door and took her hand, kissing it lightly and said, "Hey beautiful." His arms came around her waist and that was all that needed to be said before Byron embraced Jillian and began placing kisses on her eyes, forehead and then her lips. Jillian thought she would melt into his arms right there at the car and they hadn't made it to the front door. Thank God he held her tight and close. The kiss lasted so long that the driver said, 'good night' on his own and drove off. Byron continued to kiss Jillian and maneuvered them both to the front door, waved the driver goodbye with one hand and closed the door with his foot. A hunger like this, food wouldn't suffice and eventually, kissing wouldn't do either. The nearness of their bodies, the touch of their hands and the connection at their mouths was guaranteed satisfaction enough for right now or was it? Tonight seemed to shift some things for them both. Jillian tried not to think and live in the moment. All Byron could think is, 'she's in my house and I really don't want her to leave.' The sudden cough of someone else in the room broke the kiss and directed Byron's attention to the opposite side of the room. A very pleasant gentleman and young woman were waiting patiently in the doorway.

"Mr. Randolph, everything is to your specifications. We are going to excuse ourselves. Have a good night."

"Thank you Eduardo and Maria. Before you go, I would like to introduce you to my girlfriend, Jillian Forrester," Byron didn't look at Jillian to gauge her reaction. Jillian tried not to act surprised and remained calm at the new title. Her insides were jumping up and down. From *Steve Harvey's* movies and book, she realized that Byron had suddenly categorized their relationship and declared how he felt about her to other people. Eduardo and Maria walked quickly toward Jillian smiling from ear to ear. Jillian put out her hand and said, "Hello, so nice to meet you both."

They returned Jillian's handshake and said, 'nice to meet you' simultaneously and left as quickly as they had come.

Byron turned toward Jillian kissed her again quickly and said, "Hungry?"

"Starved," Byron led her on a quick tour of the living room, down a short hallway to the very large kitchen and the adjacent dining room. Everything was beautifully decorated and a single long stem red rose was at her place setting. Jillian offered to help, but Byron assured her that he was going to serve her tonight. After everything was placed on the table, Byron took Jillian's hand, prayed over the food and their time together. When he finished, Jillian said, "Thank you so much for everything. I feel like Julia Roberts in the 'Pretty Woman' movie."

Byron smiled and said, "You are welcome and I just had to see you tonight."

Jillian blushed, but really couldn't respond. Byron was happy that he had pleased her. They talked about work, how great everything tasted, how beautiful the house looked and everything in between. There was soft jazz playing in the background. Byron knew that Jillian loved Jonathan Butler and had his Pandora channel playing in the background. When, "sing me a love song' began to play, Jillian's eyes closed and she began to sing along.

Byron stood and said, "Dance with me." Any excuse for Jillian to be in his arms and especially while her favorite song was playing. They swayed to the music until it stopped.

"I think that we have been here before," Byron said as he was continuing to hold Jillian.

"This time we are not standing out in a room filled with people dancing to our own beat instead of the band's tempo."

"I think that is what we do together, dance to our own beat. I hope that we will be dancing to that beat a long time."

"Me too." He pulled back from their embrace to look in her face.

"I have a proposition for you and I don't want you to panic. I have to be in Cincinnati for a meeting at 9:30 in the morning. I thought that you might stay here for the night and then leave with me in the morning. We can stop by your place for you to change clothes, pick up your car and be in time for work." It was amazing that Jillian was quiet because there were a million things racing through her mind. She was a grown woman and she could stay in a man's house without sleeping with him. She had done it before, but remembered that his parents were there too. It was late and the thought of Byron on the road going to Cincinnati, driving back to Dayton and going back in the morning was silly.

Byron continued, "Now, before you say anything, I have a six bedroom house so just pick one." Byron would love for Jillian to pick his bed, but knew that she wasn't going for that until a ring was put on her finger. Jillian was that kind of woman and he appreciated it.

"Okay." Jillian said while remaining unusually calm.

"Okay? You sure?"

"I am sure. I do need something to sleep in and a toothbrush."

"Well, I have to confess that I already thought of that."

"Oh yeah?" Jillian smiled.

"Yes." Byron walked away and came back with a shopping bag that contained an oversized Bengals jersey, toothbrush and other amenities.

"So you were just sure that I would stay?"

"No, I didn't have a clue that you would stay. I left the receipt in the bag just in case you didn't."

"I am not perfect, innocent or without flaws. Yes, I do have my principle, faith and morals, but you kind sir, are tempting me to forget all about those principles. "

"I understand and will follow your lead. In the meantime, you can have the second master suite adjacent to mine. There is a bath, TV and anything else you need right in that room. Everything, but me." Byron smiled that sideways smile that said, 'I could be there if you wanted.'

Jillian smiled back. "Right. I confess I would love that too, but not tonight. Can I help you clean up your kitchen?"

"No, the housekeepers will take care of that in the morning."

"We can at least clear the table and put the food away. Come on handsome, let's put those muscles to good use in the kitchen."

Jillian and Byron worked well in the kitchen together cleaning up and putting things in order. Byron grabbed the bag of clothes and held Jillian's hand as they took the short walk down the hall to the guest suite. He kissed her hand, forehead and lips in a way that said, 'I am only down the hall if you change your mind.'

"Good night beautiful."

"Good night to you too and thank you again." Left alone, she put the bag on the bed and took a short tour of the guest suite. It was incredible with a California King sized bed complete with 1,000 count sheets surrounded by modern, cherry wood furniture set in a room with three beige walls and one burgundy one. The bathroom was adorned with burgundy and silver towels, silver furnishings and accents throughout. There was a fifty five inch television on the burgundy wall and the remote was positioned on the end table like so many hotels around the world. She spread out the contents of the shopping bag on the bed. She quickly changed clothes and wondered what her mother would say if she knew that she was there. She would probably be happy that they weren't on the highway that late at night and that Byron was a true gentleman. As she sat down on the huge bed feeling the comforter and sheets, she knew that sleep would come easily after a filling meal, wine, dancing and a stimulating conversation. She had just pulled back the covers to get under when there was a knock on the door, "Jillian, can I come in?"

"Yes, you can open the door, I am decent." The door swung open and Byron was wearing pajama bottoms and a t-shirt that showed off his muscles just right as he stood filling the doorway.

Byron snapped his fingers and said, "Oh, my, I was trying to catch you indecent."

Jillian laughed out loud and said softly, "Sorry, maybe another time."

"You can count on it," Byron raised his eyebrows high as he smiled. "You find everything?"

"Yep, this is a beautiful room and this bed is incredible. I suspect that these are thousand count sheets. Mr. Randolph, I must tell you that for an 'A type' personality like me this is overwhelming. You have swept me off my feet, gotten me off schedule and routine."

"I know that is a little hard for you."

"A little, but I confess, the spontaneity is exhilarating."

"I'm glad that you allowed yourself to be swept away because you are worth every minute."

"Thank you a thousand times. What time are we leaving in the morning?"

"About 7:00 a.m., because of the traffic. Do you need me to wake you or will you get up on your own?"

"I think I can manage. I have my cell phone with my charger and I respond to the alarm easily. Are you trying to catch me snoring, talking in my sleep or something?"

"Any excuse I can find will suffice."

"I see."

"As much as I love talking to you, it's already midnight. And, you look too tempting in that bed over there. I respect you, but I am still a real man. So I am going to close this door before I come across this threshold."

"Yes, Lord. Good night."

"Good night gorgeous." Jillian turned out the light and went to sleep immediately. Byron touched the door, closed his eyes and prayed to God that this woman would one day say yes and be in his bed down the hall for life.

After that night, their lives were totally intertwined. The desire to be in each other's lives on all levels only grew. Byron and Jillian were inseparable. Byron called, texted, emailed, sent flowers, candy, edible arrangements or left a message every single day of the week that he could not physically be with Jillian. When Byron's work was done, Jillian got his undivided attention. Byron rescheduled, re-appropriated and rearranged his life for Jillian. Jillian reciprocated with like passion and commitment to the relationship. She knew that Byron was a rare gift from God sent in her life to bless her. She couldn't let her fear or insecurities ruin something that she longed for all of her life.

Over the next weeks and months, they spent time in each other's home, ate at every trendy restaurant and participated in most citywide events that they could schedule between Cincinnati, Dayton and throughout the region. They attended family events and most of the concerts that Randolph Technologies sponsored. Byron's parents loved her even more than she could have imagined. Jillian's family was just as overjoyed that Byron was now a fixture in their family gatherings. Church services and/or events were even more special because each time Byron showed up with Jillian there was lots of talk amongst the congregation. Once again, one of the good guys got away.

Forrester and Randolph were already working together providing services to both their number one client which solidified them professionally. The support and excitement about their relationship was quite evident on both administrative teams. They allowed their leaders to have a love life and still be excellent in the board room.

Jillian still found time to meet with the Church Conference committees locally and on conference calls to finalize the upcoming Convention that was quickly approaching. Periodically Byron showed up at those meetings as moral support for Jillian. He sat quietly in the back so he could have a view of her, but also to get the reactions from the other committee members. Once, one of the members remarked, 'they should probably wrap up early since Jillian's boyfriend has shown up.' Jillian laughed it off and ended the meeting just a few minutes early. Amongst all of the business, church and conference planning meetings there were the holidays. Thanksgiving was held at Byron's house to accommodate both families. Christmas was celebrated as a tour of all of the family homes to exchange gifts, fill their bellies with the wonderful food of the season as well as share the joy and love that was joining their two families. Bishop and Mrs. Randolph now had a daughter and Jillian's mother now had a son.

On the other hand, Jeremy back in Louisville, could never catch Jillian long enough to get a return phone call. No matter how many messages Jeremy left, Jillian didn't give him the time of day. She knew that he couldn't hold a candle to Byron. She was busy living and enjoying her life with the man of her dreams, Byron Randolph. Byron followed the advice of Jillian's condo security guard and didn't give any space for another man in Jillian's life. When they were together, no other woman existed for Byron. Beauty and bodies fade, but the love of a good, smart, intelligent, independent, God-fearing woman was hard to find, like any rare jewel. It was love. They knew it and other people could see it too. People remarked on how great they looked together and teased about the nature of their relationship.

The year was coming to a fast close and she didn't know how long she was going to hold out. Byron had showered her with so much love, support, care and just good times over the past 3 months that Jillian was overwhelmed and overjoyed by it all. The bible says that God will go far beyond anything we can ask or think and God has truly done that for her right now. New Year's Eve was spent in church. Byron drove Jillian back to Dayton to usher in the New Year in his home. There was sparkling wine, some light snacks on the coffee table, one of the 'countdown to the new year' shows playing in the background and the fireplace was crackling with the dry wood giving the room light. Shoes were off and Jillian's head was leaning into that part of Byron's right arm that seemed designed just for her. His arm was looped under hers and laying gently on her waist. Jillian was so relaxed that she had to fight to keep from going to sleep after singing two services, a good dinner and a long drive to Dayton.

"Hey baby, are you awake?" Byron whispered into Jillian's ear.

"Yes, barely."

"I have something to tell you." Jillian sat up suddenly and looked directly into Byron's face. Inside she feared something was wrong.

"What is it?"

"It is nothing bad so breathe and relax," Byron took both of Jillian's hands in his and kissed her quickly to reassure her. He knew that look now. "I want you to know that the past few weeks with you have been the best of my life. I know that I said a few weeks ago I love you. Now, I am madly in love with you. I can't imagine my life without you in it. I enjoy our time together and making you an integral, important and essential part of my life. I need to know what you think."

Jillian burst into tears. She was silent and made no motion to do anything. She took off her glasses, held her head down shortly and took a deep breath prior to wiping her eyes. In a bold fantasy move that Jillian thought that she would definitely never make until she was married, she stood up, straddled Byron and sat down on his lap so she could look directly at him, face to face. Byron thought, 'My God, what is the woman about to do?' He leaned back, placing his arms up on the couch to give her and himself more room. Jillian leaned forward and placed her hands on the sides of his head to keep her balance prior to speaking.

"I love you more than I thought I would ever love anyone. I have been through a lot. Since you came back in my life, you have wiped it all away just like I wiped my eyes. I don't think anyone can appreciate real, true love until they've been hurt. I can't imagine my life without you in it. I am not talking about the places we have been or the things you have given me or just how you've treated me. More importantly, the love you show to me and how much you want me to be the best me possible. You have filled that empty hole and puzzle piece missing in my life. I am not perfect. I am quite sure that you are not either, but we are perfect together." Jillian took her hands and put them on each side of his face before giving him the most passionate kiss ever. Byron took a bold move as well and put his hands on her waist to bring her into him even closer. He stretched out on the coach and without releasing her, repositioned them both so they were laying down face to face never disconnecting their lips.

Byron broke the kiss first and tried to catch his breath while gently stroked her face, "Oh my, you take my breath away. I must confess that I have always loved you. I prayed that one day I would be in a position to show and tell you just how I felt about you."

"I get the message loud and clear. Thank you." Jillian said through more tears.

"You are welcome. I know that you talk about the trouble you had in the past, but I had my troubles too. I had ADHD and Dyslexia that caused me to have a lot of trouble learning in school. It is a miracle from God that I could get through college and accomplish so much academically and professionally. I always felt inadequate and not good enough for you. You were so smart, pretty, intelligent, and could sing me into a coma." Jillian laughed at that. "I always over compensated because I wasn't as smart as my brother. When I would see you at convention, I would say to myself, one day she will be mine."

"You never said that to me."

"I know. I thought it would never happen when you were dating that one guy. What was his name?"

"Roger?" Jillian thought 'how stupid could I have been to think that I would be married to that fool.'

"Yeah, him." Jillian rolled her eyes up in her head at the thought of Roger let alone Jeremy. Byron continued, "I thought I had lost my chance until I walked in your office that day."

"God's time is never ours, but here we are."

"Yes, baby here we are." The television announcer said, 'it is 11:58.'

"Hurry, get your glass so we can toast." Jillian sit up and so did Byron, but he stopped her just short of picking up her glass by saying, "Girl, we will toast later. I need to get my kiss at the stroke of midnight. Get back on this couch."

"Yes, sir." Jillian laughed, looked in his face and resumed her position of straddling his lap. There were two voices going on in her head, 'go for it' and 'you should stop while you are ahead.' Jillian ignored both voices and for once went with her heart.

"Oh my goodness girl. Look at you being a bad girl," Byron said breathlessly.

"You bring out the bad girl in me. I can't help it," Jillian said seductively with a low laugh.

"I won't tell nobody if you won't," Byron said with a sly smile.

"It will be a secret between us," Jillian replied.

"Happy New Year, baby. This year is going to be incredible because we are together. I love you," Byron said.

"Happy New Year to you too and I love you more," Jillian said.

"That sounds so good to me every time you say it," Byron replied.

Just then, the countdown started on the television, ten, nine, eight, seven, and six...

Byron and Jillian started counting down along with the television at five. They both said, 'one and happy New Year' in each other's mouths just before they kissed. The kiss started out hot as every kiss Jillian had with Byron. Something was different. Jillian realized that this was start of a new year with a new man and a new direction in her life. Her 'prince charming' had arrived. The knowledge of that made Jillian kiss him even more passionately. She explored every part of Byron's mouth with her tongue. The groans coming from Byron's throat confirmed his approval and delight. Byron knew in his mind that this 'first base' stuff was not going to be enough for him, but he would follow Jillian's lead. They were both forty years old and consenting adults. When he felt her hand come up under his shirt exploring his chest, he nearly jumped off of the couch with Jillian in his arms. The gentleness of her touch, made his manhood want to rise. He fought to control himself. Only time would tell who would win the battle.

If she got to touch, so could he. Byron ventured his hands under her top just at her waist. He thought he was going to be stopped by a hard underwire bra, but only a soft sports bra stood in his way of breast heaven. They weren't teenagers and he was definitely not a virgin so the desire to touch and be touched was as natural as breathing. If Jillian was a virgin, she wasn't acting like a virgin.

Byron was the first to break the silence, "You okay?"

"Fine," Jillian said breathlessly.

"If you want me to stop, just say so," Byron said wanting to reassure her. The silence was deafening. Jillian said nothing. She moved her lower body in closer to his bringing her heat closer to his. She put her hands on either side of his head to kiss him harder and even more intently.

Byron knew that the couch was not going to suffice for him. All of those years in the gym with squats and bench presses was about to pay off. Byron placed two hands on her behind and picked her up from the couch in one swift motion down the hall to his bedroom. He had imagined this moment all of his life. Jillian knew exactly what to do. She wrapped her legs around his waist and held on for dear life as they made it down the hallway in the dark. His California King-size bed and extra pillows in the master bedroom made the landing even more exquisite.

Byron's lips began the heavenly descent from her mouth, down her neck to the cleavage of her breasts. The scents were intoxicating. Byron smelled like a mixture of cool water and a summer breeze combined with the vanilla oils that Jillian used daily in all the right places. Jillian thought, 'thank you mama.'

Byron lips and hands were applying the right pressure to stimulate pleasure to emanate sounds from Jillian that surprised even her. This is what lovemaking is really like. Showing love, receiving love and giving back more love. They were both starved for this kind of love. The pillows went one way, their shirts went another and that bra went the opposite direction. Jillian gave herself over to Byron and he equally returned the favor. Jillian's breasts fit perfectly in Byron's hands and she screamed out when one landed in his mouth. Jillian had been touched before by someone that loved her as much as she loved him.

Byron continued to adore and pleasure Jillian's body and Jillian continued to let him. Before Byron went completely over the edge he asked one more time, "Do you want me to stop?"

"No, never," Jillian said breathlessly.

Chapter 7

The next morning was New Year's Day and a Wednesday. Both of their companies were closed the rest of the week for the holiday.

Byron awoke to Jillian nestled under his arm. He thought about how church girls had been taught about sex. Only for marriage. Byron thought, 'I hope she doesn't regret anything that happened last night because it was wonderful to me.'

Jillian rolled over and saw Byron looking down at her, "Morning," she said as she covered her mouth to hopefully, hide her potential bad breath.

"Now before you get upset, I'm sorry," Byron said it quickly wanting to be the first to get everything out in the open.

"There is nothing to be sorry about. I started it and we both finished it" Jillian said matter of factly.

"You don't regret it?" Byron asked.

"I don't regret one thing and would be ready to make love to you again, after a quick shower." Byron's body started to react just hearing those words. Jillian continued, "Jillian, the church girl, knows biblically it was wrong and I have to reconcile with God about that. On the other hand, I love you and know that you are my soul mate," Jillian answered.

"You are mine too." Byron said clearly, "Most people wouldn't understand our dilemma given that we are two, consenting and until a few hours ago, sex starved adults," Jillian chuckled and Byron laughed loudly.

Jillian added, "Just think. They always called you the bad boy. The jury is still out on that one." Jillian raised herself up on the pillows to look Byron in the eye and said, "To me, you are a wonderful, passionate loving, giving, caring, protective, sexy, intelligent and incredible human being. I will fight anybody that says differently."

"Wow, is all I can say to that." Byron said.

"I am going to take a shower and make some breakfast," Jillian said.

"Sounds great to me," Byron said and knew he had to put his next plan into action. He could hear Jillian in the shower, so he made a call.

"Patricia, Happy New Year. This is Byron Randolph."

"Yes, sir. Do you know what day this is?"

"Yes, I know that today is a holiday, but I need your help."

"What's up?"

"I need to know what type of diamond she likes. Emerald, round, pear, what?" At this news, Patricia was wide awake forgetting that she just got in bed at 6:00 a.m.

"A ring? Congratulations! I am so excited. That is awesome! We've never talked about it before, but I will find out next week. When do you want to give her the ring?" Patricia asked very excited.

"That is part 2 of the plan." Byron began to explain how, when and where he wanted to give her the ring. "I need you to keep this between us until that evening."

"I got you. I will start work on it Monday."

"Great. Thank you so much for your help. Have a great rest of the weekend. We will talk on Tuesday when I come into your office."

"See you then," replied Patricia.

Byron quickly hung up the phone as Jillian came back into the bedroom in her robe. "Hey baby. You good?" Byron asked as Jillian approached the bed.

"Yes, I am fine. Do you need to finish your call?" Jillian tried not to act suspicious, but she was a little curious who he could be talking to on New Year's Day besides his family. Oh well, she would let it go. Byron normally was an open book about most things, but wasn't going to elaborate on this call. It was a surprise. He realized that he had to cover his surprise fast.

"No, I am done. You look so good to me, come here. Wow, you smell delicious, too." Byron reached for Jillian and drew her into his arms. He kissed her lips scrumptiously to distract her from that look on her face. One thing for sure Jillian was never going to be able to hide her feelings from Byron or anyone else. Lying was never her forte and she was horrible at it. Byron had given her no reason to suspect him of anything so why make up things when they probably were nothing. Jillian quickly dressed and went into Byron's spacious and well-stocked kitchen. Eduardo and Maria were off for the holiday so Jillian was left to her own cooking skills for breakfast.

This was a New Year, new week and a new relationship status. They were now boyfriend and girlfriend. How it happened, only God knows, but it felt so good. Jillian at times, couldn't believe that she was here with Byron. He wanted to be with her every second of the day until they returned to their work schedules on Monday.

Byron loved having her in his house. He did whatever he could to make her smile. Jillian just reveled in all that he did to please her. She teased him when she could and loved making him smile in return. They talked for hours about everything and sometimes about nothing at all.

On Saturday afternoon, Jillian jumped out of the car before Byron could close the garage. She grabbed a handful of snow and hurled it at Byron when he opened the driver's car door. An impromptu snowball fight ensued.

"Now, you have gone and done it," was all Byron said before the fight was on. Snow was flying. Jillian laughed so hard, ran, fell down in the snow, made snow angels and fulfilled a lifelong fantasy of kissing in the snow. Cold and tired, some hot cocoa was in order along with a pound of s'mores at the fire place. Hot cocoa and s'mores insured more pleasure than Jillian could have imagined. Chocolate was one of Jillian's favorite things.

"Girl, you are loving that chocolate."

"You better believe it sir. I was a girl scout and had my first s'mores at camp and knew that I was in love for the first time," Jillian said with a giggle. "You know what they say about chocolate."

"What?"

"Chocolate is a girl's best friend."

"I thought it was diamonds."

"Yes, those too, but I still think chocolate is number one over diamonds."

"So, you do like diamonds."

"Of course, I like diamonds, but not more than chocolate," Jillian said matter-of-factly.

"What's your favorite chocolate bar?"

"Anything Ghirardelli, but not with coconut," Jillian said with a big smile. Byron wanted to ask Jillian what kind of diamond she liked, but didn't want to raise her suspicions. He would wait on Patricia. He definitely had a size of diamond in mind to give her. In all of the time they had spent together, he had never seen anything more than 1 carat on her hand. Byron thought, 'When I'm finished you are going to be able to see that ring across the room.'

Sunday night came much too soon. It was time to take Jillian back to Cincinnati. They were quiet in the car most of the way down I-75 South holding each other's hand the whole way. Periodically, Byron asked Jillian if she was alright, what was on her mind and kissed her hand. She said that she was fine. Inside, she knew that she had had one of her best holidays in a long time. It was time to get back to her house, company and routine. Everything was new and felt different. They had developed a pattern of being together and now, being apart wasn't going to be easy. He would only be 40 miles away. The past few days he had only been 40 inches away in that big California King Size bed next to her. As Byron pulled in the circular drive in front of her building, he stopped the car and turned toward her while in the car.

"I'm already missing you and I haven't left yet. This love thing is something else. I don't really want to leave you. I would prefer to sit on your couch, cuddle, watch the Sunday night football game instead and listen for your soft snore that you try so hard to hide." Byron said in a low tone looking deep into her eyes as he leaned on the console.

"Hey that wasn't nice, but have I snored really loud?" Jillian pretended to be offended and only slightly punched him. Byron laughed low under his breath and her touch always felt good even if it was in jest. He never totally disconnected from the embrace. His warm breath settled back on her lips long before he kissed her.

"Missing you already too, but we shall see each other on Tuesday for our follow up meeting." Jillian was still looking into Byron's eyes.

"I realize that any time I see you will be wonderful, but Tuesday is business. This right here is personal." Byron couldn't resist or say anything further until he captured her sweet lips in his. When they finally came up for air, Byron said, "You're in my heart, constantly on my mind and I love having you in my life."

"Me too. Sometimes I really want to pinch myself to see if this is really real," Jillian responded.

"Baby, I want you to always know that it's very real now and want you to know that it will be more real every day." Jillian giggled and resumed the kiss. Jillian knew if she didn't get out of this car quickly, she would invite him up and her plans of organizing her week would be shot. She reminded herself that Patricia was paid to organize her week! She was going to throw caution to the wind and ask Byron to stay.

"Come upstairs, watch the game, stay here and go back in the morning," that's all that Jillian heard herself say.

Byron kissed her one more time, put the car in drive and pulled around to the visitor space next to hers in the garage. He helped her out of the car as always and they headed toward the elevator.

Chapter 8

Monday was a blur it went by so fast for Byron and Jillian. At 5:00 a.m., Byron woke up and eased out of the bed to not wake her. He took a quick shower and dressed quickly. When she realized that he wasn't next to her, she went to the bathroom down the hall to brush her teeth to properly tell him goodbye. The proper goodbye lasted until 5:30 a.m. and included coffee which lasted until 5:45 a.m. Byron arrived to Dayton around 7. He texted her, 'I'm here and wish you were here. Love you, Byron.' She texted back while still in the lobby, 'I wish I were there too. Can't wait until tomorrow. Love you more, Jillian.'

Jillian was in love and walking on air and didn't care who knew it. Patricia knew it.

"Good morning boss lady. Looks like somebody had a great holiday."

"Fantastic is all I can say." Jillian and Patricia took just a little time to share their holidays. Jillian talked about how they spent time with Byron's family and her family as well. Jillian's eyes lit up when she talked about Byron and how he made her feel. Patricia was thrilled for her boss. Jillian had waited so long and now the relationship she wanted to complete her life was finally here.

"So what happens next? Is he the one?"

"I think so. I take that back, I know so."

"With all of the flowers, dates, gatherings with his family and him spending time with your family, you can't say that he hasn't invested anything into the relationship?"

"Right," Jillian said.

"I am sure that he is going to ask you soon. Did he drop any hints as you walked past jewelry stores?" Patricia asked.

"Girl, no. It is much too soon for that. I am just enjoying every moment we spend together. I just want to enjoy the relationship and not worry about next steps."

"Hypothetically, if Byron or your future husband would ask me about a ring, what type of ring would you like?" Patricia asked.

"I don't know." Jillian stated.

"You don't know?" Patricia asked again emphatically.

"I don't know."

"At lunch, we will know because we are going to take a quick run to Tiffany's on Vine Street and find out. I thought you were ready for a man for real. Where is your vision board with the dress, the ring, the future planned out? You're slipping boss. I need to stay on top of this situation." All Jillian could do was laugh at Patricia's antics because she was right. Just then the phone rang and it was Mr. Byron himself.

"Goodbye, I have to take this call. Hey, handsome."

"Good morning beautiful, how are you?"

"Fine now that I am talking to you."

"You are always fine to me."

"You always seem to know the right thing to say."

"That's my job, pleasing you. Are you busy or can you talk?"

"I can talk, what's up?"

"I would like to plan a little get together on Friday for our executive team and their spouses from our companies. What do you think?"

"I think that would be nice. What did you have in mind?"

"Well…," Byron and Jillian spent the next few minutes planning out a small dinner party on Friday at the Montgomery Inn on the River. Byron had notified his team already in Dayton and Jillian would let her team know that they were invited and get a count by Wednesday. Jillian continued the rest of the morning finishing her business and preparing for the rest of the week.

Patricia walked into Jillian's office at noon, "Lunch time boss lady."

"No, I have a few more things to do."

"You have nothing to do right now, but get your cute self in that coat, go out this door, down the elevator, into your car and down Vine with me to Tiffany's."

"You were serious about that?"

"I am oh so serious. Serious as a heart attack as my mother would say."

"Okay, but let me just do one more…"

"No I have your purse and you are not getting out of it." Patricia walked over and literally turned her chair around away from her desk and shoved her purse in her hand.

"By the way, I need to schedule a conference call with the Local and National Convention teams so we can wrap up things. We have less than three months until the convention is here. Byron has kept me so distracted from my convention stuff. Whew!" Jillian headed toward her coat located behind the door

"It's worth it boss." Patricia added.

"You better believe Mr. Byron Randolph was worth every minute of distraction for the entire holidays." Jillian and Patricia went down the elevator to the garage to Patricia car. Patricia drove so Jillian could continue talking without hesitation.

They walked into Tiffany's store, the sales clerk asked, "Can I help you?"

Jillian was overwhelmed by the bright blue boxes and could say nothing right away so Patricia spoke up first, "Yes, my friend and boss here is about to get married, but she doesn't have a clue about what shape diamond she would like. If her boyfriend soon to be fiancé asks, I need to know what to tell him."

The clerk said, "Well, let's look at some diamonds in different shapes and see what you think.

"Great." Patricia said.

Jillian whispered to Patricia when the clerk walked away, "I mean really, Patricia you are assuming a lot. I look real stupid in this very expensive jewelry store looking for a ring and he hasn't proposed."

"Oh it's going to happen if Byron Randolph has anything to do with it, it WILL happen."

"How do you know?"

"Are you blind? Have you been in so many bad relationships that when the real thing comes you don't even know it?"

"I guess so. I am just scared."

"Stop being scared and let's pick out a diamond."

The sales clerk returned with several rings in all shapes and sizes. The various cuts were all beautiful which made it even harder for Jillian. After trying on several rings, being teased incessantly by Patricia and comparing prices, she finally settled on a choice.

They enjoyed a fun lunch at the Millennium and then returned to work for an afternoon of more emails, calls, signed contracts and catching up on all of their work from the holidays.

"Ms. Forrester, I have Mr. Randolph on line 1." Patricia buzzed into Jillian's phone. Jillian picked up line 1 eagerly.

"Hello."

"Hey baby, how is your day going?"

"Better now that you called."

"Problems?"

"No, just a lot of catch up stuff from the holiday."

"Same here. Myron is getting on my nerves teasing me about how much I played and haven't done any work. It's the same old story and has been since we were kids. It's bad being a twin." Jillian laughed just thinking about all of their friendly banter during the holidays. Byron continued, "Is your team on board for Friday?"

"Thank you sweetie for reminding me. Hold on."

"Anytime." Byron answered. Jillian buzzed Patricia on line 3.

"Patricia."

"Yes."

"I need you to send out an invitation and RSVP for a dinner party with Randolph Technologies for the executive team."

"When, where and what time?" Patricia asked. Jillian gave Patricia all of the details. "Got it boss, I'll send out the email right away."

Jillian clicked back over to line one to Byron, "Hey baby." Jillian said sweetly.

"Say it again."

"What?"

"Baby," Byron said in a low voice that made Jillian hot all over. She loved it. So Jillian put her best 'Marilyn Monroe' voice and said, "Hey baby."

"I love it when you call me sweet, pet names. I have a feeling if I was there I could get you to call me a few other names in a minute."

Jillian laughed out loud, "You are a mess?"

"That's me."

Jillian rolled her eyes in her head and swiveled in her chair just a little at just the thought. Her insides just went flip flop and she got hot all over again. She went silent on the line.

"Jillian?" Byron asked quickly.

"Yes, I am here."

"You didn't say anything. I thought I had lost you."

"Oh no, you are not going to lose me. I am right here trying to recover."

"Glad to hear it. Sorry, I have a meeting in 10 minutes that I am not ready for. I have to stop this mutual love fest. Bye baby, I'll call you later. I love you."

"I love you more. Bye."

"You gonna make me drive down there tonight instead of tomorrow."

"I would love it, but you need your rest. Please stay in Dayton tonight. I will have nightmares about you falling asleep on the road. Baby, just call me later."

"I will."

"Thank you. Bye."

"Bye love."

Byron called back to Jillian's office really quick to speak to Patricia.

"Forrester Information Management, Patricia speaking."

"Okay, Patricia, what's the code?" Byron asked.

"The code word is Emerald, clear, white gold in 6 and three quarters. Anything else is left up to you. Over and out."

"Thanks, you are the best."

One thing about Byron Randolph, when he said that he would do something, he did it. Come hell, high water, snow, sleet or hail, he was about keeping his word. He loved Jillian. He meant it and about to prove it.

The rest of the week was filled with business meetings, brain storming sessions and research for the next project. Whenever possible, there were romantic phone calls throughout the day. Byron called early each day before Jillian left for work, during lunch and when she got home to say goodnight before she went to sleep. It was a wonderful life, but not enough for Byron. He wanted her in his house, his bed, his business in addition to his life every night.

Jillian had to catch up on work and the convention planning as well. March was just around the corner. With so much to do, why she had committed to this dinner party on Friday night, she didn't know. She was just too busy, but it was a party that Byron suggested. She would do anything for and with him. Byron didn't stop her from doing anything in her business or life. She was thankful for that, but oh was he a pleasant diversion.

Friday was finally here and everyone was supposed to meet at Montgomery Inn at 6:00 p.m. Patricia left the office at 1:00 p.m. because she had coordinated everything for the party along with the office manager at Randolph Technologies. Jillian left the office at 3:00 because she could easily get through town and get home in a few minutes.

Dressing quickly, Jillian took one final look in the mirror. The red dress hugged in all of the right places, but left room enough to eat and breath. Jillian was excited to see Byron. He had a florist deliver two dozen roses earlier with a card that said, 'Beautiful Jillian, can't wait to see you tonight. Pick you up at 5. Love, Byron.' Most people may have discarded the card, but Jillian kept each one.

The buzzer went off from the security desk.

"Hello."

"Hello, Ms. Forrester, Mr. Byron Randolph is on his way up."

"Thanks, Fred."

"Have a good night, Ms. Forrester."

"You too."

The doorbell rang and Byron stood at her door in a beautiful black tux, white shirt, no tie and a red rose in his hand. When Jillian opened the door, she took Byron's breath away. Byron stood in the doorway not saying anything. He just kept looking her up and down and down and up again. Jillian stepped away from the doorway turning her back to him so he could get the front and back view of the dress. She was trying to be slick about it, but ready to enjoy all of the compliments that were sure to come.

"Oh my goodness, do we really have to go to this dinner?"

"Well, it would be a little awkward since it was your idea and you planned it."

"Yeah, but you look so good, I want to stay in. This rose is for you."

"Thank you for the compliment, this rose and the beautiful roses earlier today."

"You are very welcome."

"You know you are spoiling me rotten right?"

"That's the intent. Come here you. I have wanted to do this all day." Byron took Jillian into his arms for a kiss that left them both breathless. The rose in Jillian's hand fell to the floor and they fell onto her couch trying not to wrinkle their clothes. At 5:30, Byron's alarm went off and he knew that he had to get Jillian in the car quickly.

"Is that your alarm?"

"Yes, it is a reminder to stop kissing you and get you to Montgomery Inn."

Jillian started laughing hysterically and said, "Ok." She found her rose on the floor. "I'll put this in a glass with some water real quick. I must get a tissue to get the residue of my lipstick off of your lips and reapply mine in the car."

"I really would love for people to know that we had been held up by your lips on mine," Byron said in a real sexy low tone.

Jillian stopped short, "please stop it or we will not get to the restaurant at all." Byron laughed out loud and locked his lips with hers. Jillian ran to the kitchen quickly to secure the fate of the rose and paper towel for Byron's lips filled with her gold lipstick. She grabbed her purse and wrap from the chair at the door and they were off.

When the elevator door opened, Fred the security guard, looked at them both and simply nodded. He didn't need to say anything to express his approval of how they looked together. Jillian smiled and nodded in return as Byron helped her into his car as usual. Byron moved swiftly through the relatively empty Cincinnati streets.

When they arrived at Montgomery Inn, there were cars everywhere with the normal crowd plus their dinner party attendees. Their car was valet parked and hand in hand, they climbed to the top of the short stair case. Patricia was there to greet them.

"Boss, you look great. You are right on time."

"Thanks so much."

"Mr. Randolph you look very dashing as well."

"Thanks," Byron replied.

They were immediately escorted to the second floor and the private dining area. When the door opened, Jillian looked around to see all of her executive staff there with their spouses or escorts. There were fifty people in attendance. There were members of the Randolph executive team whom Jillian didn't know, but she looked forward to meeting. White table cloths, fine china and beautiful floral arrangements in fall colors. Each table had place cards with the guests name and both of the company names on them. Everyone was dressed in their finest and there had been time for networking prior to their arrival. Diana was a face from Randolph that Jillian recognized right away from meeting her over the holidays as she arrived at the top of the second floor staircase. To Jillian's delight, Diana was a fifty five year old grandmother of four. Diana picked up the pace and got in step with Jillian as she entered the room and they were being escorted to the main table up front. Jillian turned to Diana and she was greeted very warmly with a hug.

Diana whispered to Jillian, "You look beautiful. You are glowing."

"Thanks so much Diana. You look wonderful as well. It is great to see you again." Diana turned quickly to introduce her husband. Jillian shook his hand and kept moving so they could get the dinner started. It appeared that Patricia had taken the lead on this dinner party, but Jillian could tell that Diana had a hand in making sure the Randolph Technologies people were in their places and mingling. Byron and Jillian greeted each person quickly as they made their way through the room. Byron touched her often while introducing her to his colleagues and staff. At other times, he was shaking hands in the crowd like a politician, but always looking back to see where she was in the room.

To Jillian's surprise, Byron's parents were in attendance at one of the front tables along with her mother, sister, brother-in-law and niece. Jillian wondered for a split second why they were all there, but family was important to them both so it really didn't matter why they were in attendance.

A few minutes later, Byron and Jillian finally arrived at their place at the table. Byron got everyone's attention with the clink of his butter knife on the glass.

"Greetings to you all. I am so glad that you all are here. It is my pleasure to officially welcome and thank everyone from Forrester Information Management and Randolph Technologies for being here this evening. We have signed contracts and have been doing business together for the past few months." Everyone in the room chuckled. "I thought it might be great for us to spend some time together socially as well. Not to mention, I have a mad crush on the CEO of Forrester." Jillian blushed madly and the entire room made sounds of approval, 'woo hoo!' 'Yes!' 'Go Byron.' "Jillian do you want to have words now or later?"

Jillian stood, "Well, I don't know how to quite respond after Byron Randolph except to say thank you so much for the welcome and I too want to thank Forrester Information Management and Randolph Technology for being here together for a night of fun, networking and great food. Let's enjoy this night! Thank you again."

Byron asked his father, Bishop Randolph to give the invocation and bless the food. He started by saying, "I am so proud of both of my sons. I am extremely proud of my son Byron for all of the wonderful changes and hopefully, addition he will soon bring to the Randolph family." There was more laughter and enthusiastic cheers. Jillian blushed again and Byron held her hand under the table. As soon as Bishop Randolph said, "Amen," the servers came immediately with trays of salad and the meal began. There was light chatter at each table and soft jazz began playing.

It was the beginning of a wonderful evening. The room was beautifully decorated for Christmas and the lights were low from the dimmer with plenty of candle light. The windows invited in the moon light that glittered off the water. There was a small dance floor that Byron hoped would be used after dinner. It was a great Friday night. As the dessert was served, Byron called the room to order again and asked the DJ to lower the volume on the music.

"Well, please continue enjoying your dessert. I really want to thank each of you again for joining us tonight on such short notice. I am glad that you were able to adjust your schedules. I want to give a special thanks to Patricia Johnson and Diana Davis for coordinating this wonderful dinner on such short notice. Can you please give them a round of applause?"

The room was filled with applause. The two ladies stood in acknowledgement of all of their hard work. "I thank them both from the bottom of my heart. I am also glad and appreciative that this could be an event for both of our work and personal families as well." There was another warm round of applause for the family members present. "I know that each of our companies had Christmas parties, but I wanted our executive staff to join us for a very special evening together tonight and Jillian agreed. I have two special announcements tonight. Before I begin, I want to thank my brother for being a great partner in business and life. We are twins and have always worked together on everything." Applause erupted again in the room. Byron continued, "Next, I would like for Jillian to join me on the dance floor."

All eyes were on the couple as they moved to the farthest edge of the room. Jillian had no idea why Byron wanted her on the dance floor, but she would soon find out. "What I am about to say Jillian has no clue about. First, our companies are NOT merging into one, just in case it may have crossed anyone's mind. We are partners to serve a major client and that is it." Jillian looked at him and nodded in agreement as Byron continued his speech. Just then Byron bent down on one knee. Jillian looked down in amazement. "My second and foremost reason for you all being here tonight is to witness this special moment in my life. I do want to merge our lives together." Byron looked up into Jillian's eyes that were filled with brimming tears. "Whether you know it or not, I have loved Jillian Forrester since I was ten years old. We played, ran through the halls of many hotels getting into trouble at conventions all across this country." The room filled with laughter again as Byron continued, "I have waited all of my life for this moment and in front of all of these people and our families, Jillian, will you marry me?" The women in the audience began the 'aw.'

Jillian burst into tears and managed to say, "Yes, Byron Randolph, I will marry you." The audience applauded the loudest of the night with echoes of 'yes' or 'go Byron!' and 'go Jillian' clearly in the background. Byron pulled out a blue box, opened it and there was a six carat white gold, emerald cut ring.

The light caught the glimmer of the ring and it reflected on the walls of the entire room. Everyone in the room noticed it. When Byron put the box on the floor, he reached for Jillian's hand and placed the ring on her finger. It fit perfectly as he took her in an embrace and a kiss that sent the entire room into a swoon. The DJ started playing 'At Last' by Etta James. Byron took Jillian on a tour of the dance floor and many other couples joined them after a few minutes.

"Did I surprise you?" Byron whispered in her ear, when he released her lips.

"Yes you did. So that was what you were on the phone about on New Year's Day?"

"Guilty." Byron was planting little kisses all along Jillian's neck while she talked. It was distracting Jillian. She wasn't dancing any more. Jillian felt like she was floating on a cloud.

"You also called my office back again after we talked on Monday to get my ring information from Patricia. I saw the caller id from my office. Don't try to distract me." Jillian continued.

"I am doing my best, but I am still guilty." Byron said into her ear.

"Lord you are doing an excellent job. What was I going to say next?"

"I don't know, but know that I love you."

"I love you back, but oh, I remember now. I will have to spend a lifetime paying you back for surprising me tonight and sneaking around behind my back to get information about what I like and don't like." Jillian said.

"I look forward to it. There will be much pleasure involved I assure you. I love you so much."

"I love you more." Another kiss resumed as the song came to an end.

When the song ended, they were both surrounded by family. Bishop Randolph continued to slap Byron's back and tell him how glad he was for him and the family. Myron was happy as well. He said 'congratulations' over and over. Jillian's mother was in tears hugging Jillian tightly and whispered in her ear the ultimate, 'your father would be so happy and proud of you.' Mrs. Randolph hugged and welcomed her to the family as well. It was a grand night. Jillian and her sister, Monique had a good cry because of all of the nights of complaining that she would never get over 'what's his name' and get married. It was a touching, emotional and happy night for all who were invited. Jillian was glad that it was Friday night because she knew that she would get no sleep or perform well if tomorrow was a work day. Other members of both companies came to congratulate both Byron and Jillian on their engagement and introduce themselves. Everyone in the room could see the love between Byron and Jillian and spread throughout the room. The music continued and there was a call for the DJ to play 'Cuban Shuffle.' A line dance was to ensue and all had fun crowding in on the very small dance floor. There were different levels of experience with the dance, but great fun was had by all. Most people danced until around 11:00 p.m. and some began to leave because of small children, babysitters and they were just tired from the week.

Patricia walked over to Jillian while she waited for the last few people to leave. They looked each other in the face as only two best friends would do, not as boss and employee and cried hugging each other tightly. No words needed to be said. Jillian was thanking Patricia and Patricia was so happy for Jillian. Jillian prayed that she could return the favor for Patricia one day and if the young man sitting next to her at the table tonight was any indication, happiness would soon come to her.

"I am so happy for you." Patricia broke the silence and said through a flood of tears.

"I am so thankful for you. You have been a part of my life from the beginning of my business, the personal lows and highs, but now, a new chapter in my personal and business life." Jillian responded through the same flood of tears.

"You have reached the next pinnacle of your life. I am so glad to be right here to see it."

"I am happy and angry with you for not telling me. I wouldn't have been able to get any work done the rest of the week."

"That's why I didn't tell you." Both women found a stray napkin and wiped their eyes amidst the laughter of that moment.

"Jillian let me see the ring again." Patricia stated.

"Here you go girl." Jillian gladly put her hand out for Patricia to see it. Patricia turned Jillian's hand gently so that it glimmered in the soft light at the restaurant.

"Is it as beautiful on my hand as it was in the store?" Jillian asked.

"It is even more beautiful because on your hand it gives the ring true meaning and not a mere piece of jewelry in the store." Patricia's statement was straight from the heart and warmed Jillian's heart just hearing those words.

"Thanks so much again. There is one more thing that I want you to do for me," Jillian said still holding Patricia's hand.

"What's that?" Patricia looked down at Jillian waiting on instructions.

"I want you to sit down and write out your dreams for yourself and let me know what I can do to help make your dreams come true."

"To be honest, I am living my dream right now helping you. I really don't have anything else that I am passionate about. If I think of it, I will let you know."

"That's fair."

Just then Byron walked over to them both and sat down in a nearby chair. He could tell the genuine, mutual, love and respect that these two women had for each other. They had been through a lot together. They had built a strong, powerful company together. They were friends as well as co-workers. He said nothing for a minute to give them a chance to recover. Patricia broke the silence by saying, "Well, Byron. She is all yours."

"No, Jillian is ours. Thank you Patricia for all that you did tonight. It was excellent."

"You are quite welcome sir. I am so happy for you both I want to burst." Patricia was now assured that Jillian was marrying the right man.

"Thanks again," The DJ was packing up his equipment and the house music was coming from the speakers. A smooth jazz tune was playing and one of Byron and Jillian's favorite.

Byron turned to Jillian and asked, "Can I have just one more dance?"

"I would love to," Jillian said.

After Byron took Jillian in his arms, he said, "I must warn you now that I will find any excuse or reason to have you in my arms, you touching me or I am touching you. I'm just saying."

"That sounds fantastic to me," Jillian replied. The song ended, the next and the next song ended before they left the dance floor.

"Are you ready to go love?" Byron spoke directly into Jillian's mouth.

"Yes, baby I am," Jillian replied without breaking their physical contact. There was one longer kiss and then they left. "You are an amazing kisser."

"I practiced all of my life for my wife. All the best kisses I saved for you."

"Ha, I love it. That one right there made me kind of dizzy and I have had no alcohol." Jillian recovered from Byron's intoxication and managed to find her purse and headed toward the coat room to get her wrap. She would always have a fondness for Montgomery Inn and never forget this night.

Chapter 9

The weekend was filled with getting used to the idea of being engaged and the new ring. Jillian looked at the very large ring on her finger all of the time. Whether it was in the shower, washing dishes or just driving down the street, she would just stare at the ring for periods of time. One time she cried out loud because she bumped the ring against a wall as she was walking down the condo hallway. Byron and Jillian spent the weekend together, planning and preparing for the next steps of their new life together. Over breakfast on Sunday morning, Byron thought he would clear the air by saying, "I am going to leave the wedding plans up to you."

"I really want for us to plan our wedding and our entire life together. I value your opinion even if I may not agree."

"I appreciate your honesty, but the wedding is up to you. I love you no matter what. Give me the day, time, the tux and I'll be there with bells on."

"Stop before we don't make it to church and I ask you to take me back home."

"I'll leave that up to you," Byron smiled with a mischievous grin and raised his eyebrows quickly. It reminded Jillian of when he would pull one of Pauline Richmond's ponytails. She would run to her mother and Sis. Richmond would run and tell Sis. Randolph who would whip Byron. Oh there were so many whippings for Byron.

"Well, I am tempted, but I can't wait to show off my man, my ring and my smile."

"Well, let's go!" They left the *Pancake House* and arrived at church right on time. Byron was seated down front and Jillian went through the back to the choir room to remove her coat and prepare to sing. She was met by her two friends Linda and Pamela.

"Girl, is that what I think it is?" Linda asked.

"What do you think it is?"

"An engagement ring?" Pamela asked.

"Yes, Lord."

"Hallelujah!! When did he ask you?" they both exclaimed.

"Friday night at our company dinner!"

"Oh my goodness! I am so happy for you. That ring is lighting up the whole room it is shining so bright." Linda said.

Suddenly, the choir director brought the room to order, "Can we draw our minds in and prepare for worship this morning? We are glad to see you Sis. Jillian and from the commotion realize that congratulations are in order. Have we set a date?"

"No. I just got engaged on Friday."

"Bro. Byron Randolph I suspect."

"Yes, Bro. Byron Randolph is correct."

Jillian's girlfriends sent a note to have the engagement announced during church announcements on Sunday. The announcer had Jillian and Byron both to stand and let the audience see them. There were congratulations from many as well as evil stares from single women throughout the congregation. Jillian had watched many get engaged and marry before her. It was now her turn. She and Byron were all smiles.

On Monday, when Jillian came into work, Patricia greeted her with a huge smile.

"There she is the future Mrs. Byron Randolph!"

"Thank you Patricia. I am still trying to get used to everything!"

"Get used to it boss. You have worked hard and prayed hard for a good man and God sent him." The phone rang, "Watch this boss lady." Patricia told Jillian right before she picked up the phone, "Forrester Management, this is Patricia, the administrative assistant to the future Mrs. Byron Randolph! How can I help you?"

Jillian smiled really big and laughed under her breath at Patricia's antics. There was silence on the other end of the line. "Hello, Forrester Information Management can I help you? Hello?" The line was silent and then a dial tone. Patricia hung up the phone and said, "I don't know who that was maybe a wrong number."

"Oh well, we have a lot of work to do today. We don't have time for wrong numbers." Jillian headed toward her office.

"Right, I'll get my iPad and I'm right behind you."

Jillian and Patricia continued their work day preparing for the week's business as well as planning for the future of Forrester Information Management.

"She's engaged? She can't be. I haven't had a chance to even go to lunch with her yet!" Jeremy yelled at the four walls of his office in an outrage.

His secretary poked her head in, "are you alright sir?" She was just standing there striking a pose in the doorway trying to be alluring to Jeremy.

"No, I am fine. Close the door!" Jeremy said brashly. He didn't pay any attention to his secretary who was always trying to get his attention. He knew that he could sleep with her anytime. He was enraged that his opportunity to get Jillian back was over. The money, power and position in her life would be taken by someone else and Jeremy knew that he couldn't change it. Jeremy knew that he wasn't going to give up just yet. He didn't care who she was engaged to he would find a way to either get her back or get even.

It was Tuesday evening and Byron and Jillian were conference planning after dinner at her condo. "Thank you baby for stepping in to help." Jillian said with papers spread all over the coffee table and living room floor. The Conference was next week and their lives would be in a busy whirlwind.

"You are welcome. I had no idea until the Duke Energy Convention Center called that it was Randolph Technologies' scheduled turn to handle the audio/video and duplication for your, or rather, our convention. Now you have an inside track on the engineering team for the conference."

"It is wonderful. God always seems to work things out for me during convention time."

"What's next?"

"I have my 'to do' list for the conference and Forrester will be fine for the week. Patricia can run that office with her eyes closed and we are always in constant communication," Jillian and Byron continued to go down the list as the phone rang, "Hey Patricia, what's up?"

"Boss, you need to get back to the office right away."

"What's up?"

"I just got a call from security at the office. It looks like somebody has tried to break into the offices. The alarm went off and it scared them away."

"Why didn't they call me first?"

"I gave them my number as the contact person just in case it was something I could handle. I think that we are going to have to increase security."

"On my way."

"What's up baby?"

"It looks like a break in at the office."

"Let's go," Byron got his jacket and keys while Jillian grabbed her purse. When they arrived at Forrester, there were police officers outside and the security guard greeted them at the door. "Ms. Forrester, I am sorry I stepped away to go to the bathroom for just a minute."

"The door was locked wasn't it?" Jillian asked

"Yes, but the person was trying to use a crowbar or blunt object to open the back door and the alarm went off. That is an older security door and with a little more effort could have been opened."

"We'll get that door changed in the morning. Did you see anybody on the video camera?" Jillian asked.

"Yes, but everything the person had on was black including a full head and face black mask to hide their identity." Their conversation was interrupted by a police officer. He had just come from the back of the building having talked to the Forrester Security officer earlier.

"Ms. Forrester, this is Officer Bernard from Cincinnati Police Department. I explained to him what I just told you." Officer Bernard shook Jillian's hand.

"Ms. Forrester it is good to meet you, but certainly not under these circumstances."

"I understand. What do you know?"

"No more than your security officer has told you. It appears that it was just an unsuccessful attempt to get in."

"Were there any finger prints?" Byron asked.

"No finger prints. The person probably used gloves. The person was alone because if there was someone else, they could have gotten in when your security officer went to check out things. I have to ask you, Ms. Forrester. Do you have any business or personal enemies that you can think of?"

"No, not that I know of specifically. I usually don't have people walk up to me and say, 'I hate you, I'm going to break in and steal from your company.' So, I really couldn't pinpoint any enemies." Jillian was frustrated, scared and sarcastic. The officer seemed to understand and so did Byron. "I am sorry, but I am angry that someone would try to do this after my company has been downtown all of these years." Byron was nearby with his arm around her for comfort.

"Baby, it's going to be okay. They are just trying to get all of the information they can so they can catch the person," Byron spoke low to encourage her as she cooperated.

"You are right Byron," Jillian apologized to the officer. "I am sorry officer that I over reacted, but you can understand me being upset."

"You are perfectly fine. We ask these questions to cover all of our bases. It could range from a homeless person, someone looking to sell something for drugs or you could be a target. From the look of the person, they were trying to be professional, but not an experienced professional or they would have been successful. I have one more question. Have you had any prank or mysterious calls lately?"

"There have been a few calls that someone didn't speak on the other line when my assistant answered. I really didn't think anything of it. Our phone number could easily be a wrong number."

"Have there been any major developments in your life in the past 3-4 months?"

"Yes, some wonderful things. My business is expanding. I just got engaged and have this great man in my life. I haven't crossed anybody that should make people angry." Jillian smiled at Byron and he placed his arm around her waist to bring her in closer as she spoke.

"Ma'am, all of those things that you just said would make somebody else extremely angry and come after you with a vengeance. I would be careful and take the necessary precautions. A report of our visit will be on file. Here is my card just in case, you can think of anything else or any other security breaches happening, contact me directly."

"Thank you," Byron answered first while shaking the officer's hand. Jillian was still shaken from the news that her good fortune would cause someone to want to see her or what she loved suffer harm.

"Thank you, officer," Jillian said politely. Byron helped her in the car and when he was seated broke the silence again.

"Baby, you alright?" Byron asked softly.

"No, I am not alright! This is crazy! Who! Why? I am sorry, I didn't mean to yell, but I am so furious right now it makes me scream," Jillian was clearly overwhelmed by it all.

"I understand. I would be yelling too. Especially, when you don't know exactly who is targeting you. You remember me telling you that I always take care of mine. You are mine, I love you and this is killing me to see you upset. I want to do all I can to help," Byron reassured Jillian.

She grasped Byron's hand as she said, "Thanks sweetie. You being here is a great help. I am trying to remain calm, strong and not get scared. My dad used to say that there will always be people who won't be happy for you when you were blessed no matter how hard you work for whatever you got." Byron took Jillian's hand to his lips for a quick kiss. He hadn't started the car so they were sitting there staring at the windshield thinking about the events of the night.

"I think that you should get a plan to combat this and any future attacks against your company," Byron said.

"Okay. I guess first, we need a new door. I will get that ordered immediately. Second, I'll meet with the security team first thing in the morning. What else do you suggest?"

"You should trace any of the missed or blank calls. In addition, you need to increase security as well. Only one security guard is not going to be enough security at night."

"You are right. Do you think that this person is going to target me personally at my condo as well?

"Maybe. We can't be too sure."

"We have good security in my building, but I will notify them of the potential problems."

Byron stayed with Jillian that night. They didn't call either of their families to worry them, but they comforted each other through it alone. Sitting on her couch, listening to smooth jazz by candle light and watching the night lights felt right. Shoulder to shoulder and hand in hand, through the good and bad times. That's what people in love do. Jillian knew that she had someone who would face the future with her as her partner, knight in shining armor, lover and eventually husband, together. Byron double checked the hallway and front door, twice, before coming to bed to hold Jillian as she slept. In his arms, Jillian knew that she could sleep. In his arms, Jillian was at peace. Byron remained on guard duty the rest of the night.

In Louisville, Jeremy Garrett was getting an update from Mickie on the break in at Forrester. "So what happened?" Jeremy Garrett asked Mickie.

"I was able to damage the back door, but the security guard came too quickly when the security alarms sounded. I got out of there," Mickie said.

"Man! You went alone. You are clumsy. I thought you could do something. I paid you good money and you botched the job. I thought you were a real criminal. You are just cheap. Forget it. I will get someone else!" Jeremy exclaimed.

"Wait, I can..." Mickie stammered.

"You can what?" Jeremy asked

"I can get you a professional man. I am just a stick up man or break in man. There is somebody who can get the job done. His name is Dynamite and he literally blows up places."

"How much?"

"It's going to cost you at least 100 g's."

"$100,000! Are you kidding me?! I am not trying to do that much. I just want to scare a person a little bit. How about a small fire?"

"Well, that should be about 5 g's."

"That sounds more like it. How do I get in touch with him?"

"His number is 513-522-5071 and I will let him know that somebody from the 502 will be calling soon. He can be found at the MOTR Pub most nights seated at the bar. Just tell the bartender that you are looking for Dynamite," Mickie said.

"Cool," replied Jeremy

"Now, about my finder's fee," Mickie stated.

The phone went silent and it was over. There was no use calling the number back because the caller never used the same number twice. Mickie knew that it was time to report to Dynamite that someone would be calling him.

What next?

The next day, Jillian and Byron met with her security manager at her condo and explained her situation. After that short meeting, Byron walked her to her car, kissed her thoroughly and didn't leave until she was safely on her way to the office. Byron called Patricia and made sure that one of the guards walked Jillian into the building upon her arrival. Her parking space was close to the door, but not at the door. He was not taking any chances. When she arrived at the office, the guard appeared at her door and walked her inside the building.

At 2:00 p.m., Patricia went to lunch and the phones rang directly into Patricia's voice mail. Normally, Jillian didn't answer her own phone, but today she did.

"Forrester Information Management, Jillian Forrester speaking, how can I help you?"

"Wow, she answered her own phone finally."

"Can I help you?"

"This is your old friend, Jeremy."

"Jeremy who?" Jillian asked. Jeremy had to fight the anger that was rising in his throat. He pushed it down with a slick chuckle under his breath and a cough.

"Jeremy who? I am Jeremy Garrett, the one-time love of your life."

"Love of my life? Are you kidding me? I only have one love and it is certainly not you."

"Is it Jesus?"

"Yes, him too. What do you want Jeremy? I am busy."

"Well, I thought we could have lunch sometime when I am in town. You know I moved closer to you in Louisville."

"Yeah, I remember you mentioning that the last time, but I am not interested in having lunch with you."

"Well, I want to help you celebrate."

"Celebrate what?"

"Your success in all areas of your life."

"Oh you mean expanding my business."

"Yes, that too." Jeremy knew that he had said too much. The phone line was suddenly silent. He remembered that Jillian was smart.

Jillian thought 'how would he have heard about her engagement? She also thought about him saying that she finally answered her own phone. Why would she be answering her own phone? She had an administrative assistant who answered her phone.' Jillian changed the tone of her voice, "Jeremy, well, if you want to help me celebrate, how can I reach you? Is this your cell number, home or office?"

"This is my cell number." Jeremy knew that he would have to change the number soon. Jillian wrote down the number quickly.

"Okay, when I have a minute, I will give you a call and we can have lunch."

"Sure. What day is that going to be?"

"Let me check with my calendar when my assistant comes back from lunch."

"Cool."

"Have a great day. Bye."

Jillian hung up the phone and called the police officer to trace his cell number. She also asked that that number be compared to her company's phone records she had turned over to them earlier in the day. The next call was to Byron and she told him about the call. She also told him what she did once she hung up from talking to Jeremy.

"Go Jillian, handle your business. I think you may be on to something. Jeremy Garrett in Louisville, KY at United Engineering. I'll check up on him from my end."

"Be careful. He's a geek, but even geeks can go crazy too."

"You are right. I'm a geek that is crazy about you and this Jeremy must be crazy, if he thinks he will threaten you and get away with it. I'll see you tonight. I love you."

"I love you more." Jillian hung up the phone and smiled to herself realizing that she had a man to help her through this. 'Thank you Lord,' she whispered. With Byron, she felt like she could conquer the world.

When Byron hung up from Jillian, he called Myron. "Myron."

"Hey brother what's up?"

"I just want to know the status on our little/big project."

"We are almost done. The furniture will be delivered and installed tomorrow. The carpet is down. The servers are in. The hardware was done a while back. We need to get our signage up, which will be delivered next week. The company was nearby in Springfield."

"Great. What about the living quarters?"

"The top floor is almost ready for you as well. The furniture for it will be delivered this weekend. What are you going to do about the Dayton house?"

"I am going to keep that as well. I am going to be staying close to Jillian until we are married. With so much going on, I can't be going back and forth. We've got to catch this person, see the convention through and keep Jillian calm and safe."

"This is terrible, but this problem too will be solved. Listen, don't you panic too. You have to be strong for Jillian."

"I know. I have waited so long to be with her and now to have somebody targeting her is making me a little crazy."

"Just hold on and work with the police to help them solve this."

"Thanks for everything. You are the greatest brother."

"I am your only brother. You are so lucky to have me."

"Yeah I know. One day I want you to love someone as much as I love Jillian."

"I will, but right now I have to help you. I can't be in a relationship while trying to help you."

"Thank you. I love you man."

"Love you too. Hold on and be safe."

"Good night."

"Good night to you too."

Chapter 10

The week of the conference was finally here. Byron stood watch over Jillian like a hawk. Jillian hadn't heard back from the police with any major developments only that they were still working on everything. Jillian couldn't afford to worry about Jeremy or anybody else who could be trying to sabotage her or her company. She had too much work to do. On Friday, she picked up Sis. Jamison first and then they went for a light breakfast.

"Baby, let me see that ring again."

"Here you go."

"Baby, that boy loves you. The ring is beautiful."

"Thanks so much. I love the ring and him too. It has taken some time to get used to it, but I am learning."

"He was a booger when he was younger. Lord, have mercy do I remember." Sis. Jamison smiled and laughed at the thought of seeing the identical Randolph twins coming to convention with their parents. "It didn't matter how many whippings he got from his father, he just kept on doing stuff. Well, I guess he finally grew up and matured to be a nice young man. He had a good teacher in his daddy, but kids don't always follow in their parent's footsteps."

"You are right, but he is great guy. I had almost given up hope on finding a husband and especially a good one."

"There are some good ones still out there, but you young girls have to pray for God to send them and don't go looking for yourself."

"You know Sis. Jamison, he told me that he has loved me since we were children."

"What took him so long? You guys aren't babies."

"I know. He said he needed to get himself together first and then pursue me. It was amazing and coincidental that he came into my office that day."

"Nothing is coincidental with God 'chile. God knew that Byron was the man for you. God arranged for you to meet at your company that day. I love how God works."

"Me too."

"Have you heard any more about your trouble?"

"No ma'am. The police say that they are still working on it. What that means, I don't know."

"Leave it in God and the police's hands. You have work to do and purpose to fulfill."

"Yes ma'am."

They continued to talk until Vernice finally sent Jillian a text message that she had just landed. Jillian paid for the meal quickly and they headed back to the airport. They arrived in baggage claim just as Vernice was gathering her luggage. Jillian timed it perfectly and they didn't have to circle around the airport too many times before Vernice came out. Vernice was dressed in her usual Chicago style, full length fur coat, boots, sweater and jeans because they had a late snow come through the night before. Vernice was her best friend. They all grew up together along with Byron and Myron running those same convention halls. She stood six inches taller than Jillian at about five foot nine and looked like a model headed to the next gig. On the other hand, Vernice was so down to earth, friendly and sensitive. Vernice cried easily whether at a funeral, good commercial or movie. They didn't have to talk everyday but when they saw each other, they picked up right where they left off.

"Hey Vernice, girl." The two friends hugged tightly.

"Hey Jillian. How are you all doing?"

"Just fine now that you are here," Jillian replied.

"Hey Sis. Jamison. How are you?" Vernice asked.

"Fine now that you are here baby. We can get this convention underway and done right. I got my two mentees who are going to take this convention to the next level." Sis. Erma Jamison said.

"Jillian you hear her trying to retire again?"

"Yeah, I hear her, but she knows that we can't do it without her," Jillian said.

"Alright girl before you start the car, I have to see the rock and I am not talking about Jesus. Your sister called me and told me the news since you have been too caught up with your fiancé to call."

"Well Vernice get them Chicago sun glasses ready because the Cincinnati gleam on this rock is going to blind you. Bam!" Jillian stuck out her hand toward the windshield to give Vernice a good look.

"Girl that is beautiful! Awesome. Go Jillian. I am so happy for you. It makes me want to cry. Just think, you knew Mr. Right all of the time. Byron Randolph, the booger."

"That's what I called him Vernice, a booger," Sis. Erma said.

"Don't ya'll be calling my baby a booger! He is a full grown, sexy, smart, spoils me rotten, man! He is mine! Hallelujah!" Jillian screamed.

"Excuse me, look at Jillian defending her man, instead of Byron, the booger,'" Vernice teased and then laughed out loud.

"Well, I am glad to hear and see that you are so in love. I can now mark that prayer request off my single and needs a great husband list." Sis. Jamison proclaimed.

"Yes, ma'am and Hallelujah again," Jillian rejoiced.

"Now, you can just move me up higher on the list," Vernice jumped in to place her order.

The three women continued to enjoy the reunion as Jillian drove to their downtown hotel. Each one was settled in their rooms and made plans to meet later. There were meetings and preparations for a walk through of the site the next day.

Jillian was checking her email when she got a call from Byron. "Hello."

"Hey baby how are you doing? Is everything okay down there?"

"Hey sweetie, everything is fine here right now. Vernice and Sis. Jamison came in and we have been having fun until the real work starts."

"They've been checking out your ring?"

"Yes, sir and can't believe that I am engaged to Byron Randolph, the booger."

"Booger! Is that what they called me? I guess it could be worse. I was terrible back then." Byron laughed under his breath.

"Do you want to mention to Myron that Vernice is in town?"

"Listen to you, Ms. Matchmaker. He will be there on Friday to hear Papa preach. We will let nature take its course like it did with us."

"Oh is that what nature did? Take its course. Oh, I just thought you were mesmerized by my beauty and couldn't help yourself?"

"That too." Byron said making Jillian chuckled that sexy laugh that made you want to get in bed and turn the lights out.

"What are your plans for the evening?" Jillian asked.

"Well, since you are secure in the hotel with some company, I am going to go back to Dayton to check on my house and get some things. I will spend the night there and come back tomorrow for the joint walk through meeting. What time does it start again?"

"It starts at 11:00 in the morning. I am in room 415 just above the main ballroom."

"Cool. Be careful baby and I will call you later. Bye and I Love you."

"Love you more. Bye."

"Mickie you did well. This should reduce your time considerably." Mickie Brown was at the police station and they were removing the recording device on his phone. This was the third person who had been recorded making a deal to get Dynamite to do a job through him. Twenty years was too long for him to stay in prison. He was doing the police more good on the street than locked up. It was a hard life for a snitch. He couldn't trust anybody, but it was either the cops or the streets. Mickie was taking his chances either way.

"Great. How much time did it take off?"

"I don't know. I will have to check with the judge. We will put in a good word for you. Now, when is this guy going to call?"

"Some time soon. I don't know exactly when, but it should be soon."

Meanwhile in Louisville, Jeremy figured that he would give this Dynamite a call. He would get his revenge one way or another.

"Yep."

"Hello, can I speak to Dynamite?"

"Speak."

"I was told that you help people take care of things." Jeremy didn't have a clue what to say. He really wasn't a criminal just greedy.

"Depends on who it is, what they want done and how much."

"Well, I am a friend of Mickie's. I need a small fire and I have $2500."

"Well, any friend of Mickie's is a friend of mine. Mickie said its $5,000. Are you trying to stiff me man or are you a cop? I'll hang up right now."

"No, don't hang up. I am not a cop and I can get the money for you."

"That's more like it. Start talking."

It would soon be all set. Since Jillian didn't want to give Jeremy what he loved, he would take away something that he was sure that Jillian loved.

Saturday arrived and all of the important players for the Christian World Fellowship Convention were in place at the convention center for a logistical meeting.

There were light snacks available and Sis. Jamison, Mother Ruby Williams, Jillian and Vernice approached the refreshment table at the same time.

"Erma, it is so good to see you. I am glad that you made it to one more convention," Mother Ruby Williams said as she approached Sis. Erma Jamison.

"Likewise Ruby," was the only thing that Sister Jamison said as she continued to put food on her plate not even looking up in Sister Ruby's direction. Jillian and Vernice noticed how cold Sis. Erma was to Mother Williams. Sis. Erma was very friendly to the other members of the team. She stopped, hugged and spoke to them warmly, but not Mother Williams.

"Erma, are you ever going to let me live that down?"

"Ruby, I am here to handle business. I will work with you all week long. I love you because God commands it, but that doesn't make me have to like or trust you."

"Erma, I have tried to say sorry so many times. What else do you want me to do?"

"You can't do nothing about the past, but you can do something about the present and the future by staying away from me."

Under her breath, Jillian said to Vernice, "What was that all about?"

"They have a history." Vernice answered.

"History of what?" Jillian asked.

"Not getting along." Vernice replied.

Just then Byron approached the table picking through the fruit and grabbing a bottle of water.

"Everything okay, baby?"

"Yes, it's fine, love."

"No, it's not. Tell him Jillian." Vernice said as she picked up her own bottle of water and returned to her seat.

"Good to see you, Vernice and thanks for telling me the truth. My love doesn't want to tell me everything. What's wrong baby?" Byron looked at Jillian sideways. She wasn't totally focused on him and appeared very distracted.

"Vernice is right it's not alright. The oldest two people in the room don't get along."

"Who?"

"Mother Williams and Sis. Jamison."

"Excuse me, but who does get along with Mother Williams?" Byron asked and Jillian had to laugh at that statement.

"You are right. She can be a hand full," Jillian continued to smile.

"I love that smile. See, that's my other job to put a smile on your face."

"What's your first job, the media?" Jillian asked.

Byron looked Jillian directly in her eyes and said, "No, to love you so good you never say stop."

"Lord, help me today with this man here." Jillian whispered under her breath as she closed her eyes and let them roll up in the top of her head. Her knees felt weak and she almost had to hold on to table before she fell to the floor. "I better get this meeting started or it will never get started. We'll both get in trouble, caught up in one of our hotel rooms."

Byron laughed under his breath and said, "That's later baby, much later."

Jillian returned to the conference table and officially called them to order, "Welcome everyone! If you would all take a seat, we are going to begin. Well, Welcome again to the 100th Christian World Fellowship Convention. I know that you are saying to yourself, 'it's finally here.' Those are my sentiments exactly. We have been planning for a solid year and it is now here. Hallelujah! We are going to begin with prayer and then on to the business at hand."

The meeting went well. The convention department officers and organizational teams would be arriving on Sunday so the rest of the day and evening was spent making sure that things were setup and ready to go.

Jillian received a text that said, 'I need to see, hold and kiss you soon or I will faint.'

'Lol. We can't have that. Where and when? Are you done setting up?' Jillian texted back.

'ASAP. Room 2220. They are still setting up, but I am setting my own thing up right now.' Byron texted back.

'See you in a few.' Jillian texted once more before she headed to the shower, changed clothes, touched up her ponytail and headed to room 2220. Byron was the only person with a room on that floor for now. Room 2220 was a three bedroom suite. He would be sharing it with his parents and brother when they arrived. Byron had the suite to himself. Jillian pushed the doorbell. Byron opened the door wearing a blue sweater and jeans. He looked scrumptious. Jillian had the same idea and changed into a comfortable knit pant suit in warm lilac. He closed the door slowly, but never taking his eyes off of Jillian's face. His intense stare always made Jillian feel warm all over and inadvertently, she would drop her head to regain her composure.

"Hello beautiful."

"Hello, handsome. I hear that there is an emergency here in room 2220."

"You hear correctly."

"How can I help?"

"The patient needs a little more care. It hurts right here." Byron had his index finger gently tapping his lips. Jillian went into Byron's arms gladly for a kiss that showed how much she was hungry for him more than anything set on that big dining room table. She had missed him for the past two days. He had been her protector, security guard and comforter for the several days since the initial break in attempt at her office. He kissed her mouth thoroughly and placed

285

gentle kisses on her eyes, nose, both cheeks and forehead.

He held her close for a long time then released her to say, "I have missed you."

"I've missed you more." Jillian replied while catching her breath.

Byron kept one arm wrapped around her waist as he escorted Jillian to the beautifully set table. "I know that we are both going to be busy and won't get to spend as much time together over the next few days so I thought I would do something special tonight." Jillian leaned her head over onto Byron's shoulder.

"This is beautiful. You are such a romantic and I love it. Thank you so much." Byron pulled out her chair and Jillian was seated.

"You are so welcome." The room was lit with candles, jazz was playing in the background and room service had been delivered. There was a vase filled with 2 dozen roses and one rose was at Jillian's place setting. The dining room table was next to the windows where you could see the downtown lights, the stadium and the river in the distance.

"When did you find time for all of this?"

"The beauty of technology and I had an accomplice, Vernice, so I could surprise you."

"I will have to give her something a little extra in her thank you gift this year."

"Yes, you should. She is so happy for us."

"I know and I want her to be just as happy one day.

"Me too."

Byron and Jillian enjoyed their meal filled with more great conversation. When they were finished, Byron ordered hot tea, hot chocolate for Jillian and coffee for himself. Jillian was looking out the window as Byron and the server settled the bill and the dishes were collected. Byron brought the cup of hot chocolate to Jillian, "thanks." Jillian replied as she continued to look out the window.

"My pleasure. What are you looking at?"

"Nothing in particular just the beautiful scenery."

"Me too. The scenery is wonderful from where I am standing too." Byron never took his eyes off of Jillian as he watched her looking out the window. Jillian turned her head slightly to see that Byron was not watching the stars, lights or river, but her.

"Byron Randolph you are truly one of a kind. I just want you to know how blessed I feel being loved by you. You spoil me rotten. You have far exceeded anything that I ever prayed for God to send me in a boyfriend, soul mate or husband." Suddenly tears started to form in Jillian's eyes and slowly run down her face.

"Oh baby, don't cry. You deserve it so much. I would love to choke all of those other guys who hurt you. My job now is to love you so good that you forget anyone before me. This booger considers it his pleasure to love you and receive your love in return."

Jillian laughed out loud at that thought. "That's what they call you, but I call you my love." Both cups were placed onto the credenza and their arms encircled each other in a hug and sensuous kiss. Byron wiped the tears from Jillian's cheeks with the napkin from the serving tray. Byron broke the kiss and took Jillian by the hand.

"I need you on the couch while I ask you something. Get your cup and come with me." They each picked up their drinks without releasing each other's hand and settled on the couch. Byron continued, "I confess that I want you in every way that a man wants a woman every single solitary day. I know we have a lot going on right now, but I don't just want to be your man, I want to be your husband. When do you think would be a good time to make you mine forever?"

"Wow, I don't care, in my heart, today." Jillian laughed through more tears. "In my mind that is not doable. Well, this is March, should it be summer or fall? Which is better for you?"

"Tomorrow is better for me, but realistically, summer. Let's go with July 4th weekend."

"That's fine with me. I will start planning next week."

"Okay, another big question for me is, honeymoon. Where have you always wanted to go?" Byron asked.

"Maui."

"That didn't take a second thought."

"No, because the first time I went I was with family. I promised myself that I wouldn't go back without my husband. It was too beautiful, romantic and pleasurable a spot to just share with family. I wanted to be with my husband and make love on beaches, in huge beds and in Jacuzzis multiple times," Jillian illustrated.

"Okay, young lady, stop that right now. We must change the subject because there are three bedrooms in this suite that I could choose for previews of our honeymoon." They both laughed under their breath. "If July 4th is good for you, it is great for me." Byron stated.

"Perfect. About July 4th, tell our families or keep it?" Jillian asked.

"Let's keep it to ourselves for now. I need to get with Myron and then start planning for Maui. I can't wait to see you in a bathing suit as well as your birthday suit."

"You never stop do you?"

"No, never." They both laughed.

"Lord, help me with this man right here. Well, I am going to have to start working out so I can build up my stamina."

"Only for stamina. I love your body just like it is." Byron gave Jillian that sideway wink that always made her happy and just a little bit nervous all at the same time. Byron walked Jillian towards the door and put both hands around her waist to turn her toward him.

"Stand right here and let me get my key so I can walk you down to your room."

"That's not necessary, I can go alone."

"I know you can go alone, but you are not going alone. You are my precious, beautiful fiancé and I don't want anything to happen to you. I love you and I am a real gentleman."

"I love you more." Byron put his shoes on and headed to the door. When he got to the door and went to open it for Jillian, she pushed him against the door and kissed him with such aggression that he would have fallen on the floor if he hadn't held the door handle. When Jillian finally released his mouth, she said, "Thanks for walking me to my room."

"I think we both may have to go on that work out plan to be able to handle each other." They both laughed again at the very thought of their future together.

When they arrived at her door, another door across the hall suddenly opened, "Hello you two. Sis. Jillian, I have been calling you and calling you. I now know where you have been."

"Hello Mother Ruby." Byron and Jillian said simultaneously.

"Sorry Mother Ruby, but I left my phone in my room."

"You know after all of these years, you are still hanging around this Randolph boy. That is clearly amazing."

"Well, Mother Ruby, Byron is not just the Randolph boy, but he is my fiancé."

"You know somebody said that, but I just couldn't believe it. I had you married to one of the Bishops and not just one of the Bishop's sons."

"Yes ma'am. What did you need from me? Is there an emergency?"

"You know I'm old and forgot now what it was. If I think of it, I will give you a call."

"Yes ma'am."

"Good night you two don't stay out too late."

"Yes ma'am."

Jillian unlocked her door and walked in with Byron right behind her.

"Now, I know why Sis. Erma is angry with her. She is so irritating." Byron said with a grimace.

Jillian said, "Right," as she walked over to the adjoining door of Vernice and knocked. "Vernice!"

"What, Jillian are you alright?"

"Girl, you got on clothes?"

"Yes, pajamas, why?"

"Byron is in here. Come on over." Vernice put a robe on and came over to Jillian's room.

"Hey Byron, did you guys have a good time?"

"Yes, until Mother nosy Ruby opened her door meddling with us. I still feel like I did when I was 10 years old and she was always getting me into trouble."

"What did she want with you guys?" Vernice asked.

"Nothing. She lied and said she was old and forgot." Jillian said.

"She already knocked on my door and said she wanted to know what time the van was leaving from here on tomorrow for the airport. I told her and she said she was gone to bed." Vernice said.

"Gone to bed my eye. She is here to meddle with everybody. Be careful. That gives me just a little insight as to why Sis. Erma is angry with her."

"Wow that is amazing. You just never know people until you work with them." Vernice stated.

"You are right. Well, I am going back to bed and let you guys say goodnight. See you sometime tomorrow, Byron." Vernice said.

"Thanks for all of your help Vernice. I owe you one."

"Glad to help. You just owe me a reference to a good man."

"I will try to fill your order." Byron said.

"You do that. Good night, to you both." Vernice added.

"Good night, Vernice."

Byron reached for her hand as they moved toward the door. "Now, where were we? I think you had me pinned against the door like this and your mouth was on mine like that and your hands were doing delicious massages on my back headed to my, yep just like that. Umm, yep I think that's where we left off." When the kiss ended, Jillian said, "Thank you so much. Don't ever stop knowing the right thing to do or say to get me back on track."

"If that kiss right there helped you get back on track, I'll gladly accommodate you any and every time, beautiful lady." Jillian giggled before stepping away from the door so Byron could finally walk out of it.

"Get ready for bed and I will talk to you tomorrow. We have much to do. Love you."

"Love you more." Byron closed the door behind him and headed back to his room. He almost stopped by Mother Williams' room to give her a warning, but out of respect for his parents, he didn't. Byron whispered a prayer, 'God, I thank you that you chose me to love Jillian.'

Jillian changed her clothes quickly and got into bed. She whispered a prayer, 'God, I thank you that you chose Byron to love me. I thank you that you didn't allow me to get my choices. Amen.'

The next day, the real work began. There were very few hiccups and everything was running smoothly. All of the team was taking care of their responsibilities with little or no assistance from Jillian. All of the regular attendees arrived early on Sunday through

Tuesday which included Byron's parents. It was always good seeing the Randolph's. Now that she was engaged to Byron, she felt a part of their family. The younger people and families usually waited until Wednesday evening or Thursday morning to begin arriving. Bright and early on Thursday morning a blast from the past arrived, Roger Hart.

Because Jillian was at the table at the time, Roger walked right up to her, began talking and didn't notice she was on the phone. She was talking to Byron who was going out to get lunch. She had just finished giving him her order when a loud voice came across the lobby of the convention center.

"Jillian Forrester! It has been a long time since I have seen you." Jillian had grown accustomed to the delegates speaking to her all week so she looked up, but didn't hang up the phone right away.

"Who is that yelling at my baby?" Byron heard the loud voice and was concerned.

"I don't know sweetie, but let me call you back." Jillian hung up the phone from Byron and placed her phone on the table.

"Hello, can I help you?" Jillian looked in the man's eyes and almost thought she saw a ghost. Standing in front of her was Roger Hart, the cheater. The man who left her heart in a million pieces and she had sold the white wedding dress on eBay. She looked him square in the eyes without a flinch of anger or nervousness and said, "Roger is that you?"

"Yes, it's me Sis. Jillian. How are you?" Roger looked into her eyes looking for anger, but saw none.

"I am fine. How are you?"

"I am doing well. Welcome to the convention."

"Thank you so much. I am glad to be here. My family and I are happy to be able to come to the convention this year."

"Family and I?"

"Yes, the wife and the children are in the bathroom and should be coming out any minute. I just wanted to see if you were still on staff and to say hello." Just then six children of all age ranges came running up to Roger yelling, 'daddy, daddy!'

"Wow, are these all your children?"

"Yes, these are all mine. They range in age from twelve to two years old."

"I don't seem to see the two year old."

"Well, she is probably with my wife and the stroller."

"Congratulations to you and your family."

"Hold on, I want you to meet my wife." Suddenly a very haggard, tired and medium size framed woman approached the table pushing a stroller. Her hair was in a slightly un-kept bun and she looked like she needed to be on a vacation by herself and not with Roger and these very energetic, six kids. Roger turned to her when he saw the stroller and the kids separated so the mother could get through the crowd.

"Honey, I want you to meet an old friend of mine, Sis. Jillian Forrester. This is my wife, Judy Hart."

"Sis. Judy it is a pleasure to meet you." In Jillian's mind, she thought, 'so this is the woman that he slept with and got pregnant twelve years ago. Wow.'

"The pleasure is all mine," his wife had to almost yell because of the screaming of the baby in the stroller.

"You have quite a family here."

"Yes, they keep me busy and I am never bored," she said as she corrected one child while looking around to make sure that all were accounted for. She felt sorry for the lady. Roger's wife didn't smile, but simply nodded her head in acknowledgement. She looked so tired she wanted to give her a room to herself. Jillian wondered whether she really signed up for the life that she was now living. Jillian realized that those tears that she cried over Roger those years ago were for nothing. Roger breaking her heart was the best thing that ever happened to her.

"Well, I pray that you have a wonderful convention."

"Thank you and good to see you," Roger said.

Just then Byron walked up with their lunch. He saw the young man, his wife and children walking away.

Byron said under his breath, "Who was that?"

"Roger Hart and family."

"That wasn't the..."

"One and the same." Jillian said through clinched teeth and low for Byron's ears only.

"Wow."

"Wow, is right."

"He slept with her over you?"

"Yep."

"Let's go eat and celebrate." Jillian broke out into laugher which made them both laugh. Byron got the lunch, Jillian got her purse and she nearly skipped to the office to eat.

"You took the words right out my mouth."

Later that day, Jillian met with the musicians to go over a solo that Bishop Randolph requested for her to sing on tomorrow night. At the Thursday night service, she thought she saw Jeremy Garrett in the audience. She hoped that she was wrong, but she wasn't. For the second time that day, an old relationship came back to haunt her. Bold as ever, Jeremy walked right up to the table right after service.

"Well, well, isn't it Sis. Jillian Forrester."

"Yes it is." Jillian wasn't giving any expression to her responses. She was trying to hide her anger, fear and irritation for a man who she suspected was trying to destroy her company.

"I finally get to catch up with you in your real element, church."

"Yep." Jillian tried to remain calm and indifferent while Jeremy talked. She wasn't at the table alone.

"Well, rumor has it all over the convention that you are engaged."

"Yes, I am."

"Can I see the ring?"

"Yes." Jillian gladly flipped her left hand with the six carats blazing in the building light.

"Wow that is some kind of ring. Who is the lucky man?"

"I am." Byron saw Jeremy approaching Jillian and walked rapidly to the table just in time. Byron had seen that face in a picture forwarded from the police so many times he would know Jeremy anywhere. He would have to call the Detective shortly to let them know that he was in town. Byron had to fight the impulse to take his fist and beat him to a pulp. Instead, Byron placed his arm around Jillian's waist as her comfort and protection, but his restraint. He was sending a clear message.

"You are engaged to Byron Randolph? One of the Randolph twins! I would never have guessed." Jeremy laughed like it was a joke. His joke was met with a blank stare from Byron and Jillian.

"Well, guess again," Byron said looking Jeremy straight in the eyes without flinching or smiling.

"Congratulations Byron, you are one lucky man." Jeremy put out his hand toward Byron, but Byron never released his arm around Jillian. The coldness of his stare and full body stance let Jeremy know what he was truly up against.

"No, I am the luckiest man in the world."

"Jeremy is there something that you need from the coordinating or hospitality staff?" Jillian asked.

"No, I think I am fine."

"Well, if you will excuse me there are others who need our help. Have a great convention." Jillian stared Jeremy down until he left the table.

"Okay, well, I'll be going." As Jeremy walked away he thought, 'you don't even know that tomorrow this time your place will be burning to smithereens.' He quickly looked at his watch and realized that he had a meeting to attend.

Byron whispered in Jillian's ear, "breathe baby just breathe. It will be fine. I am here to protect you. The police assured me that it is just a matter of time before they catch the bleep, bleep, and bleep. I will call the Detective right now and let him know that Jeremy is here in town." Jillian helped another attendee while Byron made the quick call. When finished, Jillian quickly returned her attention back to Byron.

"I didn't think I could, but I believe that I have found another reason to love you more." Jillian said looking at Byron with as much fire as her eyes could muster.

Byron came close to Jillian's ear again and said, "I feel the heat baby and can see it in your eyes, but right now is not the time and I can think of a much better place." Jillian laughed as she walked away knowing that he was watching.

Byron and Jillian entered the office after their duties in the lobby and noticed that Vernice was there on the phone. She ended her call just as they came in, "Hey, you two. It looks like everything is fine on my end for tonight."

"Vernice, you about done? Byron and I are going to call it a night."

"Yes, I am about done, but I need to check on one more item with the engineers for in the morning. Once I do that, I am going to call it a night. Go ahead and turn in because you have had a long day today."

"Anything I need to check on with my team?" Byron asked.

"No, I am just double checking with my own eyes. Any real problem, I will give you a call," Vernice said as she headed to the door. The door opened suddenly and who bumped into her, but Myron.

"Excuse me," Vernice said apologetically.

"I am sorry, excuse me," Myron replied. Byron and Jillian watched the chance meeting and quick exchange between Myron and Vernice. They stopped and sat down at the leaned in closer to watch what would happen next.

"Vernice is that you?" Myron asked.

"Yes, it's me, how are you Myron?"

"I am fine." Myron looked at Vernice up and down seeing how beautiful she still looked after all of these years. He then looked directly in her eyes.

'Yep, she still looks great after all of these years,' Myron thought. Vernice suddenly started adjusting her clothes and pressing down her hair with her hands. They forgot that Byron and Jillian were still in the room.

Byron leaned over to Jillian very quietly and whispered, "Well, look at this?"

Jillian smiled wide and replied, "Hush, I want to hear and see how they handle this." They both chuckled under their breath at the awkward and casual interaction continued.

"Well, Myron, um Byron said that you would be in town today. How has life been treating you?" Vernice asked.

"Life is going well. I can clearly see that life has been treating you very well," Myron replied.

"Thank you so much. I am headed out and hopefully, I'll see you again."

"I hope so too," Myron held the door open for Vernice as she exited and continued to hold the door and watched her as she walked away.

"Earth to Myron, oh earth to Myron," Byron stated as he and Jillian laughed out loud now that Vernice was gone. Byron loved to tease Myron and this was as good a time as any.

"What did you say?" Myron turned his head back in the direction of them both.

"Earth to Myron is what we said my brother. I haven't seen you this out of it since Angela Simpson grew breasts in the fourth grade." The laughter increased.

"Oh shut up. You two have been holding out on me. Why didn't you call me Byron and tell me that Vernice still looked great and that I should get here sooner this week?"

"Oh, no brother, you had so much work to do I didn't think that you had time for anything or anybody, but work. You've still got a couple days to get close to her. Maybe you can ask her out?"

"Maybe so. When does she leave Jillian?"

"You're in luck Myron, not until Monday."

"Thank God." Myron replied.

"Wow, my brother has something else to interest him besides technology. You better start working on your game plan." Byron continued to tease.

"Will do. I am a little rusty, but I think I still can sweet talk a woman," Myron answered.

"Myron just be yourself. Vernice has been through a lot so honesty along with the Randolph charm would be most appreciated." Jillian encouraged.

"Jillian, baby remember that you have the best twin as your man, but if Myron needs some tips, I will be happy to help him out," Byron teased.

"Funny. You guys heading out?" Myron asked while giving that side smirk to his brother.

"Yep, I am beat and ready for bed," said Jillian.

"I am going to walk Jillian to her room and then call it a night as well. What are you about to do, Myron?"

"I think I am going to hang here until Vernice comes back. It is empty and she may need a body guard for all of that beautiful body of hers." Myron smiled at them both as they exited the office.

"Now, you are talking. The rust is falling off your game. Enjoy and talk to you later. You got your key right?" Byron added.

"Yep, I stopped by the desk before I came in. Thanks brother and Jillian, good night," Myron replied. Several people stuck their head in the door to look for Jillian, Vernice or another one of the conference team, but only Myron remained.

The door opened again and Vernice entered, "Where is everybody?"

"They left about an hour ago to turn in for the night. I thought I would hang out and wait until you returned. It is a ghost town around here and I didn't want you to walk out alone," Myron said.

"Thanks Myron. You are such a gentleman."

"Yes, it runs in the Randolph family. You are working kind of late?" Myron closed his iPad to give Vernice his undivided attention. It felt like he had waited his whole life and now had his chance with Vernice.

"Yes, well, we take turns shutting down the convention for the night. Tonight was my night."

"You need help doing anything?"

"No, I think I have it. I just need to get my things and clear out." Vernice was gathering her things, organizing the desk and putting on her jacket.

"Are you hungry?"

"A little."

"How about some waffles at the Waffle House across the bridge?"

"A hot waffle with syrup sounds really good right now."

"Let's go."

Vernice picked up her purse and bag looking back to double check. Myron had his iPad, phone and keys which was his whole world.

"I'll get the light." Myron said while holding the door as Vernice walked out and he turned off the light with the opposite hand. "I came late so I was able to get a parking space right across the street." They were only a few feet from the convention center's main entrance.

Myron drove the short distance across the bridge to the Waffle House in Northern Kentucky and it was crowded. There were two seats at the counter, but they declined them. Myron wanted a booth because he didn't want to look at the side of Vernice's face, but directly into her eyes. It may be a minute before he would see her again and he wanted to cherish every moment. They kept the conversation light with no serious subjects or talk of horrible events of the past. Instead, they laughed, teased, talked and ate hot waffles for more than two hours. Myron even left his iPad in the car, in the trunk, of course.

At three a.m., Myron thought it best to let her go and head back to the hotel. After paying the bill and settling back in the car, Myron turned to Vernice as he drove across the bridge, "Thank you so much for spending time with me. I hate eating alone."

"Thank you for asking me. That was delicious and you are great company I might add. Who knew that Mr. Technology could make me laugh and bring me to tears," Vernice said.

Myron pulled to the front of the hotel to let Vernice out before he went to the parking garage. Myron got out and helped her out of the car. "Thanks again. I had a great time," Vernice said before she went inside.

"Me to," Myron responded. Myron saw her as he entered the lobby and was instantly concerned, "Is everything okay, Vernice? Did you forget something?" Myron asked as he approached her while she was seated on the couch.

"No, I have everything and I'm fine. I just wanted to wait on you." Vernice said.

"That was unnecessary, but thank you." Myron was touched. He thought, 'yes lord you are fine.'

They walked toward the elevator and Myron asked, "What floor?"

"The fourth floor." The elevator ride was short, but still gave them just a few more minutes alone before parting. Myron walked Vernice to her door.

"Here I am. Thank you again and see you later." Vernice said as she put the key in her door.

"You are welcome and see you later." Myron waited until Vernice's door was closed and he heard the latch on her door. Myron walked away and thought, 'I think I still got it.'

As soon as Vernice's door closed, Jillian opened the dividing door. She stood in the doorway wiping her eyes and asked, "Vernice where have you been?"

"What are you doing up?" Vernice asked while turning on the light.

"Girl, I can't sleep, but four to five hours at a time. Byron stayed a little while and then left around midnight. You are not getting off that easy. Where have you been?" Jillian insisted.

"Out with your future brother in law," Vernice said and Jillian's flew wide open. Jillian opened the door wider and ran to leap on Vernice's bed like they did as teenagers. Jillian picked up a pillow and put it to her chest, "Myron? Until 4:00 a.m.? How did it happen? Where did you guys go? Tell me everything," Vernice jumped on the bed as well grabbing another pillow and they both sounded like they were at a slumber party.

"Okay, Okay! He was still in the office when I came back from my walk through. He asked me if I was hungry and what about Waffle House. I said that a hot waffle sounded good and then we left."

"Until nearly 4:00 a.m.?"

"Yep. Just talking, eating and talking some more about nothing really."

"What do you think?"

"He is a gentleman. He opens doors, paid for the check, he's polite and made me laugh. He seems out of practice like me with dating. He is a hard working brother. He's laid back and so am I. He was smooth and very complimentary. I think that he is attracted to me which you know in my past has been an issue."

"No, you have always been attractive. You just listened to that crap your ex told you about how you dressed and looked to him. You and I know that you are gorgeous."

"You are right. I have had to tell myself that over the years. I am attractive, but just not to David's father," Vernice said with a little sadness.

"Now, you know my sister you are preaching to the choir over here about being attractive. I have had my own issues, but Praise the Lord that Mr. Byron Randolph has cured me of that horrible low self-image disease for life. Glory!" They gave each other high five across the pillows and smiled thinking of the hope, promise and excitement.

"I better get out of here and let you get a few hours of sleep from your date tonight," Jillian teased.

"Girl, it wasn't a date," Vernice stated.

"Yes it was. You just didn't know it. Since you did the late walk through tonight and had a breakfast date, I will take care of everything this morning. We should be good with the day's activities until the lunch break. Sleep in," Jillian said.

"Thanks girl. It wasn't a date, but I am very sleepy. I will be down around 11:30 with bells on," Vernice smiled.

"Yes, a cute dress, make up on point and a big smile just in case, Mr. Myron Randolph comes through." Jillian reiterated.

"You got that right. Get out."

"Alright sweetie. By the way, I am happy for you."

"You know I am ecstatic for you. Have the wedding plans started?" Vernice asked.

"Yep, in my head and keep the July 4th weekend open. Nothing is on paper yet. I've got to get through this first. Night or morning or whatever this is. Love you."

"Right. Love you too." They both laughed again and Jillian left Vernice's room with a smile. Jillian got back in her bed hoping and praying that happiness was coming into Vernice's life as well. Jillian whispered, 'Jesus bless Vernice.'

The last day of the conference was busy from start to finish. Jillian woke up around 8:00 a.m. and hit the ground running. Fortunately, Byron and Myron were great helpers to assist her and Sis. Erma with coordinating since Vernice was catching up on her beauty rest. Byron was keeping a close eye on Jillian to be whatever she needed. The police had called him early this morning and notified him that they suspected that there would be an attempt on Jillian's business sometime this weekend. Jillian being at the conference was perfect to keep her busy and out of harm's way.

Myron was waiting to see Vernice for the first time since last night's outing at Waffle House.

"Why you keep looking at the door Myron?" Byron asked.

"No reason."

"Yes, there is a reason. You are looking for Vernice to come in. By the way, what happened last night? I didn't hear you come in." Byron asked.

"Nothing really. We just went to have a quick bite at Waffle House." Myron stated.

"Oh, are you holding out on your brother. You had a date? The first one in about ten years." Byron teased.

"No, not ten years, but close," Myron said and they both laughed.

"How did it go?" Byron pressed.

"I had a great time and I think she did too. I thought she would be here by now," Myron said.

"She is trying to catch up on her sleep," Jillian interjected. "You kept her out until 3:30 a.m."

"You dog! 3:30 am! What were you doing?" Byron exclaimed.

"Nothing, just talking, laughing, eating waffles and enjoying the company of a beautiful woman," Myron replied.

"That's my brother!" The two high fived and laughed out loud.

"Brothers, excuse me, but I am trying to handle a conference here. Are you two done yet?" Jillian said with a smile trying to appear irritated.

Byron bowed slightly, "Sorry baby we are done. I am your humble servant, what do you need?"

"You are so cute and I'm getting distracted." Jillian shook her head slightly to regain her composure. "Okay, I'm back. I just got a call from Sis. Erma that there is a problem with the laptop in the Room 115 and they can't get the PowerPoint to play. The session starts in about 15 minutes. We can't be late today with any sessions. Which one of you in the IT department wants to go take care of that?" Jillian asked.

"I'll go. Room 115, IT department to the rescue," Myron said as he headed out with his iPad and phone.

"Thanks Myron. Text Byron if you can't get it to work in time."

"No, Jillian. It will work. I'll make sure of it." Myron was taking the ten steps to the doorway and with his hand on the door handle pulled it and who appeared, but Vernice. Trying to make sure that she didn't fall, He reached out with both hands that landed right under her elbows and very close to her waist. The connection made Vernice almost jump out of Myron's grasp.

"Excuse me, Vernice. I'm sorry. Are you okay?" Myron asked.

"Yes. I didn't realize anybody would be pulling the door when I was ready to push it open." They stood and looked into each other's eyes for a slight minute. Vernice looked down to make sure that she hadn't dropped anything on the ground. It made Myron look down too, but his eyes came back to her face much slower. He wanted to take in every beautiful inch of her and breathe in her fragrance.

"We keep doing this for some reason. By the way, you look beautiful this morning," Myron said.

"Thank you," Vernice smiled shyly.

"Oh Myron, don't get distracted. Room 115 remember. IT department to the rescue," Byron teased.

"Thanks Byron," with a snarl at his brother, "I am on my way." Myron turned back and leaned into Vernice for her ears only and said, "Will you be here later?"

"Yes." Vernice walked into the room with a smile on her face. She wore a beautiful green dress, navy heels and a navy bag to match. Her jewelry was a combination of the colors of spring to bring out the richness of the dress.

"Great," said Myron as he exited.

"That dress is beautiful Vernice. You look stunning girl," Jillian complimented. Jillian knew that she had spent years getting her wardrobe, hair and make-up right to match her job, lifestyle and budget.

"Thanks girl," Vernice replied.

"Vernice you do look very nice." Byron commented as well. "So what do you think of my brother? Jillian told me that he kept you out rather late or early this morning."

"I had a great time with your brother. We talked and laughed for a while in the Waffle House. He is fun," Vernice was looking out into nowhere special with a slight smile from an inside joke that she didn't want to reveal.

"I was knocked out sleep so I didn't hear him when he got in because it was so late. That's a great sign. I'm glad that you two went out even if it was for waffles and bacon. Would you be inclined to go out with him again?" Byron probed.

"Sure if he asked me," Vernice said.

"Well, if he doesn't ask you out again by the end of this weekend, I believe I will have to help him out," Byron said smiling.

"What do you have in mind?" Jillian said smiling slightly at Byron.

"You'll see," Byron replied.

"Well, I will leave that to you, Mr. Mastermind because we have too much to do until the end of this conference, right Vernice?" Jillian said firmly.

"Right boss," Vernice said with expression.

The conference schedule was packed and things were moving speedily without much problem. Byron was keeping a close eye on his phone as well as Jillian. He never thought it possible, but his love for her grew by the moment. Byron was so proud of her he could almost bust. She deserved a rest after this was over. Patricia would have to continue being in charge of

Forrester for one more week. He was about to do his own kidnapping of Jillian next week. His father, Bishop Randolph, would be the closing speaker tonight, his one true love would be singing a solo, his brother and mother were present and all was right with the world.

"Jillian," said Byron.

"Yes Byron," Jillian replied.

"Do you want me to place an order for some light snacks and fruit so you can at least eat a little before tonight?" Byron asked.

"That would be great Byron. Thanks love."

Byron leaned in close as he said, "You can get anything out of me if you always love me."

"I plan on doing that night and day for a long time," Jillian said low and slow. Byron kissed her quickly on the lips and rubbed his lips together slowly savoring the moment like a fine steak or dessert.

"No, no none of that. We have too much work to do Ms. Jillian and Mr. Byron," Vernice scolded.

"Sorry, couldn't help myself," Byron smiled. "I am going out to make some calls to give you ladies some quiet and peace to finish up, but I will be back in an hour."

Byron left out of the office and while walking toward the door, Myron approached him in the hallway so he asked, "Is everything squared a way for the sessions this afternoon?"

"Yep, you know the IT Department always has it covered," Myron replied proudly. "Where are you headed?"

"I am going to make reservations for the Omni for brunch on Sunday. I know that there is a wrap up session tomorrow at noon so we have room service at the hotel tomorrow night. I was going to include Vernice unless you have met somebody else in one of these workshop sessions in the last two hours?" Byron stated.

"No, my brother, Vernice is the only one I want to spend time with," Myron said emphatically.

"Great. We are all set. Can you keep an eye on Jillian for me? I promise to be back in about an hour."

"Sure."

Just then the phone rang. "Mr. Byron Randolph?"

"Yes, it is."

"If your girl sings tonight, she'll be dead by morning." The phone went dead and Byron's world crashed in on him.

Myron was still standing by and saw Byron's face. "What's up brother?"

"Somebody called and said if Jillian sings she'll be dead by morning."

"What? That can't be. Did you recognize the voice?"

"No!"

"Is there a number listed or is it private?"

"Private, of course. I'm just wondering should I tell her or don't tell her."

"Tell her."

"Why tell her and ruin the night? She's been practicing. Her name is on the program. Dad definitely wants her to sing. This is crazy! She already has somebody trying to destroy her company and now this! Help me think Myron."

"First, Byron calm down. You are no good to anyone panicking. Why don't we call the police and notify them and see what they suggest."

"That's a great idea." Byron dialed the number to the station and asked for Detective Martin. Myron stood by for moral support for his brother.

"Martin here."

"Detective Martin this is Byron Randolph, Jillian Forrester's fiancé. I am calling because I just got a call from someone threatening to kill Jillian if she sings tonight. What do you advise?" Byron asked.

"Is your cell phone listed?" Detective Martin inquired.

"No," Byron stated.

Detective Martin paused only for a second, "That narrows the suspects. This latest threat could be an attempt to take us away from her building which is most prominent. The private number is not traceable by you, but of course, it is traceable by us. I have your cell number and will let you know what I come up with." Byron gave Detective Martin his private cell number and the tracing back to the last 5 minute call began.

"I would feel better if someone was watching Jillian closer, but I don't want to alarm her," Byron said.

"According to our sources, the snitch says that the attack on Ms. Forrester's building is tonight. I will send two plain clothes female officers to the convention center to keep an eye on Ms. Forrester. Do not alarm her, but keep things going there as normal as possible. She is aware of some danger so to heighten the danger level is totally unnecessary. They will check in with you upon their arrival at the convention center," stated Detective Martin.

"Thank you so much. I greatly appreciate all of your help and I want this to be over with soon," Byron added.

"So, do we, Mr. Randolph, so do we," Detective Martin replied.

Byron hung up the phone and realized that this whole situation was getting more complicated by the minute.

"Byron, what did the Detective say?" Myron asked very concerned.

"He said that it could be a diversion and that they were sending over two plain clothes female officers to keep watch tonight just in case. They are tracing my phone and will let me know if they come up with something," Byron reviewed.

"That's great. Are we to tell Jillian about the call?"

"No, he advised for us to keep going through the evening as normal."

"Good."

"I was headed to make arrangements at the Omni, but I think I will sit here in the lobby and take care of that. Myron can you go in the office and keep guard until I get back?"

"Happy to. Keep the faith. This is going to work out and we will get to the bottom of this."

"I sure hope so."

The evening continued on as scheduled. The two female police officers introduced themselves to Byron in private with Myron's help and acted as volunteers to assist Jillian the remainder of the day. Sound check was spectacular and all was set for service that evening. The people gathered dressed to impress and all of the special guests were seated in their places on the stage. The program started on time and it was now time for the speaker. Bishop Francis the oldest Bishop in the convention introduced Bishop Randolph who took the podium proudly.

"Thank you so much Bishop Francis for your wonderful introduction. You and I have been friends for more than 30 years and I am thankful that you are with us tonight. I am also proud to have my twin sons and my lovely wife with me tonight as well. Would they all three stand?" At Bishop Randolph's words, Byron, Myron and their mom stood from an area off to the left side of the platform and turned to a roaring applause from the crowd. "I am even more proud to introduce the soon to be newest member of our family, Sis. Jillian Forrester." The crowd gave another round of applause in congratulations to them both, "My son Byron and Jillian will be married soon as you can tell by the beautiful ring he has placed on her finger. We have all enjoyed this conference spearheaded by Jillian, but at this moment, I would love for her to bless us in song before I preach."

The two female police officers took their positions looking like ushers more than officers.

Jillian took the microphone, the band played and she sang beautifully the entire song without an incident. Byron stood and held his breath the entire time Jillian sang. He enjoyed every minute of her singing. He smiled as he showed her support, but that warning phone call was still in the back of his mind. He wouldn't be happy until Jillian sat in the seat next to his on the platform. When she finished and sat down, Byron held her hand for the duration.

The service ended, a prayer was prayed for safe travel. People greeted each other with smiles, hugs and handshakes. The Conference was over and Byron's phone rang.

"Mr. Randolph, if you and Ms. Forrester could come to the station we have two suspects in custody." It was the voice of Detective Martin.

Byron got Myron and Vernice's attention who were standing nearby. "Myron will you and Vernice take care of things until we get back. Jillian and I have to head to the station."

"Got it brother, take care of Jillian. If you need us give us a call. Praying that all goes well," Myron said.

"Thanks," Byron said and he got Jillian's attention and brought her in close to him. "Baby, the Detective just called and we have to go to the station."

"Now? What about…?" Jillian asked.

Vernice and Myron jumped in, "We've got this. Take care of your business."

"Thank you Vernice and Myron. Love you both," Jillian said nervously.

"We love you too," Myron said on both of their behalf.

Jillian grabbed her purse, jacket and with her hand in Byron's headed to the loading dock parking lot to leave quickly. Bishop Randolph noticed Byron and Jillian leave and asked Myron, "Is everything alright with Byron and Jillian?"

"It will be dad, very shortly, it will be," Myron said emphatically.

Jillian and Byron made the short drive to the police station hand in hand. Byron broke the silence first, "Baby we are going to go through this together. I love you and I am right here for you the whole way."

"Thank you so much. I love you even more right now," Jillian turned to face him.

"By the way, you sang like an angel tonight," Byron added with a smile.

"Thank you. This woman has felt like the devil was chasing her these past few weeks. I hope all of this ends tonight," Jillian said.

"Me too, me too."

Chapter 11

Byron and Jillian entered the police station and asked to see Detective Martin. Detective Martin greeted them and led them to a private room to discuss the entire situation.

Detective Martin began, "Ms. Forrester, we arrested two people with the charge of attempted burglary and arson as well as criminal threats, conspiracy to commit fraud, burglary and arson. Here is what we believe happened. Jeremy Garrett contacted Mickie Brown regarding hiring an arson. Mickie Brown contacted our undercover officer who spoke with Jeremy Garrett and arranged to pay our officer Andre to burn down your building. Andre and Jeremy arranged to meet outside of your building to exchange money and he was arrested on the spot. Now, Ms. Forrester, I don't know whether Mr. Randolph told you or not, but he received a call today with a death threat against you to happen while you were singing tonight. I sent two female police officers to be on the ground just in case something happened."

Jillian turned to Byron and asked, "Why didn't you tell me?"

"I was trying to protect you," Byron said.

"I understand and don't agree, but understand. When I calm down, I will thank you later," Jillian said with a slight frown. "Detective Martin you said two people. Who is the other person? Did you find out who called Byron?"

"Yes, Ms. Forrester, it was your assistant, Patricia Johnson who made the call to Mr. Johnson and threatened your life. We traced the number back to a phone purchased by her," Detective Martin said.

"My assistant! Are you kidding me? Why? Why would she? I trusted her! She practically runs my company when I'm there and away! Unbelievable!" Jillian exclaimed. Jillian wanted to cry, but was too angry to cry. All of those years working together, lunches, dinners, saving, nights, days and weekends to pay her a good salary. Now, she betrays me? Jillian couldn't imagine.

"Wow. I didn't know that Patricia was in on it too," was all that Byron could say. He was as shocked as Jillian.

"Can I see her?" Jillian asked.

"Yes, if she agrees to see you," Detective Martin said. He called the holding area to ask if Patricia Johnson would agree to see Jillian Forrester. Jillian's mind was racing fast. 'Will she see me? We have seen each other for 10 years, five days a week and now she has to be asked if she will see me?'

Patricia agreed to see Jillian and Byron, hopefully, to somehow explain. Detective Martin walked Jillian and Byron to the interrogation room and they sat down and waited for Patricia. When Patricia walked in still with jeans and a t-shirt on, her eyes were pointed toward the ground. She was still handcuffed so the officer removed the handcuffs and she sat down in a chair at the table.

Jillian was sitting at the opposite end of the table. She leaned in against the table and asked one question, "Why?"

"I was jealous. I have no real reason other than jealousy. Jillian you have been good to me. You have asked me over and over about my goals, school, love and life, but I wanted what you had. Jeremy called the day after you went out with Byron. He was asking if you were seeing someone. It wasn't my place, but I told him yes. He was upset and furious at the thought of you being with someone else. He was angry and I was already angry. It had been so long since I had a date so I was furious. He caught me on the wrong day. He explained his plan and I knew it was wrong, but I agreed to go along with it. I didn't know the person that we had contacted was the police," Patricia said flatly.

"After all we've been through, you thought burning down Forrester was a good thing to do. Jealousy! I have been lonely for years! I have had no dates for years even when you had dates galore! I have worked my butt off. Gone to school and sacrificed much. No matter how much someone else has, nothing in me has ever wanted to sabotage or destroy what they have! How did you get that evil?" Jillian said emphatically.

"I don't know Jillian, but over time it just happened," Patricia said looking directly at Jillian.

"So what was the death threat for?" Jillian finally asked.

"It was just to scare you," Patricia said.

"Scare me! Thanks a lot considering all of the responsibilities I had this week at the conference. Really! Fortunately, I have a wonderful man in my life who saved and protected me from that scare. So you were jealous of what I do at church too?" Jillian asked.

"Yes," Patricia replied quietly.

"Honey there are tons of churches you could have gone to and helped. This is beyond my understanding," Jillian said in disgust.

"I realize that someone like you will never understand someone like me. I finally know now that I will never have what you have in business, education or life. I was just jealous. I have to pay for my jealousy instead of working hard to have my own life," Patricia said clearly without any anger or venom.

"No, you will never have what I have because you were supposed to have your own! Just to think I was a little jealous inside myself because I wasn't as tall as you or naturally slender like you. Today, I take all of that back and I'm proud to be me!" Jillian paused a second and added, "Do you realize that your jealousy has landed you in jail for a while? You will also have plenty of time to think about all that you have done and how you will live your life and not someone else's," Jillian stated.

"Yes, I know and hopefully, one day you can forgive me," Patricia said.

"Oh, I will forgive you because I don't want any malice, anger or hatred in my heart. I have too much life to live and love to give for that. By the way, besides helping to burn the place down, did you sabotage anything else at my company?"

"No, all the systems are in place and working fine. I have limited access because of the additional layer of security. I knew I could be found out easily if I did something to interfere with systems. You have paid me well so I never stole any money. Your accountant would have found me out anyway. I know that sorry will never be enough, but I am truly sorry," Patricia stated.

"Yes, you are sorry. More than that, you are a great disappointment to you and everyone who has known you. I will move forward with my life with love and laughter in my heart. You on the other hand have a lot of growing to do. Goodbye Patricia." Jillian ended the conversation by sitting back in her seat and turning her head.

Patricia started to speak again, but the Detective signaled for the guard and she was escorted back to her cell. When she left, Byron spoke first, "What happens now Detective?"

"She is given a lawyer if she can't afford one and they both will come before a judge to determine the next steps. Do you wish to see Jeremy Garrett, Ms. Forrester?" Detective Martin asked.

"No, I have no desire. I have a wonderful evening to continue, a business to reorganize and a life to live out to the fullest," Jillian said emphatically. "If you need me, Detective Martin, you know how to reach me." Jillian picked up her purse, Byron took her hand and walked out of the interrogation room.

"So what's the game plan pretty lady?" Byron asked as they walked out the front doors.

"Well, first this," Jillian stopped, stood on her toes and wrapped two arms around Byron's neck kissing him thoroughly. She didn't care. She was alive. Byron wrapped his arms around her waist and brought Jillian in as tight as possible to return the favor. No matter what happened next, she was here, loved and wanted.

"I wasn't ready for that, but so glad I was here," Byron said with a huge smile while still embraced.

Jillian laughed which was a great relief, considering the previous few minutes in the station. "Thank you for everything. I love you more than ever."

"No problem. I love you too. What's next?" Byron asked while gently stroking her back.

"Let's go join our friends and family and celebrate." Jillian said.

"Right, but first, I have to get one more taste of this," Byron kissed her one more time, gently. This kiss said I love you and I also cherish you.

Jillian and Byron walked hand and hand down the street to not only their car, but to a brand new day and season filled with hope, faith, more family, love and prosperity.

Made in the USA
San Bernardino, CA
27 March 2016